Rescuing the Rain Man

Praise for the Award-Winning Buffalo Springs Series

"This book did not disappoint. I love how Amy writes, so heartfelt, twists and turns to keep people real and engaging, short chapters, and great story. Great characters that work together to make a small town better for all."
Desert Fire, Mountain Rain, Rose on Amazon

"Amy does it again. Another great book full of wonder, family, small town life, travel, adventure, followed by disillusionment, deceit, trickery, distrust, disappointment, ending with triumph, trust, faith, and love.
Under the Summer Moon, Amazon Reviewer

"We are proud to announce that SAPPHIRES IN SNOW by Amy Schisler has been honored with the B.R.A.G. Medallion (Book Readers Appreciation Group). It now joins the very select award-winning, reader-recommended books at indieBRAG.!"
Sapphires in Snow, Indie B.R.A.G

Praise for The Award-winning Chincoteague Island Books

"I can already see the Hallmark Channel movie!"
Island of Miracles, Anne, Goodreads

"[Amy] draws you in to the lives of her characters…she paints the picture so eloquently it's almost like you are there.
Island of Promise, Cindy, Amazon

"The romance was pure, refreshing, and beautiful, completely believable and just the right level of sweet. At the same time it was heady and exhilarating–in short: it felt like falling in love–and I was delighted by it."
Seeking Tranquility, Jessica Castillo, Catholic 365

Also Available by Amy Schisler

Novels

A Place to Call Home
Picture Me
Whispering Vines and The
Good Wine
Summer's Squall
The Devil's Fortune

Chincoteague Island Trilogy

Island of Miracles
Island of Promise
Island of Hope

Chincoteague Sunsets Trilogy

Seeking Tranquility
Seeking Sugar and Spice
Seeking Space and Time

Buffalo Springs Series

Desert Fire, Mountain Rain
Under the Summer Moon
Sapphires in Snow
Rescuing the Rain Man

Children's Books

Crabbing With Granddad
The Greatest Gift
A Very Loud Christmas

Spiritual Books and Bible Studies

Stations of the Cross Meditations for Moms (with Anne Kennedy, Susan Anthony, Chandi Owen, and Wendy Clark)
A Devotional Alphabet
Meet the Saints from A-Z, A Children's Introduction to the Saints
Clothed With Strength and Dignity: Women of the Bible
Sowing the Seeds of Faith: Inspiration from the Garden of Saints
Meditating on the Mysteries of the Rosaries (Joyful, Luminous, Sorrowful, and Glorious)

Rescuing the Rain Man

By Amy Schisler

Copyright 2025 by Amy Schisler
Chesapeake Sunrise Publishing
Bozman, Maryland

Published by Chesapeake Sunrise Publishing
Amy Schisler
Bozman, MD
2025

Dedication

To my parents. I am the person I am because of the people you are. I love you.

One

Cooper eyed the ledge and made a quick assessment. Could he make the jump? Was it safe? Was his equipment properly rigged? It was going to be close, but experience told him he could do it.

"Cooper, don't do this," Lucy urged. "The rest of the team will be here soon with the equipment. They can rappel down from the other side. It's not worth the risk."

"They can't get to her from up there without someone else being down on that ledge to guide them. You see how it juts out right above. Heck, I don't know how she even got there."

"Help! Please! I'm scared, and the bleeding won't stop."

Cooper's heart sped up, not from the cries for help, but from the adrenaline that began racing through his veins. They'd found her, and she needed help. There was no time to waste. No more seconds could tick by as he analyzed the situation or waited for the others. It was now or never.

Lucy grabbed his arm. "Coop, if anyone should go, it's me."

He shook his head. "Have you ever made a jump like that?"

He waited while she assessed the distance between the ledges before she shaking her head.

"I'm on my way," he called to the woman, Lacie Grey, who had been missing for three days. She'd identified herself when they heard her screams and answered, and he'd felt relief wash over him. But that relief soon disappeared when he realized she'd gone over the side of the mountain and was perched perilously on a jagged ledge on the other side of the canyon. Cooper would have to rappel down and then jump across the chasm, hoping he could fit on the narrow ledge beside her with his first aid kit and climbing gear.

With a silent prayer that he could make it, that she wasn't too badly hurt, and that a member of his team would find a way to help them up, he took a breath and began his rapid descent. Rocks loosened and fell each time his feet hit the wall, but he made it to the ledge just above and opposite where Lacie was huddled.

"I'm going to jump over to you," he told her as he unbuckled his harness. "Don't move."

She looked down to the racing water below.

"Can you make it?" Lucy called from above.

Cooper nodded without thinking. He had to make it. There was no other choice. Even with help on the way, there was no telling how long it would take them to arrive or how badly hurt she was.

"I'll make it, Lacie. Stay where you are so I have room to land."

He hoisted his first aid pack higher onto his back, inhaled deeply three times as his thoughts automatically pleaded, *St. Bernard, pray for us*. On his last inhale, Cooper made the leap, crashing onto the ledge, gripping the side of the mountain as his balance wavered. He clutched the rock wall and steadied his breathing until he was ready to let go and turn to Lacie. Her pants leg was covered with blood, and a bone protruded through a tear in the fabric.

"I tried to use part of my shirt as a tourniquet, but I couldn't get it as tight as I wanted it."

"You did the right thing. Even if you didn't stop the bleeding, you probably slowed it down. How long ago did this happen?"

"Not long. An hour, maybe. I heard you calling me, and I tried to follow your voice. I guess I wasn't paying attention to where I was going. I fell from up there." She pointed to where Lucy waited.

"How did you end up here?" he asked, reeling with disbelief.

"I, I don't know. I just did. Lucky?" She shrugged.

Cooper winced. Lucky was an understatement. Visions of another woman on a similar ledge, one who hadn't been so lucky, filled his mind, but he couldn't go there. He focused on Lacie, whose voice was weak, her breathing shallow. She was close to going into shock from the blood loss.

"Coop?"

He picked up his radio and answered as quietly as he could, turning away from the young woman. "She's okay. Protruding tibia. Sizable loss of blood. Shock imminent."

He carefully removed his backpack and knelt beside her. Dried blood was caked in the dirt around her, and blood continued to drench her pants but wasn't gushing. He checked her pulse, assessed her pupils for signs of head trauma, and took stock of her condition. She was shivering, but not as much as she could've been. He checked the temperature of her skin. Just as he thought, shock was imminent.

"You're lucky. Temps are dropping tonight, so you would've suffered from hypothermia. The nights aren't as cold as they have been, but the weather is unpredictable around here. No telling how cold it could get. Can you feel your fingers and toes?"

She nodded. "Pretty much. They've been numb at night, but I've been wearing gloves and warm hiking socks. I tried to keep moving as much as possible."

Cooper grunted his approval before he gently began cutting away her pants.

"I'm going to try not to hurt you, but I have to see how bad this is."

"It's okay. Go ahead and—" she gasped and clutched his arm. Cooper felt her rapid breaths on his face, smelled her stale breath.

With as much tenderness as possible, he removed the fabric but left the wrapping she'd secured around the bone and wound.

"I had an extra shirt," she said between gasps as he tightened the tourniquet. "The gauze I had was for small scrapes and minor injuries. I didn't have anything—" she grunted in pain. "To wrap it with."

"You did a good job." He wasn't lying. She'd done just what he—and every other EMT—was trained to do. "Do you have first aid training?" He needed to keep her talking and focused on anything but the pain.

"I used to be. I was a Girl Scout when I was growing up and volunteered at a camp when I was in high school."

"Well, it shows. You did everything right."

"Everything except watch where I was going."

He didn't argue with her, and he didn't add that the worst thing she did was go hiking alone. He knew she knew that already.

"Any allergies to medicine?"

She shook her head and said, "No."

He nodded.

She winced as he added more bandages to the wound. He wrapped them around the bone, trying not to move it but applying enough pressure to stabilize the tibia. He gave her credit for being tough and composed.

"Now what?" she asked as he sat back and breathed a long sigh, her voice fading.

"I check on the rest of the team." He pulled his radio from his pack and called for a location.

"We're almost to you," Lance answered back. "About a hundred yards or so. How's she doing?"

"Better than expected, but she's got a protrusion of

the right tibia. Significant blood loss. She's awake, lucid, and stable, but shock is setting in."

"Copy. See you in five. Is Lucy with you?"

"She's still above. It was tricky getting down here."

"Copy that. We'll assess once we arrive."

Once the team was there and made a plan for getting the Stokes basket down to the ledge and up again, it took less than twenty minutes to get Lacie up on firm ground and dosed with a mild sedative. Lucy, their medic, was monitoring her until the chopper arrived. The authorities had been notified, and her family was being called. Cooper told Lacie goodbye and gathered the gear he'd left above when he rappelled down.

An hour after finishing his paperwork, Cooper sat at the bar in Rick's and nursed a beer. It had been one heck of a day.

***

"How's the patient?" Dr. Joe Blake asked Amanda. They stood in the first-floor breakroom.

"Better. Lucy had her stable by the time the helicopter arrived. She's a good medic. The ambulance will be here soon to take her to Mountain Home. She's going to need surgery." She paused and looked at Joe. "What made her think it was a good idea to hike in that area alone?"

Joe shrugged. "People do it all the time."

Amanda leaned against the counter in the room Joe had converted to a break room. She admired all he'd done to turn the centuries-old house into a clinic. It was as state-of-the-art as it could be, considering they were in a very poor town far from any large medical center, while still maintaining a cozy, comfortable feel. That was thanks to their ability to obtain funding as well as the keen eye and skill of local interior design student, Cindy Kline, and local carpenter, Stan Higgins. Amanda had been Joe's partner in the medical clinic for almost three years and much preferred working at this small-town clinic to the chaos of the busy Nashville hospital.

"How's Helena feeling? Any better?"

"Not really. She's tough, though. And she knows it's almost over. She's tired all the time, her feet are swelling, and she's eating nonstop, but nothing abnormal." Joe chuckled. "And she likes the excuse to eat anything and everything."

Amanda scoffed. "Joe, that's terrible."

"But true. She knows I love her no matter what, and it's nice to see her not worry about her weight for once."

Amanda shook her head. Helena was one of the most beautiful women she knew, and Amanda wished she wasn't so paranoid about being a couple sizes larger than she thought she should be. As far as Amanda was concerned, Helena was just right. So many women were much too thin.

"Keep telling her that, Joe. And don't let her compare herself to Andi. They may be sisters, but Andi is a former Navy SEAL with a serious exercise regimen."

"True. And we know how Helena feels about her body, which is beautiful by the way. She was so anxious she was going to have twins and never be able to shed the weight. I worry about her."

Amanda's irritation grew, not at Helena but at society. "You tell her that maternal weight gain with twins isn't any more than with a single baby. The babies gain the weight, not the mother. And she's going to need to be healthy to feed both babies, so the weight should be the last thing she worries about."

Joe's eyes widened. "Hold on. What did her last sonogram show? She didn't tell me—"

Amanda laughed. "No, she's not having twins. I'm just saying, if she ever does have twins, she has nothing to worry about."

"Phew. Okay. You scared me. Although, there was nothing like growing up with a twin, and I wouldn't trade it for the world."

Amanda saw the pain in his eyes and knew not a day went by that he didn't think about Jeremy.

Before she could muster some inadequate response, Joe looked at his watch. "I'd better get going. We're having dinner with Andi and Wade tonight."

"I'm right behind you. Have a good night, Joe."

"You, too, Amanda," he called as he headed upstairs where their offices were.

Amanda checked her own watch. She hadn't prepped anything for dinner, and she was starving. She'd drop by Rick's and pick up a burger to take home. Her mouth watered as she walked upstairs to her office to grab her purse. A burger was just what she needed.

***

"Hey, Dr. Pierce. How are you tonight?" Cooper heard Rick say to the doctor on the other side of the bar.

He knew Dr. Pierce a little from dropping off people at the clinic, and she was friends with his brother, but he didn't know her well. She had long auburn hair twisted into a braid that was beginning to loosen so that strands curled around her face. She had hollows under heavy-lidded eyes and must have had a long day. It occurred to Cooper that she may have treated Lacie. He wondered how the young woman was doing. He considered asking, but he was too tired to move from his barstool, and he didn't want to yell across the bar.

"Hey, long day?" Dale laid his hand on his brother's arm.

"Not really. Just another day on the job."

"I heard. Nice rescue. I heard she's going to be okay. She needs surgery for the leg and was dehydrated, but otherwise, she's in good condition. She was lucky."

"Would've been luckier if we'd had a dog. It's taking forever to get the approval."

"Red tape, I'm sure. And funding."

"I've footed the bill for the training and the adoption." He smiled at his brother. "Living rent-free has its perks."

"Evening Chief. What can I get you?" Rick asked Dale.

"Nothing, thanks. Just wanted to check on Cooper."

Cooper felt the usual irritation toward his older,

sometimes meddling sibling.

"I don't need checking up on," he said, not shielding his annoyance.

"I didn't say you did. I saw your truck in the lot and thought I'd let you know what I heard about the girl." He gestured to the beer sitting in front of Cooper on the bar. "Though this is becoming a habit. Having a beer or two after a rescue."

Irritation was replaced by anger. "You trying to say something? Because last I checked, I'm a grown man, well over the age of twenty-one."

Dale shook his head. "Just an observation. You and Trudy still on the outs?"

"We broke up. And it's been weeks. End of story. Not that it's any of your business."

"She's a nice girl," Dale said.

"Yeah, she is, but she's way too young for me. It just wasn't right." He turned to look at his brother. "And how about your love life? Want to share who you're dating these days?"

A look of hurt crossed his brother's features, and he knew he'd crossed a line, but he didn't apologize. Dale held Cooper's gaze for a moment, then shook his head.

"I heard about the rescue. Where she was when you found her. Heard she fell over a cliff onto a ledge." He paused before asking, "You okay?"

Cooper looked away and swallowed before shifting his gaze back to Dale. "Yeah. I'm okay, and I'm sorry for what I just said. That was uncalled for."

Dale nodded. "It's fine. But I mean it. I really was

coming by to check to see how you're doing. That couldn't have been easy for you."

Cooper shrugged and took another drink. "It's part of the job."

Dale stared at his brother for a few moments. "Look, for what it's worth, you did a good job. I'm proud of you. But I'd be a lot happier for you if you had somewhere to go besides a bar and someone to go home to besides me and my kids. I know today must've been hard, and I'm sure it brought back a lot of memories, but I hope it reminded you that you're good at what you do. You save lives. And you deserve to be happy."

"Do I?" Cooper looked at his brother, knowing the answer already, and knowing that he and Dale disagreed on what that answer was.

"You need to let it go, Cooper. Move on. You've spent enough years blaming yourself."

"Yeah, so I've heard. Thanks for the advice." He took another swig of beer. "Don't you have kids to get home to?"

Dale watched him for several moments before speaking. "Don't stay out too late. I don't want you waking them when you get home."

Cooper stared ahead, not looking at Dale. "I won't be long."

Dale stood there for a few minutes more before turning to go. "Don't drive. Call me if you need to. See you later."

Cooper waited until Dale was gone before he placed a handful of bills on the counter and headed toward the door. He shouldn't have said anything to his brother about dating. That was low. Ruth had been gone for almost three years, but Cooper knew Dale was still devoted to her. She was the love of his life, and cancer claimed her too soon.

The evening was cooler than when Cooper first entered the bar. April was almost here, but March had yet to become a lamb, and it still felt more like winter than spring. Another long, cold winter had come and gone, and Cooper was still alone, as he should be. Dale thought he knew what was best, but Cooper didn't deserve happiness or someone to go home to. All Cooper had to go home to were nightmares about a rescue gone wrong, a day he could never get back, a decision he could never change.

***

"This meeting of the Southern Comfort and Aid Society is now in session," Andi said, raising her glass and clinking it with the other women at the table.

Amanda clinked her red wine with Helena's sparkling water and took a sip.

"How are things at the library?" Amanda asked.

Helena groaned. "We aren't getting enough money from the county to purchase all the books being requested. Now that there are a few rentals in town, and businesses are attracting tourists, more people want to use our services. But the town can't afford to give us a anything, though, so I'm spending my weekends going to thrift shops and yard sales trying to build up the inventory, but new releases are few and far between."

"What about grants? Have you tried finding any that support libraries in low-income areas?"

"I'm filling them out, but we don't seem to be getting any." Helena sighed. "And they're getting ready to open that new bookstore on the other side of town, which could be the death of us."

"I don't think so," said Melanie, a nurse at the clinic. "Even with the town growing and people bringing in a little more money, most people don't have the extra money to buy brand new books. Not at the prices they sell for these days. That bookstore will do well with tourists, but you won't lose your base. Besides, you're the only place in town with free internet access and all those programs you run. Even if the bookstore holds a story time, they can't host all the other meetings you do."

"Yes, but the AA group and quilting clubs don't pay to use our meeting rooms, so there's no income there."

"Can Wade and Jackson find the funds?" Melanie asked. "After all, they know lots of people with money. That's what their business is all about."

Andi shook her head. "Their business is about investing in the town, not funding the library."

"What's the difference?" Amanda asked. "Isn't investing in the library the same as investing in the town?"

"She's got a good point," Helena said, elbowing her sister.

"Okay, enough talk about money and investing. I

hear enough of that from Jackson," Cindy broke in. "I've got a new client who wants me to redesign her main bedroom and bath, and I need help convincing her not to go with red and black wallpaper."

All the women groaned and began offering Cindy advice. Amanda sat back and listened, knowing this was out of her wheelhouse. She smiled as she gazed around the table. The women were locals and newcomers, fresh college graduates and established career women, childhood best friends and new additions to the fold. Yet they were all friends, all women who came together to support each other, give advice, lend a hand to help or a shoulder to cry on. These were the women who had welcomed her into their inner circle, and she couldn't be happier than she was at this moment. With her job at the clinic and friends like these, she had everything she could want in life.

***

"Really?" Cooper could hardly believe his ears. He looked at his phone as though they must have the wrong Cooper Mackenzie. "How soon can I get her?"

"You can pick her up today if you want. She's ready to go. The department's already approved it."

Cooper pushed back his chair and leaped to his feet, pumping his fist in the air.

"Finally. I'm on my way." He headed to the sheriff's office, knocked, and opened the door without waiting. "Just got the call that we have a dog. They said you already approved it. I can't thank you enough."

"Don't thank me. You've earned it." Sheriff Beverly Wilson grinned at him. "Go get your girl."

Cooper's cheeks hurt by the time he got to the training facility in Fayetteville. He hadn't stopped smiling the entire way. After showing his credentials, he tried to be patient as he waited to be called.

"Officer Mackenzie?" He stood and looked toward a woman standing by an open door. Suddenly nervous, he wiped his hands on his pants. What if this didn't work? What if she wasn't a good fit or didn't take to him? What if she wasn't good with kids? That was a deal breaker.

"Here," he answered after tamping down his doubts.

"Hi, Officer Mackenzie. I'm Wendy. I'll be working with you and Scout." The blonde, ponytailed woman reached out her hand, and he took it, shaking it vigorously.

"Cooper, please. Did you say Scout?"

"Cooper," she said with a smile. "And yep, Scout. We didn't even name her. I think she has a destiny, Cooper. Come on back."

He followed her, greeted by a wave of barks as they walked between two walls of cages. They stopped near the end, and Wendy turned to Cooper.

"Here she is. She was a rescue. Came from a pretty bad situation, but she has survival instincts and has already proven her intelligence. The shelter recommended her to us right about the time we got the approval from Sheriff Wilson."

Cooper frowned. "Rescued from a bad situation?

How is she with kids?"

"They said she's great with kids. She's just a little… we'll say rambunctious, but that's a great quality with SAR dogs because we want her excited every time you take her out on a job."

"I live with my brother and his kids. You think that's okay?"

Wendy nodded. "I think she'll be fine. She's a good girl." She turned and changed the tone of her voice as she looked in the cage. "Aren't you, sweetie? You're just the best girl."

The dog eyed him warily. She looked like a lab, a well-bred one.

"Is she a purebred?"

"We think so. Yellow lab. Loves to play fetch." Wendy opened the cage door. "Come meet your new best friend, Scout."

The dog scooted away and glued herself to the back wall of the kennel.

"Oh, come on, honey. It's okay. He's one of the good guys."

"What's wrong?" Cooper asked, beginning to doubt this was going to work.

"It's not you. She's afraid of the uniform. But she has to get used to it. Here." She reached into her pocket and pulled out a dog treat, then handed it to Cooper. "Give her this."

Cooper took the bone-shaped treat and reached his hand inside the cage. "Hey, there, Scout. This is for you, girl."

After a moment, Scout leaned toward his outstretched hand and sniffed the treat and then his fingers before moving on to his hand and arm. Cooper carefully stooped down, so he wouldn't seem as threatening, and talked in a low, soothing voice.

"Good girl, Scout. It's okay. We're going to be good friends. Come on, girl. You can take it."

Scout looked past his hand to his face and locked eyes with him. He understood the fear and questions they held, and he smiled, letting her take him in.

Tentatively, she licked the treat then gently took it from his hand.

"Good girl, Scout. Good girl. Want to come out and play?"

After a couple more treats, the dog stood and slowly stepped out of the cage. She sniffed him some more before nudging his hand onto her head for a scratch.

"She likes you," Wendy said. "Now, time for some training."

Four hours later, Cooper pulled into the driveway where two very excited children were jumping up and down, eager to meet the new member of the family. He'd asked Dale not to be in uniform so Scout could get used to him in plain clothes first. Cooper explained the rules to Suzy and Jamie and reminded them that Scout was not a pet, but they could play with her and help with her training as long as Cooper was there, too.

When Cooper got into bed that night, Scout walked around her bedding three times before settling down. Cooper smiled and told her good night. By the time the sun was breaking through the curtains, Scout was stretched out beside Cooper in his bed.

***

The clinic was crazier than ever all week. Amanda couldn't wait to go home on Friday and do absolutely nothing. She prayed for a no-event weekend, but that rarely happened. Her phone buzzed on the way to her car, and she answered with a smile.

"Wade's meeting with Eric to discuss some questions Eric has as the new mayor. Wade said he'd help him out. Alicia and I are lonely. In the mood for pizza and a glass of wine?"

"Always," Amanda said. "I'm leaving work now. Is five minutes too soon?"

"Never. Come on over."

"Need me to pick up anything?"

"Nope. We're all set. See you soon."

Amanda drove straight to Andi's house. Though closer in age to Helena, Amanda was drawn to Andi from the beginning. They quickly became the best of friends, and Amanda was grateful they were in each other's lives. Andi was the first real best friend she'd ever had.

The first thing Amanda did when she got inside the house, besides giving Andi's golden retriever, Boomer, lots of love, was take off her shoes.

"I don't care how comfortable the shoes are in the morning. Nothing feels good by five." She gave Andi a hug and took a seat at the table where she began playing peek-a-boo with Alicia. Andi's daughter was almost two and just graduated to a booster seat.

"I hear you. I don't know how other women wear heels all day. Boomer, leave Amanda alone," Andi said to the eight-year-old golden retriever who was nudging Amanda for more attention.

Amanda felt herself relaxing already, and it was more than the wine. She felt a real kinship with Andi, and it was impossible not to feel good inside this beautiful old house. The large rooms with floor-to-ceiling windows, walls filled with books, and family portraits lining the staircase turned the farmhouse into a home.

"Were you busy today?" Amanda asked. "It looks like a lot of folks were in town."

"We were. It's going to be a beautiful weekend. Lots of hikers and campers out and about."

Amanda frowned. "Which means I won't have a nice, quiet weekend."

"Rough week?" Andi handed her a glass of wine.

"Let me put it this way, I hope this is a freshly opened bottle."

Andi laughed. "It is, and since you're the only one drinking, there's plenty more. I tried to get Helena to come over, but she and Joe had plans, not that she can drink either."

"Yeah, Joe said Helena was looking forward to a night at home."

Amanda smelled the pizza as soon as Andi opened the oven door. Her eyes were fixed on the pie as Andi carried it to the table, her mouth salivating.

"I didn't know how hungry I was until you opened the oven."

Andi laughed. Once she was seated at the table, they said grace and dug into the pizza.

"I saw the books being delivered to the bookstore today," Amanda said after downing almost an entire slice.

"Helena is still a nervous wreck about it, but don't all towns have a library and a bookstore? Cities have a library and dozens of bookstores. When I was at the Academy, I think there were only a few in Annapolis, but I remember Baltimore had tons. And San Diego has at least a dozen. I could spend hours at Bluestocking and never look at my watch. Or my phone. Which says a lot."

"I think there's so much more to the library than just shelves of books. She runs programs and has all those computers, and how many book clubs check out books from the library? Plus, she partners with the schools since they don't have librarians anymore. Whose smart idea was that anyway? No school librarians? Crazy."

"I agree, but the bookstore will still compete, I'm sure. Except they won't have librarians and probably not the school partnership, but who knows?" Andi stopped and answered Alicia's fifteen questions before continuing. "I get why she's nervous, but there will always be people who don't want to buy books. Maybe a few special ones here and there, but for books you're going to read once and then be done with, why buy them when you can get them from the library?"

They moved on to talking about other things

happening in town, the new businesses coming in, and the two hotels that seemed to crop up overnight. They were small, but they were always full, fueled by their proximity to the national park.

Amanda noticed Alicia rubbing her eyes. Her angelic face was covered with sauce, and Amanda couldn't help but smile. She never wanted marriage or kids, but lately, she thought her friends' kids were the greatest things on earth.

"I think this little one is ready for a bath and bed," Andi said. "You want to stick around until I get her down?"

"You know, I'd love to, but it looks like I may not get much rest this weekend. I'd better go home and get however much sleep I can."

She hugged Alicia and gave her a loud kiss. Alicia returned the affection with a sloppy, open-mouthed "kiss" on Amanda's cheek. They said their goodbyes, with more love for Boomer, and Amanda headed out.

The night was still cool for late March, but there was the distinctive, sweet scent of verbena in the air. Spring was coming, and Amanda was ready for it. She inhaled deeply and closed her eyes. Wade and Andi's farm was magical, and Amanda loved everything about the fields, the long, fruit tree-lined driveway, and the gardens that Andi's mother spent a lot of time grooming. She often said it was like spending time with her beloved friend, Blanche Montgomery, once again.

Wade and Andi had a rich history in this town. Their families went back generations, and they had more friends than they could count. Most of them, happily married and beginning to have kids. Amanda had all that, too, back in Nashville, including the family with the big house that went back generations, but nobody in Buffalo Springs knew about that part of her life, and she wanted to keep it that way.

Two

Cooper's phone buzzed, pulling him from the first deep sleep he'd had in over a week. He and Scout had driven to and from Fayetteville every day, giving and receiving signals, running drills, and learning how to work together. It wasn't as much exertion as performing rescues, but it was just as exhausting. They were getting high marks, though, so it was worth it.

He'd taken Scout on a couple night calls, but they didn't require her help—a cliff diver collided with another diver mid-air and needed to be airlifted out, a boater was rescued when his kayak overturned and was washed down river, an intoxicated teenager drowned after jumping from a cliff and not resurfacing, and an older man drove his car over a steep embankment and wasn't able to be saved. Cooper couldn't wait to go to bed and hoped for an uneventful night.

He turned in early. Dale and the kids were doing homework, and it was still light outside, but he craved his bed.

Hours later, Cooper was jolted from sleep. He reached for his buzzing phone and tapped the screen, accepting the call and putting it on speaker as he sat up and rubbed his eyes.

"Cooper here."

"Cooper, we've got a lost child," He recognized Sheriff Wilson's voice. "Wandered off from the tent after her parents fell asleep. The family is camping for the weekend. Mom is frantic. Dad is out looking, but it's dark, and he doesn't know the area."

Cooper let a low moan escape his throat as he tossed back the covers and stood. "Oh, not a kid."

"Yeah, a little one. Time is of the essence, and we need you, Cooper, and your dog."

Cooper was already pulling on his jeans.

"What about my team?"

"Call them. Whatever helps us find this little girl."

Cooper heard the worry in the sheriff's voice. He thought of his niece and how they would feel if she was missing. He crept down the hall.

"Dale, you asleep?"

"I was. What's up?"

"I got a call. Lost kid. Buffalo River Campground. Thought you might want to know." Dale didn't have anything to do with most of Cooper's calls, but sometimes, especially when kids were involved, Dale wanted to help, too.

"I'm up. You call Mom?"

"Nope. Can you?"

"On it."

Cooper went back down the hall to retrieve his shoes. His bed partner was sitting up, panting, and her tail wagged at a breakneck speed.

"Party time," he told her. "This is not a test. Let's see what you can do."

He pulled a shirt over his head and headed toward the bathroom. In under ten minutes, he and Dale were giving their mother a kiss on the cheek as they walked out the door.

Cooper and Dale met the sheriff at the entrance to the campground.

"No sign of her. She's five. The mom thinks she went in search of a bear cub they spotted when they were hiking earlier. She's obsessed with bears."

Cooper blew out a long breath. "Let's hope the mom is wrong."

"You've got this, little brother. Come on." Dale patted him on the back as they headed toward the anxious family, and two more trucks pulled in front of the welcome center.

Sheriff Wilson introduced them. "This is Officer Cooper Mackenzie, Chief Search and Rescue Responder in this area, and his brother, Dale, chief of police in Buffalo Springs. Cooper's going to lead the search to find Evelyn."

Cooper shook their hands. He asked several questions, gathering information about the child. "Do you have anything that smells like Evelyn? Clothing, a favorite stuffed animal?"

The mother nodded. "Yes, just a minute." She retreated to their tent and returned holding a sweatshirt. "This is what she was wearing today. She's in pajamas now. Her shoes are missing, but she doesn't have her jacket." The woman broke down in tears, and her husband put his arm around her.

Cooper took the shirt and held it out for Scout. "Here, girl. This is Evelyn's. We need to find her, okay?"

Scout sniffed the shirt then gave a short, sharp bark, her tail wagging at top speed.

"I'm going to take this with me. We'll be back with your daughter."

He turned to brief Dale and his team, instructing them each where to go. He told Dale to stay with the parents. As a parent, himself, Dale could empathize with them, and he was always calm under pressure.

Cooper let Scout off her leash. It was still dark, but the moon was almost full, and they had already lost too much time. Scout put her nose to the ground and began sniffing. She circled the campsite several times before sitting by a trail and giving her sharp bark.

"Good girl, Scout. Let's go." The dog headed down the trail at a quick but efficient pace, sniffing the ground as she went.

"Evelyn!" Cooper called. "Can you hear me? Your mommy and daddy are looking for you." He listened but only katydids and tree frogs answered him back. He called again, and an owl responded. Cooper smiled. It was as if the animals were calling, too, trying to prompt the little girl into answering.

After thirty minutes of searching and calling, Cooper was beginning to worry. Scout continued sniffing, but every now and then, she stopped, circled the area, and then turned down another trail. Cooper wanted to have confidence in his new partner, but in his mind, he was certain they should have found her by now. How far could a five-year-old go in the dark on her own?

He knew how easy it was to get lost in the woods at night, how easily one could get hurt out here, and how close the river was to the campground, but could she really have gotten that far? A chill ran down his spine at the thoughts racing through his mind. He called again, louder, and he heard the fear in his voice. A nighthawk answered this time, and then the woods fell silent.

The lack of sounds unsettled Cooper as they walked quietly through the woods, the soft wet leaves uttering none of their usual crunches. The silence was deafening. He'd never experienced this before. Not even a single chirp of a cricket could be heard, but then…

Scout barked, and her tail went crazy. She looked to Cooper for a command, and he almost yelled, but forced himself to keep calm as he was trained to do.

"You've got this, Scout. Go!"

Scout took off, and in the silence of the night, Cooper heard a small mewing, like that of a newborn kitten. His heart began to hammer, and his senses went on full alert. He followed Scout, who had picked up her pace. He heard the mewing again, and this time, he knew it was a child crying.

Scout ran right to a hollowed-out tree and sat on the ground, her tail wagging even more. Cooper approached cautiously and softly said, "Good, girl, Scout," before leaning toward the tree.

"Evelyn, is that you? Can you answer me? My dog and I are here to help you. She followed your smell all the way here. Your mommy gave us your shirt, so Scout knew what you smell like."

He took a breath and continued, "I know I'm a stranger, but I really did talk to your mom and dad, and they told me some things about you. I know you're five, you love bears, and you've been camping your whole life. I also know you're brave, and you're not afraid of the dark. Your mommy and daddy would really like for you to go back to the campground. They're worried because they couldn't find you. Will you let Scout and me take you back?" As he spoke, the crying stopped.

"Am I in trouble," a small voice asked.

Cooper smiled. "Well, I can't promise that your mom and dad won't be upset you left the camp, but I promise they'll be relieved that you're okay."

"I'm not supposed to go with strangers."

"That's a really good rule. My name is Cooper, and you're Evelyn, so we aren't total strangers, but you're still right to be careful. What if I call your dad and let you talk to him?"

There were several beats of silence before Cooper saw a small shape emerge from the tree, the moonlight illuminating strands of blonde hair around Evelyn's face.

"Can I pet Scout?"

Cooper smiled at the little girl covered in wet leaves and dirt. Her blonde hair stuck to her face.

"You sure can. She loves kids."

After a few moments of petting Scout, Evelyn turned to Cooper. "Can I talk to Daddy?"

"I'm calling him right now," Cooper told her as he waited for Dale to answer. After a brief assurance that she was okay as far he could tell, he handed her the phone.

Cooper smiled as he listened to Evelyn try to explain that she had wandered off because she needed to go to the bathroom and thought she was big enough to go by herself, then she saw a deer and followed it.

She began to cry as her father spoke on the other end of the phone. She nodded at whatever he said, then handed the phone back to Cooper. He told her father they would be back soon and disconnected. He sent a message to the rest of his team.

"Are you hurt anywhere? Can you walk?"

"I'm not hurt, but I'm scared I'll get lost again."

"How about you hold onto Scout's collar? She won't let you get lost." Evelyn nodded and took hold of the collar. Cooper praised Scout before they headed back to the campground. It wasn't until they were walking through the trees that he realized the symphony of night music had resumed and accompanied them through the forest.

***

"Sorry to do this to you," Cooper told Dr. Pierce when she met him at the clinic. It had started to drizzle, and the once-bright moon was hiding behind a cloud

"It's fine. Part of the job. It's my night on call." She unlocked the door and turned on the lights.

"The family will be here any minute. I'm sure the little girl is okay, and Lucy checked her out on the scene, but her parents wanted her to be seen by a doctor." He looked around the clinic with the same awe that hit him each time he was there. One of his classmates grew up in this house. Cooper had attended birthday parties and sleepovers here. He'd thrown up downstairs when he was fourteen and they were being reckless and stupid.

"I can't get over how different this place is. From the outside, it's still the same house I visited as a kid. From the inside, it's an amazing medical facility."

The doctor nodded and dropped her umbrella into a tall, metal can. "I'm pretty amazed myself. Joe had been here a year when I joined the practice. It was awesome then and is even better now. Of course, after the fire, we made some big changes."

They heard a car, and both turned to look through the window.

"It must've been a nightmare for her parents," the doctor said.

"You have no idea," Cooper told her, all too familiar with the feeling of having a loved one lost in the mountains.

She looked at him with questions in her eyes, but he

turned away. He had his demons to live with, and he didn't share them with anybody. Too many people around knew about them already.

"I told Dale I'd meet the family here so he could get home. Mom's with the kids."

"That was nice of you. I know Dale appreciates all your help."

"Yeah, well." He shrugged. "As soon as the intros are done, I'm heading home, too."

"That's fine," Amanda told him.

After Cooper introduced the family to Dr. Pierce, he said his goodbyes. Before he made it through the door, a small pair of arms encircled his legs. He gently turned and looked down at Evelyn. She gazed up at him with large blue eyes.

"Thank you, Mr. Cooper. And Scout. Thank you for finding me."

Cooper felt his heart melt. He bent down and wrapped the little girl in his arms. She was the same age and size his niece was when she lost her mom, so he attributed his sudden churning of emotions and the moisture in his eyes to that fact.

He let her go and told her to never wander off again. She nodded and promised, and Cooper made a hasty retreat before he revealed even more about himself than anyone had a right to know.

***

Amanda yawned as she slipped back into bed. She'd

alerted Joe and their office manager, Dotty, that she would be in late, so she didn't need to be at work until noon—that was the deal she and Joe had when one was called in overnight. She might sleep until eleven. It wasn't that she was at the clinic long. Evelyn was fine, and the exam was quick and easy, but being awoken in the middle of the night, dressing, hurrying to work, and having to be at the top of her game didn't make settling back down easy.

After locking up and driving home, Amanda tried to calm herself enough to go back to sleep, but she felt wired. She made a cup of chamomile tea, but Amanda was still wide awake by the time she finished the cup while reading a chapter in the cozy mystery Helena recommended. Her mind didn't want to turn itself off. She kept thinking of that little girl, of the fear her parents must have felt, and about the man who rescued her.

Amanda had known Cooper since she first arrived in Buffalo Springs. They were often out with the same crowd. His brother, the chief of police, was best friends with Joe and Wade, and Cooper had gone to school with Helena. He was a great dancer—not that she'd danced with him—and was often taking a turn on the dance floor with one of his former classmates who all seemed to be in love with him. He dated Trudy for a few months, but that seemed to end without drama. He laughed out loud, on the rare occasions he laughed, smiled when he found something to be funny, and enjoyed being part of the crowd—at least he seemed to—but Amanda knew nothing about him other than his family and community ties. The few words about the converted clinic were the most she'd ever heard him say about his personal life. What was his story?

Giving in to another yawn, Amanda closed her eyes and began drifting off to sleep. Cooper's kindness to the little girl was the last thing her mind conjured before the Sandman arrived, but by morning, Amanda had forgotten all about her late-night, wandering thoughts.

***

Cooper dropped into bed and drifted off to sleep. His body was accustomed to almost anything, and sleep came naturally whenever he needed it. That wasn't always the case though. There was a time when he didn't sleep at all. He couldn't avoid the flashbacks to the scene that was always before him, the tortured thoughts that ran through his mind, and the ripping open of his heart.

He wasn't too proud or too macho not to seek help, but even the pills his therapist had prescribed for him didn't help. The only thing that made the difference was work. The more he worked, the more he could try to make up for what happened, for the mistakes he made, and the better he slept at night. Every time he saved a life, he thought he was one step closer to forgiving himself. Only, forgiveness never came.

When the therapist suggested he was ready to move on, to develop a serious relationship, he stopped seeing both the therapist and the woman he was dating. He would decide when and if the day ever came when he was ready to think about something serious. So far, it hadn't happened, and he didn't think it ever would. He'd tried dating, and it led to nothing. The only time he felt anything at all was when he was on the job, when the adrenaline pushed him to do what needed to be done to save whoever needed saving.

Cooper was good at his job. He'd been recognized more than once by SAR, the county, and even the state, but he hated the limelight and tried to maintain his personal privacy as much as possible. He knew what needed to be done to save anyone who was lost, injured, or in danger. What he didn't know how to do was save himself.

***

It was one of those evenings where the sky looked like a Michelangelo masterpiece, reminiscent of the sky on the Sistine Chapel. The clouds billowed on a giant canvas stretching across the vista, and Amanda could almost envision God and Adam lying with their hands reaching toward each other.

She loved these kinds of evenings, this kind of sky. One could look at that sky and know there were no imminent storms, no haze of humidity, just peaceful, pink-tinged clouds, hanging over the pink and orange horizon of the setting sun. On nights like this, Amanda was able to convince herself that everything was perfect in the world.

Things were pretty good in her own world. She had

a nice life. Just not the life she had when she lived in Nashville with its many bars, restaurants, and nightclubs, endless entertainment, and a stream of cowboys—or cowboy hopefuls—flooding every sector of the city and of her life. Where her family's name and influence could open any and every door.

Here, there were a dozen or so men within range of her age, many who were quite older, and most were married or attached to their high school sweetheart for many years. Helena managed to catch the one eligible newcomer to the town, and as Amanda's boss, Joe was off limits anyway. And the last thing Amanda needed or wanted in her busy life was a man to throw her off balance.

Amanda was in awe of Joe, and she knew he admired her intelligence, calm under duress, and knack for picking up things many doctors might miss in a cursory examination. But that was as far as things went between them. Joe had been in love with Helena since the first time he laid eyes on her, and the feeling was mutual. Sometimes, Amanda wished she had someone to look at her the way Joe looked at Helena. But then she thought of all the hours she put in, the middle-of-the-night calls, the exhaustion she experienced most evenings, and she knew she didn't have room in her life for love or even dating. And she had no desire to be tied down by marriage and children. Her career kept her busy and satisfied enough.

She was content as she walked down the sidewalk, that masterpiece of sky overhead, but continued thinking about her life and family back in Tennessee. Her father was larger than life, a brilliant surgeon and rising star at Vanderbilt University Medical Center from the time he was a student there, and Amanda grew up wanting to do nothing less than continue his legacy.

Of course, being a general practitioner in a small-town clinic wasn't exactly living up to that goal, but goals changed, and within a very short time, Amanda knew she wasn't cut out to be a big city doctor. Nor did she want to live in the shadow or the world of her family. She liked the ebb and flow of the quiet clinic where she was almost anonymous and could go from an annual checkup to a long labor and delivery, and then on to assessing a stroke victim. Joe had done the town justice by creating a clinic that had the means to handle just about any medical need, and he aligned himself with doctors and hospitals who were always ready to accept any patient at Joe's word and trusted that his diagnosis or presumption was within the inner ring if not the bullseye of the medical dart board.

"Hello, Mrs. Swanson. How are the twins feeling today?" Amanda asked the thirty-something mom of six when they met outside the Save-A-Lot.

"They're much better. Thank you. I'm so glad it was nothing more than a spring cold. Ever since the world fell apart, I panic every time someone sneezes."

Amanda frowned. "Maybe you should talk to someone about your anxieties. I can set you up—"

"Oh, no need for that. I got plenty of people around to talk to. I just don't want to go through that again."

Amanda forced a smile. "None of us do." She'd begun to wonder if Jess Swanson needed professional help. She always seemed to be at her wit's end, but maybe having six children did that to a person, especially one so young.

"Well, if you ever need anything, please don't hesitate to call or stop by the clinic. We have wonderful counseling services now that Bethany has joined our medical team."

The woman grimaced. "Thanks, but I'm good."

Amanda watched as she walked away, irritated that there was still a stigma attached to getting professional help for one's mental health.

"Amanda, just the person I was hoping to see."

As she turned, Amanda saw Helena coming out of the store, her arms full of bags.

"Can I help you?" She rushed over to her friend.

"No, I've got them. Thanks."

"Are you sure?" Amanda noticed how the bags were perched over Helena's protruding stomach.

"Yes, I'm parked right there." She gestured with her head, and Amanda followed her to the SUV parked in the first space in the lot.

"At least let me get the door for you." Amanda opened the hatch and reached out to prevent the bags from falling as Helena slid them into the back of the vehicle.

"Thanks. So…" Helena blew blonde, corkscrew curls out of her eyes. "Joe and I are having an end-of-winter celebration this weekend, and we'd love for you to come." She looked up and frowned. "Hopefully, the rains don't last. Tonight's a beautiful night, but the weatherman says the next few days will be a washout. Let's hope Saturday is clear. Can you make it?"

Helena often talked like that, moving from one topic to another without taking a breath. Amanda was used to it and smiled.

"That sounds like fun. I wonder why Joe didn't mention it at work today."

Helena smiled, her eyes twinkling with glee. "Because he doesn't know about it yet. But once he does, he'll be all for it."

Amanda laughed, knowing Helena wasn't wrong. "Okay, then. What can I bring?"

"Your delicious potato salad that nobody can ever get enough of."

"I'll make a double batch," Amanda promised.

"Great. Andi's going to bring a pie, of course. She doesn't know that either, but she will."

"Your sister's pies are reason enough to be there. What else do you need?"

"Absolutely nothing. Everyone will bring something, and it will all come together perfectly."

"Well, you are the town's queen of organization, so I don't doubt you."

Helena grinned broadly. "Thanks. Now, I've got to get these groceries home and put away before tonight's meeting. It's almost April, and Memorial Day will be here before you know it. We've got to get working on the parade and decorations before time gets away from us."

With a quick goodbye, Helena was in the car and pulling into the street. Amanda was exhausted just listening to her. Even several months pregnant, Helena hadn't slowed down.

Amanda found herself thinking about the party as she opened the front door to the little house she'd bought just off Main Street. She supposed all the usuals would be there, and that was fine with her. The longer she lived in Buffalo Springs, the more she fell in love with the town and its citizens.

***

A scream broke the silence of the first clear evening, and Cooper went on high alert. He jumped and ran toward the house only to be knocked out of the way when the back door flew open and two menaces to the community ran into the yard. Then the barking started as Scout leapt and twirled, tying to be part of the game. The barking and screaming continued until Cooper felt he and the neighbors had had enough.

"Hey!" he shouted. "What the heck is going on here?"

Suzy came to an abrupt halt, and Jamie skidded to a stop behind her. Both turned their eyes on their uncle. Scout immediately laid down and covered her eyes with her paws. *Where did she learn that?* Cooper wondered, suppressing a grin.

"He took Angelina," Suzy said indignantly.

"She took my Switch," came Jamie's defiant reply.

"Because he wouldn't give me back Angelina."

"I don't have your stupid rabbit."

"You do, too. I know you took her."

The level of animosity went higher with each response.

Jamie shook his head. "I don't care about your rabbit. I just want my Switch back."

Cooper looked from one to the other. He knew they were stir crazy from all the rain, but he was exhausted and didn't want to deal with their restlessness.

"Suzy, give Jamie back his Switch."

Suzy crossed her arms with the handheld gaming device clutched to her chest. She vehemently shook her head no and pursed her lips.

"Not until he tells me where Angelina is."

Through gritted teeth, Jamie told her, "I don't know where she is. I told you that. You just won't believe me."

Cooper sighed. "Bean, why would Jamie have your rabbit?"

"My rabbit has a name, and he took her just to bug me."

Twelve-year-old Jamie rolled his eyes but spoke calmly and lovingly to his sister, more mature than most kids his age. "Suzy, I didn't take her, and I wouldn't take her just to bug you. You know that."

Suzy narrowed her gaze at him. "Then where is she?"

Cooper shook his head. Kids! Why did anyone want to deal with this? He looked at his nephew, a good boy who always looked out for his sister and never made waves.

"Any idea where your sister's rabbit might be hiding?"

"No. None. Honestly. I wouldn't take her rabbit. I know how much it means to her."

They all knew. Though Suzy, at eight, was too old to carry her rabbit everywhere, they all understood her need to have the stuffed toy close by. Suzy's mother had given her the rabbit right before she found out about the cancer. Even three years later, Suzy struggled with her mother's absence. She acted and talked much younger than her age, and she attached herself to any adult who looked her way. She was in therapy, but Bethany said Suzy needed to let go in her own time.

"When is the last time you had Angelina?" Cooper asked.

"This morning when Grandma was here."

"Suzy," Jamie said in a calm voice. "Didn't you spill milk on Angelina when you were eating lunch?"

Cooper tried not to crack a smile at Suzy's serious, thoughtful expression.

"Yes, and then Grandma told me to go outside and play while she cleaned her off."

Jamie looked up at Cooper and nodded. "I'll be right back."

He headed into the house, and Suzy spun around, close on his heels. Cooper and Scout followed them through the kitchen, down the hall, and into the middle bathroom where the laundry closet was. Jamie opened the dryer and stuck his head inside.

"Aha," he proclaimed triumphantly as he pulled the pink ball of fluff from the dark interior of the dryer. "Mystery solved!" Jamie declared as Suzy grabbed the rabbit and hugged it fiercely.

"I'm home!" Dale called from the front of the house.

"It's about time," Cooper muttered. "Coming!"

They trudged down the hall, and Dale greeted them with a curious smile.

"What's going on?" he asked.

"I'm never, ever having kids," Cooper said.

"That bad?" Dale frowned, following his brother to the kitchen, not disguising the humor in his voice.

Cooper shook his head. "No, but I'm not cut out for this. Too much drama and too much mess."

"No comment," said Dale, eyeing Cooper's dirty hiking boots by the door.

"Hey, I moved in to help you out. I pick up after myself. Most of the time."

"But you don't do much else."

"Who needs to with Mom here all the time?"

"You drive me crazy."

"But I'm good at keeping dinner hot. Let's eat," Cooper said, pulling the already hot casserole from the oven.

"Sounds good. Then we can talk about your disdain for kids and your lack of help around the house."

Cooper rolled his eyes and told the kids to set the table. They did so without protest. He supposed they weren't so bad after all. He had to admit, Jamie and Suzy were pretty special, and he loved them fiercely.

Three

Saturday morning sun had given way to afternoon showers, and Amanda pulled the hood of her raincoat over her head as she headed toward the door, potato salad in hand. Joe and Helena's house was typical of a small-town house with a front porch with a white picket fence. There was nothing on the outside that made it stand out. However, the inside was remarkable.

The Tuscan themed kitchen alone was extraordinary, and Amanda never ceased to be amazed that Joe had designed it himself. The marble countertops gleamed in the sunlight—when there was sunlight—that streamed through the three windows fanning the large farmhouse sink. The deep windowsills were laden with pots of herbs, and between huge drawers and large cabinets were a double oven and a gas stovetop. A very large refrigerator was nestled between floor-to-ceiling pantries. There was even a bread warmer beneath the cooktop. Wooden beams lined the ceiling where recessed lights shone down on the counter. Flowers adorned the beautiful wooden table that Joe had refinished himself after reclaiming it from a yard sale he and Helena stopped by. It made Amanda's kitchen look even older and shabbier than it was.

After dropping off her potato salad and being shooed from the kitchen by Joe and Andi—ironically, Helena didn't know her way around a kitchen—Amanda made her way to the large, stonewall gathering room which opened to an enormous, covered patio. Helena's brother, Jackson, was flipping steaks on the grill while his fiancé, Cindy, gave him a hard time about overcooking them. Already prepared gardens were ready to be planted with veggies and flowers.

"Hey, Amanda," Helena called. She held a tray of tall glasses filled with what Amanda suspected was Southern Comfort and lemonade, their group's signature drink. "Here you go," she said, handing one to Amanda.

"No, thanks," Amanda said, trying to hide her disdain for the drink. "I'm going to start with water."

"Suit yourself," Helena said as she walked back toward the kitchen

Suzy chased Alicia and Paige's toddler, Hope, around the covered patio as Amanda made her way over to Paige and Allie. She took a seat in one of the chairs on the patio and sighed with contentment.

"This is what weekends were made for," she said to her friends. "Even if it is raining."

"You're not kidding," Paige said. "I spent all week

putting together summer marketing campaigns for clients, and I'm so happy to be outside and not staring at a computer screen. I don't even care what the weather is."

"I'm just happy we have a good group of kids running the shop so I can down this drink and enjoy myself," Allie said, taking a long sip of her spiked lemonade.

"How are sales this spring?" Amanda asked.

"The best yet," Allie told her. "If it keeps up, I'll be able to buy out my investor by the end of the summer, but I still expect free marketing and free custom designs."

"Always," Paige promised. "I'll be happy to not have to worry about two businesses."

"I see lots of visitors wearing your t-shirts," Amanda told them. "I think the ones with Sasquatch and Gowrow are a big hit."

Allie laughed. "Who knew that shirts with a fabled wingless dragon who preys on livestock and small animals would be such a hit with tourists."

Amanda shrugged. "People love local lore."

They sat in contentment, watching the kids chase each other and inhaling the scent of the steaks and pure mountain air, while the spring shower fell just beyond their reach. Every now and then, Paige called out to the kids while her husband, Jimmy, talked college football with Allie's fiancé. Both men were relative newcomers and worked in sales and hospitality in the new hotel that opened in town the previous year.

Dale and Cooper sat at a table just inside the house, deep in conversation, and Amanda wondered what they were talking about. Before she could hazard a guess, Cooper reached into his pocket, took out his phone, and stood. He hurried to Helena and said something before quickly disappearing down the hallway toward the front door.

"Another rescue underway," Paige said.

"Is he always on call?" Amanda asked.

"Pretty much. He's the lead responder, so he's always busy. He prefers working to sitting around, so he's happy whenever he gets a call."

"Have you two always been close?" Amanda asked.

Paige made a noise of agreement. "Yeah. Everyone in our family is close, but Cooper and I are closest in age, so we've always been there for each other."

"And you're first cousins?"

Paige shook her head. "Third, but like I said, we've always been there for each other." She took a drink. "I worry about him though. He's so into his job that he never has time for anything else."

"Don't you think that's why he's so into his job? So he doesn't have time to think about other things?" Allie asked.

"Probably," Paige said. "I mean, after what happened, he's kind of kept everyone at an emotional distance. Even Dale and the kids, until Ruth passed. I don't even talk to him as much as I used to unless we're all out together, and that rarely happens anymore." She gestured to her daughter and smiled.

"What happened to Cooper?" Amanda asked.

Allie and Paige exchanged a look before Paige opened her mouth to answer.

"Dinner's ready!" Helena called. "Come on in and fill your plates while it's hot."

Paige jumped up to find her daughter, and Allie headed inside. They were both gone before Amanda could stop them.

So, something had happened that made Cooper close himself off from others. That would explain why he never talked about himself. Amanda wondered briefly what it could have been, but the topic was soon forgotten once she followed the others into the house.

***

"Two boys, Tommy and Billy, one nine and the other ten. They were supposed to be at home, but their parents were both at work, so nobody was watching them." Sheriff Wilson shook her head. "Nine and ten. Jeez. They should never have been left alone. Anyway, it looks like they rode their bikes out here and then hiked. We found one backpack by the river, soaked through. It has Tommy's name on it. No sign of the boys though."

Cooper frowned. "The river is raging today. All that rain the last few days really caused a lot of swelling."

"At least the rain is lighter today. It could be worse."

Cooper nodded. "I suppose, but missing kids and a swollen river are pretty bad no matter the weather."

When the dispatcher called Cooper about the

missing boys, he relayed the information to the rest of the team. They met at the Emergency Operations Center, quickly gathered their equipment, and assembled at the bank of the river where the backpack was found. Cooper laid out a map and went over the grid, praying someone would find the boys on high ground, safe and sound. Before they could fan out, his radio went off.

"Hikers spotted someone in the water. Looks like a kid. Moving fast." The dispatcher gave the coordinates, and Cooper sent Danny and Mike downstream on foot, following the grid pattern he laid out. Kevin and Rob would take the upper district of the park. Cooper went to the back of his truck and patted Scout, still in her crate. "Not today, girl. Next time." He gave her a treat and hightailed it to the closest open field to wait for his airlift.

As soon as he and Lucy were in the chopper, they heard from Lance who operated the drone. "I see one of them. He's holding onto a limb in the middle of the river. He's not going to be able to hold on for long." He relayed directions.

Cooper radioed back. "Can anyone get to him?"

"River's running pretty fast," Lucy said. "Danny and Mike aren't going to make it down there in time to grab him before he's forced to let go."

"Don't let anyone do anything risky," Cooper commanded. "We're on the way in the bird."

He gave instructions to Bud, the pilot, and they flew over trees and mountains, watching the water below until they saw people. Cooper zeroed in on the boy just as he lost his grip and was washed downstream. Cooper's heart leapt in his chest, like he'd had the wind knocked out of him. The chopper followed the boy's movements until he barreled into a downed tree. Cooper winced, feeling the impact in his own body.

On Cooper's command, Bud lowered the chopper, and Cooper dropped slowly from the sky, holding onto the cable that tethered him to the chopper. He kept an eye on the kid and silently asked St. Bernard to keep the boy pinned to the tree until Cooper could reach him. When his body hit the river, the full force of the water pushed him against the tree. The boy looked up at him, terror in his eyes, his face a cross-section of scratches and lacerations.

Cooper motioned to the boy what they had to do, and the boy nodded, but his face was flooded with terror. When Cooper had him secured to the tether and himself, he looked up at Lucy to pull them from the water, and they rose into the air, twisting and turning as they were pulled toward the chopper. Cooper felt a wave of relief when Lucy buckled the kid into the seat and laid a blanket over him before checking his vitals.

But they weren't finished yet.

Three hours later, Cooper sat on the bank farther down the river while a mother screamed and a father cursed the world, the heavens, and himself. One boy had been treated in the back of an ambulance before leaving for the clinic, and the other would be leaving in a black bag.

And that was the real reason Cooper didn't want

kids. He'd seen too much of this. Too many adventures gone wrong.

After all was said and done, and his paperwork had been filed, Cooper found himself huddled in a pew in a darkened church, illuminated only by the flickering, red prayer candles. With his head in his hands, he wept for the boy, for his brother and parents, and for all the others Cooper hadn't been able to save. Among them was Jessie, the one that hurt the most.

***

When she walked out into the cool, dark night from the brightness of the clinic, Amanda stopped and took a long, deep breath before opening her umbrella. She glanced up and down the empty streets and let the sound of the rain and the way it glistened in the streetlights overtake her. There was something about a light rainfall that always soothed her, and she needed soothing tonight.

She never minded being on call and pulling her weight, but it was beginning to wear on her. Her heart ached as she thought about the family she'd spent the past couple hours with. Aside from all the scratches and lacerations Amanda treated, Tommy needed x-rays, but he was hysterical, and she ended up having to sedate him. If she could have, she would've sedated his mother, too. Her keening echoed through the building like a dying animal, but Amanda couldn't blame her.

Cases like this were exhausting, mentally and

physically. The town and the area were becoming more popular, and they were suddenly in the throes of all the drama and craziness of other busy, summer tourist towns. It didn't help that their clinic was the closest to the national park and all the outdoor enthusiasts it lured. The clinic didn't have the means or the horsepower to deal with all that was demanded of it.

Amanda took a step and wobbled. She was beat from the hectic days and too many night calls. It seemed that every emergency in the past month had taken place on her night, and while she didn't blame Joe or resent his luck, she didn't know how much more she could take. They needed a physician's assistant to take a turn, but they were just beginning to take applications.

Steadying herself, Amanda made her way toward her house, her body on alert as she walked in the dark, though it was a moderately quiet town. There wasn't much crime in Buffalo Springs, though she was aware of the town's dubious past. Drug rings, shady officials, and corrupt cops had led to the town's tarnished reputation, but that had been dealt with. A few crazies here and there, including Joe's ex-fiancé, had added to the stains on the town's patchworked history, but things were much better now. Most nights, Amanda didn't give a thought to walking home after dark, but tonight, something felt off. It was probably the lack of sleep, her tired mind playing tricks on her, or the memory of the mother's wails for her child.

As she turned a corner, a hawking figure stepped into her path, and Amanda let out a scream as the man reached out and grabbed onto her. She tried to fight him, but his grip was too strong. Suddenly, a dog started barking, and Amanda was in even more fear for her life.

"Dr. Pierce, it's me," the man said, his voice vaguely familiar to her wearied mind. "It's Cooper Mackenzie. I'm not going to hurt you. Scout, heel." The dog backed off and sat.

As the blood pounding through her veins began to slow, and her heart sought a normal rhythm, Amanda let out a breath. Cooper relaxed his grip.

"I'm sorry if I scared you. I didn't see you, and I almost knocked you down." He locked eyes with her. "Are you okay? You don't look well. Do you need to sit?"

Amanda shook her head. "Sorry, I'm fine. Startled, but fine. Just tired. Really, really tired."

He nodded. "I'm sure. We've had a lot of rescues lately, and you're at the clinic all day."

She smiled. "Yeah, and I always seem to get the most patients when it's my night on call."

"I noticed that. You've had to handle all my rescues in the past month. What's up with Joe? Why are you working all the odd hours?"

She gave her head a quick shake. "It's not like that. Like you said, your rescues are all taking place when I'm on call. We're spending too many late nights and weekends together."

Through her haze of fatigue, she realized how that sounded and felt herself blush. She was suddenly grateful for the dark and shadows.

After a moment of silence, Cooper released a quiet laugh. "Well, that's one I've never heard before."

The admission made her heart pick up its pace once again, and this time, it wasn't due to fear. She took a step back and inhaled sharply.

"I'm sorry. I'm so tired. I don't even know what I'm saying. I need to get some sleep."

"You are tired. I understand. We'll get you home and in bed."

His words startled her, and she recognized the signs she should have picked up on—the glazed eyes, the hollows in his cheeks, the lazy curl of his lips. She took another step back.

"You're drunk."

He shook his head. "No, I'm not. Honestly. Sometimes I hit the bar for a drink after a rescue, but not always. Even then, it's only one, despite what my brother thinks. Most of the time, I wallow in my sorrows in a different kind of low-lit building where sinners go when they need someone to listen."

Amanda was confused. "I'm sorry. I don't understand."

He turned his head slightly, and she realized they were standing in front of the church. She'd seen him there before, inside, with the rest of this family.

"Oh," she said quietly. "I'm sorry. I didn't mean to offend you."

"Stop apologizing. That's the fourth time you've said you're sorry in the past five minutes, and you've yet to do anything wrong."

"I'm sorry—" She looked at him, and they both laughed. "I'm not sorry, I'm just—"

"Tired," he said for her. "I know. So am I. Darned tired. Let's get you home. It's late, and it's dark. I'll walk you to your house. Come on, Scout."

A sudden wave of something—she wasn't sure what—swirled through her, and she felt dizzy. She wobbled again, and he caught her. The feel of his hand on her arm only intensified the strange sensation. When he let her go, a cold shiver run through her, and she wrapped her arms around herself.

"Wow, you really are tired."

"I am." It was then that a sudden thought hit her. "Have you always had a dog?"

"No, Scout and I are new partners. She's the one who found the little girl a week back."

Amanda smiled and said hello to Scout. "I would pet her, but I'm not sure I would be able to stand back up once I stooped down to reach her."

Cooper laughed a rich, comforting laugh, and she chastised herself for misreading him just minutes before.

"Come on. Let's make sure you get home okay. It's the least I can do after depriving you of some much-needed rest over the past couple weeks." He took her free arm and looped it through his own.

She managed a feeble "thank you" as unexpected shock waves ran from his arm to hers, emanating throughout her body.

I must be more tired than I thought.

She didn't know Cooper very well, which must be

why she had these feelings. He was practically a stranger, and her body was reacting to this stranger boldly taking her arm.

When they reached her house, Cooper walked her to the door and waited for her to make it inside. She thanked him again and closed the door, locking it behind her. As she collapsed against the cool wood, she heaved a long, slow breath, letting the exhaustion take over completely. It didn't take long for her to fall asleep that night, oblivious to the tall, muscular man in her dreams.

***

On the day of the fire, Cooper awoke feeling like the luckiest man on earth. He never thought he would be the first of his friends to buy a ring, but as he sat up in bed and opened his nightstand drawer, he couldn't help but smile. The diamond sparkled in the morning light and his heart did a backflip.

Cooper and Jessie were working the same shift at the station, and the thought of seeing her made getting out of bed worth the effort. His muscles ached from the strenuous day before, but they loosened during his hot shower. He hummed a song to himself as he shaved and winked at his own reflection. He had reservations at their favorite restaurant in Eureka Springs that evening, and he hoped for an uneventful day. Or not. He and Jessie were both addicted to the chase, and it fueled their relationship.

The crackle of the radio was harsh in the quiet of the

morning. Cooper froze, his t-shirt pulled just over his head, his chest and abs exposed to the cool morning air. He wrestled with his shirt as he grabbed the radio off its charger and listened.

"Campfire gone wild," was what he heard, but the magic of Christmas morning was what he felt. This was what he lived for.

"How wild?" he asked.

"Wild enough to be a problem," his chief responder told him. He rattled off the details as Cooper finished dressing.

"Our orders?"

"Assist as needed. Possible campers still in the area. Some Boy Scouts doing an early morning hike. The fire started just before dawn but quickly gained momentum. There wasn't time to send any warnings."

Cooper knew how quickly fires spread and how easy it was to miss that opening to save lives. He wasn't a firefighter, but he worked closely with them and had friends who volunteered. Much of his training was the same as theirs, but Cooper knew how to search and find, and that's what was needed.

"On my way. Will see you all at the EOC." He hoped they'd have a full team waiting at the Emergency Operation Center Mike and Rob could already be at the scene as firefighters. Lance would be at work, and the new girl, Lucy, worked the ambulance when needed.

He raced through the house, grabbing his boots and coat. Within less than ten minutes, he was enroute to the EOC for what would be the worst day of his life.

***

"Wake up, Coop. I have to get to work."

Cooper woke, disoriented, and blinked several times. He recognized his room in his brother's house and knew that his trip to the past was over. He was grateful for that.

The pitter patter of feet pounded the floorboards outside his door, but he didn't have enough time to brace himself before Suzy was on top of him. Thinking it was a game, Scout followed suit, licking him in the face.

"Get up, Uncle Cooper. Daddy said you'd take us hiking." Suzy tugged at his arm in an effort to pull him from the bed. She smelled vaguely of sweet yogurt and coffee. Dale had given in again, indulging her with something her mother would never have allowed.

Cooper shot Dale a look. "He did, huh?"

"Yep. And he said we could take Scout."

Another look and this time, an annoyed "Hmph."

"Can we take Scout?"

"Yes, we can take Scout. She needs to learn the area anyway."

"Yay!" Suzy yelled, pulling Scout's face toward her so the little girl was lavished with sloppy dog kisses.

"Heading out," Dale said from the doorway, putting on his chief's hat.

"Bye, Daddy," Suzy said, giving her full attention to the dog.

"You're too big to be jumping on Uncle Coop's bed, Suzy." Dale leaned down and gave her a kiss, his hat shifting on his head. "Get down and go finish your breakfast." He watched her leave, then turned back to his brother. "Don't lose them."

"Seriously?" Cooper asked, only mildly annoyed. The kids could disappear faster than a chipmunk scuttling across the road. Dale gave him a hard look and left without another word.

Cooper shook his head and pulled himself from bed. He needed to shower and shave, but he knew the kids had zero patience. A splash of cold water and clean shirt would have to do for now.

Two hours later, backpacks hoisted on their shoulders, Cooper, Suzy, and Jamie scampered over the top of the rock that provided one of the best views in the Ozarks, at least in his opinion. Scout stayed next to Cooper the whole time, much to Suzy's dismay. Cooper had to remind her several times that Scout was a working dog, not a pet, but Suzy didn't understand the difference. Sometimes, Cooper wasn't sure he did either.

"Uncle Coop," Suzy asked. "Do you think Mommy can see us better when we're this close to Heaven?"

His heart cracked a bit as it did each time one of the kids asked a question about their mother.

"I think your mom can see you perfectly wherever you are."

They stood in silence and gazed across the expanse of mountains and valleys framed by a display of freshly bursting colors. Unlike the rest of the world, Cooper much preferred the view in the spring to that of the fall. In autumn, he always saw yellow, orange, and red flames dancing against the cerulean sky, and it took several blinks of his eyes before the fire was replaced by a skyline of trees standing tall in their fall glory. Now, delicate blossoms of pink, purple, and white were just beginning to show themselves on the trees, and there were no phantom flames on the horizon.

Cooper thought about Suzy's question. Could Jessie see them, too? What did she see? Anything? What did she know? Was she able to transcend space and time? Did she know, could she feel, how incomplete his life was, how incomplete he was, without her? Did she know how often she was in his dreams, the wind from the fire blowing through her hair, the way the flames danced in her eyes as she turned away, promising him she'd be okay? He'd let her go. Alone. Against his better judgement. It was his fault she wasn't there now, enjoying a beautiful springtime hike. Cooper swallowed and gave his head a shake.

"You okay?" Jamie asked, and it took a moment for Cooper to realize his nephew was addressing him.

"Yeah, I'm fine. Why?"

Jamie shrugged. "Nothing. You just looked…I don't know. Like you were somewhere else."

Not somewhere. Sometime. But the kids didn't need to know about that. Jamie was a little kid back then, and Suzy was only a toddler.

"Just admiring the view." He managed a smile and patted Jamie on his head. By next year, Jamie would be almost as tall as his uncle. Not as tall as Dale, but that would probably come in time. Cooper wasn't short, but Dale had him beat in the height department. Jamie was going to take after his father for sure.

"Better head back," he told the kids. "It still starts getting dark kind of early these days, and your father will kill me if I don't have you out of the woods before sunset."

They meandered through the national park, retracing their steps while hoping for glimpses of deer. They played their familiar game of trying to name the trees. Despite his complaints and claim that he didn't like kids, there were times in his life when Cooper allowed himself to think that they were his kids, his and Jessie's. The thought used to make his heart ache, but as time went by, he used the mind game to help himself cope with the loss of all that ought to have been. For just a few moments in time, he had it all.

When they got home, Cooper sat in the car and watched as the kids ran up the porch steps to their father. Cooper loved his niece and nephew with all his heart. He loved his brother, too. They all meant the world to him. But that didn't mean he never suffered from pangs of envy. Both men had lost the women they loved, but at least Dale had the kids. Cooper had nothing but dreams of fire and the guilt that he had failed at the one thing he was born to do.

Four

The morning sky on the opening day of the farmer's market that first Saturday of April was a brilliant kaleidoscope of rich hues in pink, purple, orange, and blue as the rising sun tumbled the colors together. Amanda shed her earbuds to take in all the sounds of the glorious morning as she marveled at the scene over the silhouette of the mountains. This was her favorite thing about Buffalo Springs. The crisp mountain air, the lush terrain, and the peaks that jutted into the clouds provided the most beautiful backdrop for her morning run. That is, on the mornings she had the energy to run.

There had been no emergencies on any of her on-call nights that week, and she felt like a human again with fast-paced days and long, uninterrupted nights. Her mood was enhanced by the news that they were beginning the interviews for the physician's assistant. Amanda was also pushing for a nurse practitioner, and

Joe seemed to be warming to the idea.

Amanda ran for a solid hour and was rounding the bend that led back into the town when she spotted the first tent being raised in the park. The weekly farmer's market was a big deal in Buffalo Springs, and opening day was always widely attended. Local artists and artisans would set up their wares in the park, and there would be food and games for all ages. The market, established by Helena and Andi several years prior, had grown substantially, but no day was bigger than opening day.

Rather than working inside, Amanda and Joe would set up an outdoor clinic along with a table displaying information about their services. It still amazed Amanda how many people in the town didn't understand the importance of annual wellness checks, mammograms, and prostate screenings. And the number of citizens who still smoked was staggering. The clinic's staff was doing its best to relay healthy messages to everyone and get them into the clinic for check-ups, but it was not easy.

She picked up her pace as she neared the street where her little house stood and gave it her all on her last push toward home. Once she made it to her front porch, she stopped and took several deep breaths to slow her heart rate before going into her stretches. She was bent in a long stretch, reaching for her right foot when she heard someone call her name.

"You're out early," Andi said with a smile as she approached.

"A run at sunrise is my favorite way to start my day."

"You and me, both," Andi agreed.

Amanda did one more calf stretch before motioning toward the door. "Coffee is next. Want to join me?"

"I'd love to, if you don't mind."

"Not at all. I'd love to catch up. My life has been crazy lately."

"Yours? Try wrestling a two-year-old every morning in between trips to the bathroom."

Amanda gave Andi a knowing smile. "Already?"

Andi nodded with a long sigh. "Yeah. Earlier than with Alicia. I had hoped to skip the morning sickness this time."

"It might not last as long as before. Every pregnancy is different."

Andi wasn't even showing yet, and Amanda had just confirmed her second pregnancy the week prior.

"From your mouth to God's ears," Andi said as she took a seat at Amanda's kitchen counter.

"Joe says Helena is starting to nest."

Andi nodded. "Yeah, which is funny to see. You know, she's not the greatest housekeeper."

Amanda laughed. "I know. But you never know. Motherhood can change that."

"Or make it worse," Andi said. "My house has never been so messy."

"Well, you are running a business, chasing a toddler, and helping Wade transition from mayor to business owner."

Amanda admired the entire Nelson family. Andi was a former Navy SEAL who now owned a sinfully good bakery, and Helena was the head librarian and consummate volunteer, heading every cause in town. Andi's husband, Wade, and her brother, Jackson, had opened an investment firm utilizing Wade's law license and Jackson's business degree to lure more investors and business owners to Buffalo Springs. They were all such go-getters.

Amanda placed a mug of decaf in front of Andi then took her own mug from under the Keurig spout and sat down at the table where she'd already placed a pint of cream and bowl of sugar.

"At least I have a nanny," Andi said. "Hopefully Joe's sister will help Helena finish getting ready for the baby," Andi said as she stirred a small drop of cream into her coffee. "I don't know what she'll do once she's on her own."

"What every other mother does," Amanda said, though her own mother had a host of help at her beck and call. "Joe said Serena's arriving in a couple weeks. He's excited she'll be staying with them for a while."

"So is Helena. They really love each other, have ever since Joe first took Helena home to meet the family. They're total opposites, but they really hit it off."

"Joe says Serena is meticulously clean and obsessively organized."

"Like I said, total opposites. Helena's good at organizing, you know," Andi said thoughtfully. "I mean, look at how well she runs the library. She's just not good at organizing her own living space. She's getting better, but their house is definitely not her workplace."

"Why hasn't she ever asked Cindy to help?"

"Cindy organized their house beautifully when they lived together, but Cindy has so many clients now, and she's still finishing her degree. She really doesn't have time to take on anyone or anything else. Plus, they've got the wedding to plan."

"Still no date?"

"No, but that might change once Serena hits town. I'm sure every engaged woman within miles will want to pick her brain."

Amanda took a sip of her coffee and offered Andi a piece of cinnamon bread. "It's from the best bakery in town," Amanda told her with a grin.

"No thanks," Andi told her. "But you just reminded me we've got an order for a fancy birthday cake that I need to get done before I start taking stuff out to our tent." She looked at her watch. "Wade and the guys did their own early morning run, and I've got to pick up Alicia. She spent the night at my parents' place. I'm sure Mama is about to text me, asking why my run is taking so long. If she knew I was pregnant again, she'd have a fit. She hates that I keep it up while I'm pregnant."

"Tell her your doctor approved it."

They said their goodbyes, and Amanda went to shower before going to the park. She was looking forward to meeting Joe's sister, the famous Serena Blake of Serena's Celebrations. She could only imagine what Serena, planner of weddings for everyone who is anyone, would think of their little town of Buffalo Springs.

Amanda was drying her hair with a towel when she

realized she should've asked Andi about Cooper. Andi would know what his story was. Dale and Wade were best friends. And Amanda was strangely curious.

She frowned at her reflection in the mirror. Why did she care? Cooper was obviously not the right person to get involved with. And she didn't exactly have time to date anyway. Still, she was curious. Maybe she'd have another chance to ask, and if not, she supposed it didn't really matter after all.

***

Cooper stretched and let his heart rate return to normal while he waited for Wade, Dale, and Joe to join him in the parking lot of the Buffalo River National Park. It was rare that he was able to run with them, and he enjoyed it, but they were all much slower than he was, even with Scout by his side.

"Did you think this was a race?" Dale asked, coming behind him and slapping him on the back.

"I wasn't racing," Cooper told him. "Just keeping up with Scout." He gave her a rough rub on the top of her head, and she licked his hand when he pulled it away.

"You were both running a race then," his brother remarked.

"Or we're just faster than you." Cooper stood and looked around. "Where are Wade and Joe?"

"Wade won't be long. He's fast, too. Joe, on the other hand, is a lot better than when he first started running with us, but he was definitely not an athlete growing up."

"Not everyone was," Cooper said, thinking about Jessie. She exercised as much as she needed to in order to be successful on the SAR team, but she hated every minute of it. If she had been better at exercising, would it have made a difference that day? He couldn't help but wonder.

Wade and Joe appeared at the edge of the woods and jogged to where they had all parked. Wade looked like he hadn't broken a sweat, but the doctor breathed heavily and was soaked to the skin.

"You okay, Joe?" Cooper asked.

Through wheezes, Joe nodded and answered. "Yep. Fine. Thanks."

Cooper grinned. "Aren't doctors supposed to be in good shape? You know, as good examples to their patients?"

Joe snarled at him from his bent over position. "Most of us aren't. Who has time?"

"You're doing just fine," Wade told his brother-in-law.

Joe stood and took a deep breath. "Wait until you meet my sister. She makes Andi look like a couch potato. She's always on the move. Running in the morning, Pilates in the evening. She never stops all day, barely eats a thing, so I don't know where she gets the stamina. She's a health fanatic on top of being a top-notch businesswoman."

"I guess she has to be on her toes and in tip-top shape with all those celebrities she works with," Wade said.

"What does she do?" Cooper asked. He knew Joe's kid sister was coming to town and staying with them for a while to help Helena, but he hadn't paid much attention to the talk about her.

"She's a wedding coordinator," Joe said, grabbing a towel from his car and wiping his face.

"Not just a wedding coordinator," Wade said. "According to Andi, she's handled some of the most important weddings of the past five years. Politicians, daughters of politicians, actors and actresses, business moguls. The richest and most famous Texans as well as others around the country."

Joe shrugged. "Yeah, that's true. But mainly, she's just my kid sister. She's as down to earth as they come. I think that's why she's so successful. She's not in competition with the brides, and she tells it like it is. She's a pretty tough cookie. And she can tone it down and put on a small, country wedding, too. Ours wasn't exactly *People Magazine* worthy."

"And she's beautiful," Wade added. "Even in a traditional bridesmaid dress, she was stunning."

"Well, she did help pick them out," Joe said.

"Wait," Cooper said, realization dawning on him. "Was she the one with long, jet-black hair and the killer body?"

Dale feigned shock. "Hold on. My brother noticed a beautiful woman? Did she pique your interest?"

"Very funny," Cooper said, rolling his eyes. "I still notice women, beautiful or not. And I don't need to be pushed into a romance."

Dale's smile faded. "I'm sorry, Coop. I'm just kidding."

Cooper shook his head and began to walk away. "Whatever, Dale. I've got to get ready for work."

"Same," said Joe. "We're setting up a tent to try to get more people to come into the clinic for regular checkups."

Cooper heard the others tell each other goodbye, but he was quiet as he caged Scout in the back of Dale's truck and climbed into the passenger seat. Of course, he noticed women. He'd even dated some of them. Dale knew that. He also knew Cooper didn't want a relationship.

"Hey, I'm really sorry," Dale said as he folded himself into the truck. "I didn't mean anything by it."

"Forget it," Cooper said grudgingly.

"No, I mean it. I am sorry. But…"

Here it comes.

"Maybe it's time you get back out there. With someone other than Trudy or the girls you went to school with. Maybe you need to start paying attention to the new women in town. I want to see you happy."

"You know, Dale, happiness is up to one's own self. You can't rely on others to make you happy." He stared out the window as he spoke. Dale started the engine and made his way out of the lot.

"You know, Coop. You should listen to your own advice. If it's up to you to make yourself happy, why are you letting yourself be miserable all the time? Why not start looking for a path toward happiness?"

"You don't get it," Cooper said defensively.

"What don't I get?" Dale shot back. "That you'd rather spend your life being miserable than try to love someone?"

"You don't get that I don't want to love anyone. That ship sailed, and I wasn't on it."

"Come on, Cooper. I know you loved Jessie and thought you'd be together forever. I know that what happened is painful. And it's not easy getting back out there. But you have to move on. You have to find a way to get over it."

"Get over it? *Get over it?* Easy for you to say!"

Cooper regretted the words as soon as they left his mouth. He looked at his brother and saw the pained expression on his face. "Dale, I'm sorry. I didn't mean it."

"Oh, you meant it all right. You think you're the only one who feels pain? Who feels helpless? Who feels like he let someone down? You think that just because you couldn't prevent what happened to Jessie, your life is over? Well, let me tell you something about life being over, little brother. Jessie may have been near death for a long time. She may have been resuscitated more than once, and maybe she isn't able to live the same life as before. But she lived, Cooper. She lived. You think that's easy for me? To know that you've wasted five years on someone you loved who lived, while I've been trying to go on living after my wife actually died? I'll say it again, Coop. Get over it. I'm tired of watching you wallow in self-pity over something neither of you could control. It's not fun, and no, it's not easy. But that's life. When are you going to start living yours?"

Dale hit the steering wheel with his fist. Cooper didn't know what to say, so he kept his mouth shut the rest of the way to town. The weight of the world pressed on him as he stepped from the car, and he knew Dale was right. He had no right to feel this way. He didn't know how else to feel. He didn't know what to say to Dale, to Jessie's family, to anyone. He'd said he was sorry over and over, but it never made anything better.

***

Amanda took a break to walk around the park, visit the vendors, and sample some sweet and savory Southern vittles. She watched Dale's kids compete in the potato sack races and stopped to check out the library book sale. Cindy and Trudy were volunteering to help Sarah and Helena with the sale.

"Where's Helena?" Amanda asked, looking around for Joe's wife.

"She's taking a break to put up her feet." Sarah placed another stack of books on the table as she spoke. "How are things at the clinic's table? Are you convincing the locals to submit to your modern medical ways?"

Amanda laughed. "We've had quite a few get their blood pressure checked and even some who let Joe listen to their hearts. Not many takers on the shingles vaccine though."

Sarah shook her head. "No surprise there."

"It's a tough sell, especially after the pandemic. Nobody seems to trust doctors or vaccines or medicine in general anymore, which is really frustrating." Amanda picked up a book and read the blurb on the back before handing Cindy a dollar. "How's Jackson? I hear you're still deciding on a date."

Cindy shrugged. "He's fine. We're getting closer on a date, but I need to finish my degree. Mrs. Baker has strict rules about that, and since she's helping me with the tuition, I have to follow her rules."

Amanda smiled. Imogene Baker was an icon in town, and she had taken to Cindy like a bear to a honey pot. "She won't steer you wrong."

"No, ma'am, she won't."

Amanda bid the young women goodbye and moved on to Jessica Swanson's tent, filled with hand-blown glassware. Her eyes went straight to a delicate, pink apple blossom on a thin piece of fishing line. Next to it was a Northern Mockingbird with every stripe of its wing carefully outlined. Jessica's works of art filled Amanda with awe.

"I don't know how you manage to make these beautiful glass objects with six kids running under foot!" Amanda exclaimed as she handed Jess the money for the blossom and mockingbird. She'd take it to her mother for Mother's Day when she attended her niece's first Communion.

A stroll around the grounds would not be complete without a stop at Andi's bakery tent or the McDowell family's farm table of fresh produce, several varieties of honey, and the most amazing combinations of flavors in their homemade jams and jellies. Amanda did a fine job of stocking her own pantry as well as picking out things to take back to Nashville for her family when she got home the following month.

Just before reaching the medical tent, she caught a glimpse of what looked like a family spat between Paige and Cooper Mackenzie. Amanda tried not to stare as the two squared off. She couldn't hear what they were saying, but both parties looked offended. Amanda wondered what they were arguing about. Not that it was any of her business, but for some inexplicable reason, she found herself wondering more and more about Cooper's past each time she ran into him.

****

Cooper had to remind himself that a slow day was a good day in his line of work. It was better that he was walking around the park, representing the sheriff's office, and not off tracking a missing person or triaging someone who was injured. He knew his job was meant to be a last resort, something most people hoped was never necessary, but it was hard to beat the adrenaline rush that coursed through him every time that call came in.

"Hey, Coop."

He turned to see his cousin heading in his direction, pushing a turquoise umbrella stroller. He gave her a hug and realized how little they'd seen each other lately.

"What's up, Paige? How are things in the marketing business?" He bent down and gave Hope a kiss.

"Good, really good. The more businesses Wade and Jackson bring into town, the more marketing clients I get. And many of them recommend me to their friends back home, so I've got a lot going on these days. How about you? Is this the new dog? Aunt May told me about her. Can I pet her?"

"Yeah, sure. Her name's Scout." She bent down and introduced herself to Scout, then allowed Hope to pet the dog.

"Everything good?" she asked again once she stood.

"I'm good. Working. Helping Dale. Training with Scout. The usual."

She gave him a once-over and frowned. "You know, there's a new ice cream parlor opening in town. I met the girls who own it. Two sisters, really nice. I think they're both—"

"Don't say it." He held his hands up in protest. "I'm not interested."

"Oh, Coop. Come on. It's been so long now. Don't you think it's time—"

"Jeez!" He sucked in a deep breath and let it out. "You, too? Mama won't leave me alone, and Dale's all in my business. And now, you, too? What is with this family?"

Paige opened her mouth, blinked, and shook her head. "Maybe we care about you, Coop. Maybe we don't want to see you spend your life alone. You could be a little gracious."

Cooper ran his hand down his face. "Yeah, I know. I'm sorry. I'm just so tired of hearing all the time about me not being happy. Who says I'm not happy? Who says I can't have a fulfilling life as a single guy with a job I love in a town as great as this? Maybe I'm freaking over the moon with happiness. Did anyone ever consider that?"

With a curt nod, Paige began to back away. "You're absolutely right, Coop. You're just the picture of happiness. I hope I can be as happy as you are someday." She turned and walked away, leaving Cooper feeling as badly as he had earlier when Dale high-tailed it from the truck without giving a backwards glance to his brother.

He knew his family was trying to help. He knew they only wanted the best for him. Maybe it was time for him to let go of the past. But the only way he could consider doing that was to face it head on.

***

"Yes, the swelling is concerning, but it's also normal." Amanda tried to relieve Helena at the clinic on Monday. "What does Joe say?"

"That I'm doing everything right. But you're my doctor, and you have more OB/GYN experience than he does."

"Well, I did brush up on that when I took this job, but if you're really concerned, I can set you up with someone in Harrison." Amanda went to the counter and picked up her iPad to look up the number.

"No, I trust you. And Joe, of course. And I still want to have the baby at home, but I'm so worried something will go wrong, and I'll need to go to the hospital."

Amanda put the tablet down, washed her hands again, and sat down in her swivel chair next to the exam table. "We're going to keep a close eye on you. Right now, your blood pressure is good. Your hands aren't swelling, and neither is anything other than your feet. You're not having headaches or chest pain, right?"

Helena shook her head. "No, nothing out of the ordinary. An occasional headache on a stressful day or when I've been staring at the computer for too long."

"And it's better if you lie on your left side?"

"I think so," Helena said, her brow furrowed in concentration.

"Okay, then. I don't think you have anything other than normal pregnancy-related edema. Let's take a look, though, to make sure everything is on track."

Ten minutes later, Amanda shed her gloves and helped Helena sit up.

"The baby is perfectly in position, and everything looks great. Here's what I prescribe. Try sleeping or resting on your left side to keep pressure off your inferior vena cava, the vein that takes blood to your heart. Keep your legs elevated as much as possible, especially at work. I know you're on your feet a lot. Let Sarah do the standing. You don't have to be at the circulation counter all the time. And you can wear support stockings if they make you feel better."

"Stockings? I don't even own a pair."

"That's fine. I prefer you wear loose pants anyway. Maternity pants or sweats but not leggings or socks with tight bands around the calves or ankles."

"These days, I can't reach my feet to wear any socks at all."

Amanda laughed. "That's okay. Just wear comfortable shoes, and not flip flops. They have no support, and I treat so many women who trip and fall because of them."

"And you think I'm still on track to deliver at home?"

Amanda patted Helena's arm. "Do you think Joe would let you consider it if there was any cause to worry? So far, I don't see any reason why you can't. And if things go smoothly with the interviews, we should have a certified pediatric physician's assistant on staff to be there with us."

Helena breathed a sigh of relief and was visibly feeling better. Her coloring was noticeably brighter than when she first arrived, and her eyes no longer held the fear Amanda saw in them when the exam began.

"Thank you so much, Amanda. I feel better now."

"Good," Amanda told her. "I'm glad I could reassure you." She picked up her iPad and began updating Helena's chart. "When does Joe's sister arrive?"

"In a couple weeks. I'm glad she's coming. I'm going to stop working when she gets here, and I'll be happy to have someone else around. The nursery isn't finished, and Joe doesn't have the time to do it. I'm worried we won't have it done in time."

"Helena," Amanda said with a smile. "Stop worrying. That doesn't help your blood pressure. It's all going to be fine. We've all got this."

Amanda meant it. Her exam confirmed that Helena should have a routine labor and delivery without any problems. Of course, there was no guarantee of that, no matter how smoothly the pregnancy went, but Amanda believed that everything was going to be okay.

She waited at the bottom of the stairs for Helena to poke her head in the office and say goodbye to Joe, and then walked her to the reception area. They embraced before saying goodbye, and Amanda watched her leave. Everything was going to be fine, and Joe and Helena would make the best parents. But that knowledge, and the depth of their friendship, didn't stop the small and surprising twinge of jealousy Amanda felt watching the pregnant woman walk away.

***

Cooper was off the following Sunday, but he had big plans for the day. He'd made up his mind he wasn't putting it off, because if he didn't go now, he might never go. The drive felt longer than it was, especially without Scout by his side. The closer he got, the more he wanted to turn around. He hadn't called ahead or alerted anyone that he was coming. He wasn't sure what was right—to give them warning or just show up and hope for the best.

The parking lot was crammed with cars, and it occurred to him that Sundays probably were popular days at a place like this. Was that good or bad? Did it mean an audience or a buffer? What would they say or do when they saw him? His knuckles were white and his palms sweaty as he released his steely grip on the steering wheel.

The first obstacle was the visitor's desk. He told the woman who he was and whom he wanted to see. To his surprise, his name was on the list, even after all this time. Why was that? He didn't know if it made him feel better or worse.

The second obstacle was his own fear. He took several deep breaths before lifting his hand to knock on the door. His heart raced, and he was nervous to say the least. Could he do this? Could he face her? What was he supposed to say or do? He let out a few short puffs of breath and raised his hand to knock.

"No need to knock."

He spun around, his heart pounding, and saw a small woman wearing scrubs. She offered him a kind smile and gestured to the door. "Just go in, young man. She'll be happy to have the company."

He nodded and then remembered his manners. "Thank you."

"You're welcome. I hope you have a nice visit."

The woman's smile and encouragement calmed him, and he slowly pushed open the door. The lights were dimmed, and the room was almost silent except for the rhythmic sound of a mechanical whisper. As he drew closer, he noted the plethora of tubes to various machines around the bed. She wore a bright colored nightgown, like something Suzy would wear, which was visible above the sheet and blanket that covered her thin body. Her arms were exposed and at her sides on top of the blanket.

He stood in silence as the ventilator continued to whisper. He didn't know if he could touch her, didn't know if he wanted to. Not much had changed since the last time he saw her, when she was still in the hospital, when she still had color in her cheeks and a shine to her hair. Now, her skin had a pallor to it that made bile rise to his throat, and her hair was limp and dull. She looked like… he couldn't bring himself to even think the words, but it reminded him of seeing his grandmother in her casket.

"Took you a long time to get here," came a man's voice from the doorway.

Cooper turned. Mr. Hopkins didn't look the same at all. He was smaller than he used to be, with less hair and many more wrinkles. He looked a good ten years older, maybe more, than Cooper knew he was.

"Yes, Sir. Too long."

The man walked into the room and stood beside Cooper. "Still the prettiest girl in the room."

Cooper nodded. "Yes, Sir." Though he thought it only true because she was the only girl in the room. The beauty he remembered—her bright smile, the way her eyes twinkled, her rosy complexion, and the confidence she exuded in any situation—was completely hidden and unlikely to return.

"I'll leave you two alone. I imagine you have some things you need to tell her." The man looked down at his watch. "Her mama's at church. I stopped going long ago." He paused and looked at his daughter. "Well, anyway, she won't be by for a good hour or so, so I'll just go down and have a cup of coffee. I'll be in the cafeteria if you need…anything."

The man turned to go but stopped and looked back at Cooper. "She hasn't been waiting for you, you know. I hope you haven't been waiting for her either. There's enough of us doing that already, and you've got no reason to stop your life just because hers stopped. That would be a waste." The man gave him a weak smile and left the room.

Cooper stood there a while longer, unsure as to why he came, what he should do. It wasn't until he tasted salt on his lips that he knew he was crying. He pulled the chair closer to the bed and sat down. Without thinking, he took her hand and caressed it, trying not to think about the way it felt—not real, as if he was touching a body in a museum, not quite like wax, but not like skin either. He sat silently for several moments before he found the words he hoped were adequate. They didn't feel like her hands. They were too soft and smooth.

"Hey, there, Jessie, it's Cooper. It's been a long time. Too long. I'm sorry about that." The words came in one long stream, and once they started tumbling from his lips, he was unable to stop them. "I've missed you. I've missed you so much." His voice cracked, but he didn't stop speaking. "I've tried to think back, to go over that day, to figure out how I could have… I wish I could have…" He wished he could stop himself from crying, but a dam had broken.

"If I had known what was going to happen, if I had any sense that I should've gone with you. In hindsight, I feel it and see it every time I think of that moment you walked away, but then… I didn't know. I would've stopped you or gone with you. Anything to stop what happened." He wiped his sleeve across his dripping nose as tears soaked his cheeks.

"I'm so sorry. I'm so, so sorry. I had plans for that night. No, I had plans for our lives. I had it all mapped out, just like one of our searches. I knew where we were going and how long it would take to get there. I knew there would be stuff in the way, things we had to go around or move or just deal with. I knew there would be rivers to cross and mountains to scale, but I was ready. I had a plan. All I had to do was ask, and all you had to do was say yes. The rest, we would work our way through just like we always did."

His words were coming in gasps, and his chest was heaving. There was so much he wanted to tell her, explain to her. "It wasn't supposed to end like that, like this. We were supposed to have a life together. Why didn't I know? Why didn't I stop you? Why, why, why?"

He buried his face in the blanket and wept, begging her forgiveness, asking the same of himself.

Cooper had no idea how much time had passed by

the time he slipped into the adjacent bathroom and splashed cold water on his face. He took one of the rough paper towels from the dispenser and dragged it across his features. He couldn't say he felt better, but he felt different in some way he couldn't quite name.

Mr. Hopkins was still in the cafeteria, a cup of cold coffee in front of him, when Cooper took a seat across from him.

"I should've come sooner. I'm sorry."

Jessie's father shook his head. "No, son. You came when you were ready. That's the way it was meant to be. What would you have done if you'd been here back then? What would you have done all these years other than sit at her side and wish she would look at you, smile at you, squeeze your hand? No, son, that's no life for a young man. And you're still a young man. Lots of living left to do."

"I don't know… how. I can't seem to move on."

Mr. Hopkins swallowed, and his eyes became moist with tears. "Don't do that, Cooper. Don't let this be the end of your story, too. Not that I'm saying it's the end. We still hope. Well, Martha hopes. Me, I'm just here because she's still my little girl." He took a long, deep breath. "But she's not yours anymore. She was at one time, and I can't tell you how jealous I was."

Cooper blinked in surprise.

"Her world revolved around me until you came along. She loved you so much. Her mama and I knew it, and we knew you loved her, too. But it wasn't meant to be, son, and that's not for us to ask why. Martha says the

Lord has his reasons. I don't understand them myself. Can't see any good reason for this to have happened, for this to still be happening. I just know that I can't drive myself crazy trying to come up with one because Martha needs me, and my little girl needs me. But you…" He pointed to Cooper. "You need to move on if you haven't already. You're a good man, and I keep hearing how there are more women in this world than men, and how there just aren't enough good men left. My Jessie wouldn't want you spending your life waiting for something the doctors are certain is never going to happen. She loved life. She loved living. She'd want you to love and live and have everything that's good in life."

He stopped and took a drink, making a face as the cold liquid slid down his throat. He pushed the cup away. "Live your life, Cooper. If you don't think you can live it for yourself, then live it for her."

Cooper nodded. "I can try, Sir."

Mr. Hopkins shook his head. "Trying ain't doing. Promise me you're going to leave here today and not look back. If you want to stop by sometime and say hello, you're welcome to. But I want you to leave here with the resolve to live, really live. Do you understand?"

Cooper closed his eyes, swallowed, and opened them again. He looked at the man sitting across from him. "Yes, Sir. I understand, and I promise."

Nodding, Mr. Hopkins reached across the table and laid his hand on top of Cooper's.

"Thank you." Without another word, the man stood and walked out of the cafeteria, turning in the direction of his daughter's room.

It took several minutes before Cooper felt ready to leave. He didn't know how he was going to do it, but he was going to honor his promise to Jessie's father. It was the least he could do for the man, and for Jessie.

Five

"Incoming!" Dr. Blake's voice rang through the halls, sending a ripple of adrenaline down Amanda's spine. She was simultaneously filled with anticipation and dread. Usually calm, Joe sounded almost frantic.

"What's going on?" Amanda asked, joining him in the lobby.

"Just got a call. Major car accident in town. A family with a pregnant mother. She's being airlifted out, but the kids need us. Not sure of the extent of their injuries."

Pregnant woman. Kids. That was it. With Helena's impending delivery, it made sense that Joe would be emotional about a pregnant woman and her children.

Sirens screamed as the ambulance pulled into view, and Amanda felt her heartbeat accelerate with each chord. She pulled on gloves and raced outside as the vehicle came to a stop.

"Multiple victims," the driver called as he ran to the

back of the vehicle and threw open the doors.

A second ambulance pulled in behind the first, and chaos reigned for the next few hours.

Once Amanda could stop to take a breath, she swelled with pride at what she and Joe had been able to accomplish at the small-town clinic in the middle of the hills.

The two young children—escaping with a few minor cuts and scrapes—had been calmed, treated, and sent home with Grandma, adorned with stickers. The father—anxious about his wife's condition—was released with seventeen stitches above his eye, a set of negative x-rays of his ribs, and a list of concussion rules. He would need follow-up, but he would be okay. They received news on his wife—medically induced coma— and the child inside her was fighting to come out but, for now, being kept safely inside her natural incubator. Both were expected to recover once stabilized.

"You okay?" She asked Joe when he emerged from their private bathroom.

He shrugged "Yeah. We did our jobs. I pray the doctors in Mountain Home can do theirs."

Amanda wondered if he was thinking about Helena and her home birth. She laid a hand gently on his arm.

"She's going to be fine," Amanda told him, thinking about both women.

Joe nodded. "I know. I'm good." He smiled warily at her. "Thanks."

Amanda nodded. She couldn't imagine what that poor husband was going through or what Joe was dealing with. She'd never been pregnant and had no idea what it was like. Andi and Helena were her first friends to be pregnant, at least when she was nearby. Her friends and sisters-in-law back home had children now, but she'd either been away at school or living here when they'd gone through pregnancy and childbirth.

For the first time in her life, Amanda felt a yearning deep inside, a yearning she didn't know she had.

***

"Well, look what the cat dragged in." May smiled and pulled her younger son into a hug when he walked through the kitchen door. "I only see you at Dale's these days. And you brought Scout! Want a treat, girl?" She gave the dog a pat and went to the counter where she had a canister of dog treats waiting.

"What brings you home?" she said, giving a treat to Scout before focusing on Cooper. She caught her breath. "What is it? What's happened? Dale? The kids?"

Cooper shushed her and smiled. "No, Mama. Everyone is fine."

"Something has happened. Your eyes are bloodshot, and your coloring isn't good. What's wrong? Are you sick?"

"I'm fine. Scout, sit." The dog sat on command. "Lay down." Scout made herself comfortable on the white and grey linoleum floor.

"Mama." He led her to a chair at the kitchen table. "I just wanted to come by and see you."

"Now you really have me worried. Since when do you just come by for a visit?"

"Not often enough," he admitted. "I need to do that more. There are a lot of things I've neglected doing, but I'm going to be better."

May sat back and let out a breath. She folded her hands on the same round, oak table where they shared every family meal since Cooper graduated from a highchair. "You've been to see her. You finally went up there."

Cooper nodded.

"Well, it's about time. Did you see her parents?"

"Only her father. I went by yesterday. Nothing has changed. Everything is still the same as when she was in the hospital five years ago. Her father said the doctors don't think she'll ever wake up."

His mother reached across the table and clasped his hands with hers. "Oh, Cooper, I'm so sorry. Jessie was such a sweet girl, so full of life."

"She was, Mama. Her father said she loved me, and she loved life." He tried to smile, but it felt bittersweet. "He made me promise I'd move on with my life. But…" He hesitated. "I don't know how."

"Oh, sweetheart, there aren't any rules or guidelines for that. You just have to be open to life. Be open to new possibilities, to trying new things and meeting new people. You need to take a few tentative steps, and before you know it, you'll be running at full speed."

"How do I know which direction to take?"

"You don't." She sat back and looked at him, her

hazel eyes full of love. "None of us has a road map that sets us on course. But we all have a compass, and it points true north." She pointed up, and he followed her gaze to the ceiling from which an antique Tiffany lamp hung.

"I wish I had a GPS that was a little more accurate."

Mama laughed. "Don't we all. But that's not the way it works. You have to be open and attentive. God is telling you what you should do, where you should go, and even how to get there, but it's up to you to hear him and follow his directions."

"But what if I don't hear him, Mama? What if I've never heard him? Never even felt him?"

Mama smiled. "Oh, Cooper, of course you have. Think about all the time you spend in the woods, all the hikes you take in the mountains. Have you ever listened to the steady tapping of the woodpecker or heard the early morning call of the whip-poor-will? Have you marveled at the sunrise or been taken aback by the sudden appearance of a mother doe and her fawn? Have you heard the babbling brook and the song of the warbler? What about the ovenbird calling, 'Teacher, teacher'? Who do you think he's calling? The creator is there, communicating with all his creatures. Why would he not also be speaking to you?"

Cooper chuckled. "Mama, I'm not sure all us creatures are speaking the same language. I might recognize those calls, but I don't understand them any more than I understand when he might be calling me."

"Oh, but he is. Trust me, he's calling. Listen to your

heart, Cooper. It won't steer you wrong."

"You know, Mama, sometimes I don't understand a word you say, but I still leave feeling like I've learned some secret, some kernel of wisdom that I need in life."

"And that's just the way it should be." She stood and went to the counter. "Now, I'm no Andi Nelson, but I make a mean pecan pie. How about joining me in a slice of pie and a good, strong cup of coffee?"

"That's music to my ears, Mama."

"Good. Go wash up, and I'll cut us each a piece while the coffee brews. Then we can talk some more about where life might could be taking you." Cooper smiled at Mama's use of the local phrase 'might could' that he'd worked so hard to stop saying.

He obeyed his mother and went to wash his hands. He still didn't know what he was supposed to do next, but taking the time to eat pie with his mother sounded like a good place to start.

***

Amanda awoke during the night to the sound of torrential rain. She rolled over and tried to go back to sleep, but a loud crack of thunder rocked the house and jolted her upright. Had she made sure all the windows were closed? She'd been so tired when she went to bed after a terribly busy day. A strong gust of wind stirred the covers, and she rushed from the bed to the window on the other side of the room.

By the time Amanda finished closing all the windows

in the old, two-story house, she was wide awake. She often suffered from insomnia, but the crazy days and nighttime emergencies had her body clock more mixed up than ever. The clock next to the bed read 4:36, and Amanda sighed with the knowledge that she was not going to be able to sleep.

She reached for her iPad, swiped through her emails, checked her appointment calendar for the next day, and opened the book she'd fallen asleep reading the night before. Almost an hour passed before her eyes grew heavy. She stifled a yawn and tossed the iPad onto the other side of the bed. She closed her eyes and felt her body finally begin to relax. When she opened them again, she still heard the driving rain and howling wind and assumed she'd been asleep for a few minutes.

The clock told her otherwise, and she leapt from bed with only thirty minutes to shower, dress, make coffee, eat a quick breakfast, and head to the clinic. She was still groggy but realized it was quite dark in the room. It was typically light outside by now.

Amanda tugged on the window shade and looked out. It was raining so hard, she couldn't see past the windowpane. The wind continued to howl, and the sky was still black. A small limb crashed into the window and Amanda jumped. Suddenly, she heard another loud boom, and the world became even darker. The numbers on the clock were gone, and the barely visible glow of the streetlights had disappeared. Amanda reached for the chain on the bedside lamp, but no light appeared when she yanked it. This was not good. There would be no hot shower, no hot coffee, and no hot breakfast.

She looked outside again and wondered how long Joe's generator would last. Would they be able to treat their patients? On second thought, would any of their patients show up for their appointments? What if there was an emergency?

The buzzing of her phone pulled Amanda from her thoughts, and she reached down and picked up the device. She slid across the screen and said hello, then waited for Joe's voice.

"Stay where you are. Don't try to get to the clinic. You probably know the power is out. The whole town is out. I've got Dotty calling everyone to stay home. The authorities don't want anyone on the roads."

"Really?" She turned back toward the window. The storm would let up soon, wouldn't it? "Is it going to keep raining like this for a while?"

"I think so. I had the news on before the power went out. It's a massive system, and the worst of it isn't even here yet. The weatherman kept comparing it to a storm back in 2017 that apparently devastated parts of Northwest Arkansas with tornados and landslides. They're predicting about two months of rain in only several hours of rainfall."

Amanda realized she was pacing back and forth and sat on the bed. "I'm guessing that's bad."

"It's bad. They expect extreme flooding, roads under water, even houses breached. Thank Heaven we don't typically have flooding here in town. Helena said Andi and Jackson spent hours last night placing sandbags around their house. Apparently, their farm has flooded in the past, being so close to the river and at the base of a mountain. Be careful, and check in with us later to let us know you're okay."

"I will. How's Helena doing?"

"She thinks I'm worried about nothing. She says 'her people' can handle a lot worse than a deluge of rain."

Amanda laughed. "I have no doubt. Okay." She let out a breath. "Let me know if you need me for anything."

"Will do. Take care." He disconnected the call, and Amanda placed the phone back on the nightstand. She had a whole day in a dark house and no idea what to do.

***

"Got it. On the way." Cooper shoved his radio back into its holster and headed toward the door. He'd been on alert most of the night, and he knew his team had been ready since the first call thirty minutes earlier, letting them know they may be needed. As soon as he saw the forecast, he was aware things could get bad. Once the rain started, he knew it would be worse than bad.

He took his phone out of his pocket and hit a number. "Lucy, we're on. Woman and child trapped in a car on 21 near Glory Hole Falls Trailhead."

"Got it, Coop. Where do you want me?"

"Meet me at the chopper in fifteen. I don't think we can get there in less than that with all this rain and flooding."

"Copy that."

Cooper called Lance and instructed him to mobilize the ground crew. The likelihood of the chopper being able to maneuver in this storm was low, but it was the victims' best bet. The ground crew most likely wouldn't be able to get anywhere near the car, but their help would be needed in other ways.

After giving his mother a kiss—his parents were staying at Dale's, knowing their sons most likely would be called out—and telling Scout to be good while he was gone, he fought the wind and rain in route to his truck.

Twenty-five minutes later, Cooper, Lucy, and Bud were in the air, but the rain and wind were fierce. The chopper's propellers, made to withstand most atmospheric conditions, were taking a beating, and Bud warned them that the torque generated by the main rotor was severely disabled by the inability of the tail blades to reach maximum thrust. They were in as much danger as the woman and child in the car below.

"Can you handle it?" Cooper yelled into his headset.

"For now, but not if the wind picks up much more," Bud answered back.

"Then let's get in and out before that happens," Cooper told him.

Within minutes they were above the car, only visible by the headlights barely shining above the rushing water. They had little time to get the victims out before the car would go under. Worse, the car was being pushed by the water, picking up more speed as it went.

"We need to stop the car's forward motion," Cooper shouted into the radio.

"Copy," Lance answered from below. "We're about a mile down, and there's already a dam in place, so to speak. You're not going to believe it when you see it. Can't guarantee the water and the car won't go over it. We can't get close though. The water is taking over the whole area."

"Copy," Cooper replied. "We'll do the best we can."

He relayed the info to Bud, and the chopper followed the car as it headed toward the makeshift dam. Cooper had no idea what Lance was using, but he prayed to St. Bernard that it was big enough and strong enough to stop the car. As he scanned the road below, the chopper jerked to the right.

"Sorry. I'm having trouble holding on, and visibility is getting worse," Bud informed him. "I'm going lower and hoping to get beneath the wind."

As Cooper kept his eyes on the raging water below, he started to make out something ahead. Lights shone from what looked like a…

"Holy…" His words caught in his throat as he focused on the so-called dam. An eighteen-wheeler stretched across the roadway, partway on its side, its headlights casting an eerie glow on the unseen road and shoulder. The water was rushing around it, and he understood what happened. How was the little car any match to the water if an eighteen-wheeler couldn't fight it?

Cooper didn't know if the person driving the truck

was still inside, but the cab was almost fully immersed. There was little chance of the driver being saved if he hadn't already bailed and found his way to dry land, but the truck just may be the instrument to save someone else. Before Cooper had time to wonder about what would happen next, the car lurched toward the truck, and Cooper said another hasty prayer to St. Bernard.

Please let them stop without too much force, and please let them be okay. Aid me in my efforts. Amen.

He made a quick Sign of the Cross and kissed the medals he wore around his neck—one, a depiction of St. Bernard, and the other, the Miraculous Medal. He might not hear the voice of God, but he would take all the help he could get from those who had.

The car hit the side of the truck and bounced back slightly before being pushed back against it by the moving water. Cooper didn't think it would hold for long. The pressure of the water and the weight of both vehicles would be too much to hold them there. He needed to move fast. He pulled on one harness and hooked the rescue basket to another. He grabbed the blowtorch and braced himself by the open door.

"Lower me now!" he shouted to Lucy who was already up and stabilized. She lowered him down, and the full impact of the rain and wind hit him as he and the basket whipped back and forth.

There would be no way to open the door, and once a window was opened, the water would rush in too quickly to save anyone. Cooper clutched the blowtorch tightly, hoping it would work, and work quickly.

The wind was abusive as Lucy lowered him toward the car, and he knew time was running out. Once he was on the roof of the car and started up the torch, he could hear the screaming from inside. There was no use yelling to the mother and daughter to stay calm or cover themselves to avoid the torch. His voice would be lost in the storm. He just had to hope and pray that things would go their way.

Once he was through the metal, Cooper threw down the torch, peeled back the roof, letting the wind rip it away, and began tearing at the ceiling with his hands. He watched helplessly as the torch flew off the top of the car and was lost to the rushing flood.

Water began to pour through the roof, and Cooper thrust his hands into the opening. waving them amid the rushing water. There was a the grasp of his hand, and he pulled as hard as he could. A child, maybe ten or so, held onto his hand and was pushed through the roof. Without letting go, Cooper managed to grab onto the basket and helped the girl inside. He buckled her in and gave the cable a hard tug. The basket began to rise, and Cooper turned back to the car. He could hear the girl's fading screams as the basket took her to safety.

The interior was almost filled with water. He plunged his arm back down into the car and frantically waved it around. Just as his thoughts began to turn to despair, there was another hand grabbing his from the coursing water. Working against the rapid flow wasn't easy, but together, they were able to fight the flood, the rain, and the wind. He pulled the woman out just as the basket returned. He quickly buckled her in, and the two were lifted into the chopper.

"How are we doing?" Cooper asked as soon as he had his headset back on.

"It's going to be touch and go," Bud told him. "But you've already done the hard part. All I have to do is fly."

"They okay?" he asked Lucy.

She was buckling in after checking on the mother. "Some cuts, possible rib injuries from the steering wheel and airbags. They went off when the car hit the truck, but the water slowed the impact. Nothing major from what I can see."

"Good." He buckled in and held his breath as the chopper turned back toward the hanger.

It was a rough ride back to the EOC, and several times, Cooper and Lucy shared a nervous look. They rescued the mother and daughter from the car, but that didn't mean they were out of danger. They stayed as close to the treetops as they could and rode out the turbulence while Bud fought the chopper's inclination to go into a spin. Once they were back on solid ground, Cooper let himself relax. At least for a moment.

***

"Pretty rough day?" Amanda asked Andi when they spoke on the phone the next evening. Amanda was still at home, still waiting for the electricity to come back on though the rain had stopped.

"To say the least." She heard Andi take a drink and

let out a breath. "Dale told Wade there were six known fatalities and maybe more we haven't even heard about or discovered yet."

"Wow! Anyone from town?" She played with her cold, leftover pizza but was quickly losing her appetite.

"An older man, Mr. Lewis."

"Oh, I know him," Amanda jumped in before Andi could say more. "We've seen him at the clinic. What happened?"

"Heart attack trying to save his cattle. That's what they think anyway. They found him in the barn, with several of the cattle, but not all of them. Some are still missing, some were dead."

"Oh, that's awful. Anyone else?" She pushed the pizza away and took a long drink of wine.

"Nobody else from town. Some kayakers who thought they could beat the rapids were washed away and found early this morning. And a little boy washed downstream and is still missing."

Amanda's chest hurt. "Another one. That one a few weeks ago was so heartbreaking. Oh, gosh. Oh, that's awful." She downed the rest of the wine.

"Yeah, and several waterways are still rising even without the rain. We're not out of the woods yet. Wade's had the police radio on since it started, and I haven't heard anything in the past couple hours, but nobody was prepared for this. Hopefully he doesn't have more bad news when he gets home."

"The weathermen sure messed up with this one. They didn't know it would be bad until the morning after it all started. I'm glad I'm not them. But you guys knew. Joe said you put out sandbags."

"Precaution, we thought," Andi said. "Wade grew up in this house and knows not to chance it."

"Good for him. Generator still holding up?"

"So far. Are you sure you don't want to come over? We have plenty of room in this big old house. Wade can stop by and pick you up in his truck."

"No, thanks. I'm fine. It can't be too much longer, right?"

She heard Andi sigh. "No promises. Until the water recedes, not all the power lines can be fixed. And some of the substations are under water."

"Great," Amanda said, standing and walking to the trash can with her paper plate. "I'm not sure I have enough wine for this."

Andi laughed. "I hear you. At least you can drink."

"True. How are you feeling?"

"Actually, not too bad. The morning sickness is better than I thought it would be. Maybe you were right that this one will be easier."

"Well, that's some good news."

"It is. But, hey, Wade just got back from helping Dale. I'll talk to you later. Okay?"

"Yeah, sure. You take care of yourself. Let me know if you need anything."

When they disconnected, Amanda went to the back door and looked out at the swimming pool that was once her back yard. Grateful that the roads weren't flooded in town and her house wasn't taking in water—yet—she settled on the couch with her iPad and began reading. At least she still had some battery left, and she always had a backlog of books to be read.

***

"We've got a landslide on Cecil Cove Loop."

"What?" Cooper said in disbelief. "Did you say landslide?'

"Roger. Possible victims in harm's way."

Cooper was alerting the team while reeling from the news. Landslides along that route were happening more frequently, but he was always surprised when they had one. Cooper, Lance, and Mike had dealt with several, but the rest of his crew had not. They were well-trained but not very experienced. Only Kevin had been there for one previous slide. He prayed the training they all had was enough.

Once they got the official call they were needed, the team met at the EOC and made their way to the campground, which was still closed due to the area flooding and provided a base of operations. Cooper quickly located his brother and other area law enforcement. Cooper brought Scout but left her in the crate in the back of his truck. He would use her if he needed to, but the conditions were treacherous, and he planned on using ATVs. The faster they did their job, the better.

"Close the road on both sides." Cooper instructed the first responders who had gathered at the site. "It's small and contained, but we need to keep it clear and shut down until the state highway crew or FEMA can assess the roadway." Several officers began giving orders.

Cooper looked around and continued. "We've got a support area at the campground, but we need an exclusion area set up around the hot zone. Nobody goes near this except my team until FEMA or someone from the state arrives. Next, we need a transitional area set up for my team to get ready for the response. We need to have our gear ready, and any other response teams will need to set up their gear and teams there as well. This area also needs a place for debris and anything we find while digging." More officers jumped in to do what they were told. "We need law enforcement outside those areas in an outer perimeter. Make sure nobody without the proper credentials gets inside that perimeter. I mean nobody. Until somebody higher up arrives, I'm in charge, and I don't want anybody getting hurt."

"I don't know how stable the slide is," he continued. "Right now, it doesn't look like it's going to move any farther down, but we don't know that."

The rain had finally stopped, and the waters were receding, but after three days of steady rainfall and swelling lakes and rivers, nothing was stable. Cooper didn't want to take any chances. If the slide continued, the road could give, and they could have more people to search for.

"Our number one job right now is to search for anyone who may have been in the way when it happened." He looked up at the mud and debris before him, unable to imagine that anyone would've been out in this flooding, but one never knew what compelled some people to put their lives at risk. He motioned his team over to a staging place in the transitional area.

"Lance, are you ready?"

Lance grinned. "You bet." The technical wizard told everyone to clear space while he prepared his drone for flight. "I've already got the monitors up and running." He gestured toward tables which held screens that were cabled to a van. Satellite antennae adorned the van's roof.

Cooper looked around at his crew. "Be alert. Look for swept-up structures that may have had people in them. Look for human limbs sticking out of the mud. Keep an eye out for ATVs and other vehicles that may have been in use by anyone at the time of the slide. If you see any movement of any kind, let me know. Once we determine if it's human or nature, we act with caution to get to them and rescue them, or we get the hell out of the way."

His instructions were the best he knew how to give. They couldn't wait for FEMA or anyone else to show up. They needed to make sure nobody needed help.

Sometime later, after FEMA was on scene but allowing Cooper's team to continue taking the lead, Lucy called Cooper to the monitors. "There. Look. It's an arm for sure. And I think it's moving."

Cooper peered at the screen. "Lance, can you get closer?" Lance moved the drone in for a better view.

"I saw it move," Danny said. "It's definitely moving."

"Let me see," said FEMA agent, Arthur Mills. He watched the monitor for several moments before nodding and turning to Cooper. "You equipped for this?"

"Yes, Sir. We're ready and able."

"Then do what you need to do to get that person out of there."

After a crew of geologists determined the ground was stable enough for ATVs to ride up alongside the slide, Cooper was ready to move. He took one ATV, and Lucy took the other. Everyone in his team was a certified EMT, but Lucy was the only medic they had, and Cooper didn't know what they'd find. They took it slow, not quite trusting the ground wouldn't give way even with the assurances of the scientists.

It took some time to find the arm, now moving slower and less actively than when they first saw it on the monitor. Then it took more time for them to make their way gingerly across the mud. Cooper wanted to remove and toss his helmet so he would have better vision, but he knew that wasn't smart. There was no guarantee the mud wouldn't give way under them, or another slide wouldn't come from above. With careful movements, he and Lucy dislodged the mud around the now-limp arm and kept digging with their hands. Any type of equipment could make the area too unstable. When they finally unearthed the man's face, Lucy felt no breath and no pulse.

"We've got to get him out, and fast," she said. "He needs CPR, a neck brace, maybe a shock. And that's just the beginning of treatment. We need him free of this mud and away from this place."

Cooper nodded. He knew her assessment was right on, as always.

They continued to move the mud as quickly and cautiously as they could until Cooper was able to pull the man free and drag him to dry land.

"Let's see if we can get a pulse and get him breathing. Then we strap and move him," Lucy said as they both removed their helmets.

Cooper immediately began chest compressions, and Lucy administered breaths until the man began to cough.

"I'll call it in," Cooper said, reaching for his radio. "Victim found and resuscitated. Pulse steady. Chopper needed. Medic on scene."

"Copy. Chopper being dispatched. Ambulance waiting for the victim."

While they waited, Lucy checked for other injuries. They inflated a stretcher and used a neck brace to ready the man for transport. Lucy continued to take his vitals.

"I think he's going to be okay, but I can't rule out any broken bones."

"If that's all he gets away with, he's one lucky man."

The radio crackled. "Coop, we got another possible victim. Two-hundred yards or so below you."

"Copy. What do you see?"

"Overturned ATV. Could belong to your guy. Could be someone else."

Cooper looked at Lucy.

"Go ahead. I'll wait for the chopper then meet you down there," she told him.

A knot formed in the pit of his stomach. He couldn't leave her alone. He pressed the microphone on the radio.

"We're waiting for the chopper. Can Danny and Rob check it out?"

"Cooper, we're closer. You need to go," Lucy told him.

She was right, but… His gut, and experience, told him not to leave her. Never leave anyone on their own. That was his rule. He could go out alone, but nobody else could. That's just the way it was.

"Danny and Rob are ready, but you're closer, Coop. What will it be?" Lance asked.

A distinct thwop-thwop-thwop sounded from somewhere above. Copper released the breath he didn't know he was holding.

"Chopper is inbound," he said into the radio. "We're heading to the next site shortly."

"Go," Lucy told him. "I'm right behind you."

He didn't like it, but he reached for his helmet.

"Go. I mean it. You're wasting time."

"I'm heading down now," Cooper told Lance.

He nodded to Lucy, stood, and put on the helmet. He gave her one last glance before he revved the ATV's engine and headed down the mountain, praying he wasn't making another fatal mistake.

***

"You want to talk about it?" Dale asked, settling on the barstool next to his brother.

Cooper took a drink and stared ahead. Scout was sleeping on the floor beside him. "Nothing to talk about."

"I was at the site. I heard the exchange. Was it because Lucy is a woman, or would you have felt the same if it had been Lance or Danny?"

"Back off. You don't know what you're talking about."

Dale motioned for a beer. "I've never known you to be sexist, so I'll give you the benefit of the doubt that it's not because she's a woman, but in this situation, I'm not sure that's entirely the case."

Cooper turned toward his brother. "Look, I didn't want to leave one of my people alone on a mountain after a fresh landslide. That's all."

"That's all? You sure about that?"

"Maybe I was just tired and worried about Lucy being tired. That was the sixth rescue we had in the past two days. You know how crazy it gets when there's flooding and the river swells. It's probably not even over yet. The river will be high for days."

"Look, Coop, I hear what you're saying, but I talked to Mom. She told me about your trip to Mountain Home. Are you sure this doesn't have more to do with that than the flooding?"

Cooper bit back a retort he knew he would regret.

"Where I go is my business, big brother. Just because I live with you—to watch your kids, by the way—doesn't mean I have to answer to you."

Dale shook his head. "Coop, I'm not trying to get into your business or check up on where you go. Come on." Dale lowered his voice to a near whisper. "I love you. I want to be there for you. Talk to me."

Cooper gazed at his brother until his defenses fell, and he accepted his brother's advice. "I know. I appreciate it. I'm just dealing with stuff right now, and I need to figure things out on my own."

"You're not on your own, Coop. You have a lot of people who care about you. Tell me what happened today. With Lucy, I mean."

Cooper shook his head. "I don't know. I've been having dreams lately, nightmares really. Seeing Jessie at the bottom of the ravine, the way she looked, lying there motionless. I thought… Well, you know what I thought. We all thought she was gone.

"Then, after, when we knew she was alive and she was airlifted out, I kept trying to figure out what went wrong, what she'd done wrong. When the doctors said she would most likely never recover, then I asked what I'd done wrong. I let her go. I let my partner go into a fire without backup."

"But you didn't. She didn't go into the fire. She went the other way, to warn people, to let them know they needed to evacuate. You couldn't have known the fire would turn, that she'd be running from it and fall. Nobody could've known. Not even your chief knew."

"It doesn't matter what we knew or didn't know. She was alone. She needed help, and there wasn't anyone to give it to her."

"Coop." Dale laid his hand on his brother's arm. "It wouldn't have mattered. If you'd've been steps behind her, you couldn't have saved her. She couldn't see through the smoke. She lost her bearings. Even if you'd been right there, you couldn't have performed any medical acts that would change the way she is now."

"You don't know that. You don't know that she'd have gone that way, that she'd have gotten lost in the smoke. I might have steered her in the right direction or seen the cliff and yelled for her to stop."

"And maybe you'd both be lying in the nursing home, hooked to machines, with little hope of recovering. Maybe you would never have made it that far. Think about what that would've done to Mom and Dad."

"What about Jessie's mom and dad?"

Dale sighed. "Look, you know how sorry I am that this happened, but you can't take all that on your shoulders. Don't you think I worry about the people I command? Of course, I do. But we all got the same training. We all take the same courses and do the same certifications. What happened to Jessie could've happened to anyone on your crew, including you. You have to stop blaming yourself."

Cooper stared at the glossy grain of the bar. "Her dad said I have to live my life, that Jessie would want that."

"And I'm sure he's right. How would you feel if the shoe was on the other foot? Would you want her to spend her entire life feeling guilty, shutting off her emotions, not allowing anyone special in her life? That's not who you are and not who she was. She would want you to live the life you planned to live, even if it's not with her."

Cooper looked at his reflection in the mirror behind the bar and took a long pull of his beer. His brother was right. Jessie's father had been right. Lucy had been right. Cooper needed to let it all go.

"Where do I start?" He looked at Dale, hoping for insight. "How do I move on after losing someone I love?"

"I'm not sure I'm the best person to ask." Dale took another drink of his beer. "So how about this? How about we help each other figure it out? I know I can do better by my kids than letting them be raised by the two of us."

Cooper laughed. "I should be insulted, but you're not wrong."

"How about we both put ourselves out there. See what happens. Deal?"

"I'm not sure what I'm agreeing to, but deal. I'm open to seeing what happens." Cooper raised his bottle to Dale's, and they tapped them together in agreement.

"Watch out, world. The Mackenzie brothers are back on the market," Dale said.

Cooper smiled at his brother. He was making a big promise, and he wasn't sure his heart was in it.

Six

Amanda stopped mid-reach for the knob. A potted tree, so tall its branches reached up to the gutter lining the roof, drew her eyes to the hand-painted quote above the door.

"Books and doors are the same thing. You open them, and you go through into another world." –

Jeanette Winterson

She smiled and opened the door to the sound of a bell jingling. She instantly felt pulled into another world, like Alice down the rabbit hole or Gulliver landing in Lilliput, Dorothy over the rainbow! She stood and marveled at the floor to ceiling shelves literally filling every space of the building. They wound throughout like a maze, curling around walls, protruding from columns, jutting from under the stairs, even flanking the staircase like a magical banister that twisted and turned as the stairs led upward. Vines ran all around, reminding Amanda of *Where the Wild Things Are*, and she half expected to see yellow-eyed monsters hanging from the wooden beams in the ceiling.

Instead of normal headers telling what each section of the store contained, there were whimsically painted quotes—wonderful, exhilarating quotes—that left little doubt about the contents of the shelves.

"A book is a garden, an orchard, a storehouse, a party, a company by the way, a counselor, a multitude of counselors." - Charles Baudelaire (Self-help).

"Today a reader, tomorrow a leader." - Margaret Fuller (Biography).

"If you don't like to read, you haven't found the right book." - J.K. Rowling (Middle Readers).

"Literature is the safe and traditional vehicle through which we learn about the world and pass on values from one generation to the next." - Laurie Anderson (History).

"I love the way that each book — any book — is its own journey. You open it, and off you go..." - Sharon Creech (Travel).

Amanda could spend all day just reading the

quotations. They made her smile. They made her think. They made her want to read everything in each section. She smiled. What clever marketing.

She found herself walking through the maze, fingering the collection, inhaling the scents of ink, leather, and paper. Some of the books were brand new bestsellers, and others were worn and well-loved. Amanda had never been in any bookstore quite like it, and though she felt bad that Helena saw the bookstore as competition, Amanda could stay inside these walls forever.

She giggled when she read, *"Some books should be tasted, some devoured, but only a few should be chewed and digested thoroughly."* - *Sir Francis Bacon* (Cooking) and laughed out loud at *"I can feel infinitely alive curled up on the sofa reading a book."* - *Benedict Cumberbatch* (Home Decor).

"Do you think this will help improve my cooking?" Dale held a book for Amanda to see.

"Hi, Dale." She surveyed the book. "Well, he is one of the world's top chefs, but I think you might want to start more basic. I'm not sure *European Quisine* is for beginners."

He laughed. "Yeah, but the kids like pasta. And there's pasta on the cover."

Amanda leaned closer and frowned. "A very fancy pasta dish. I think you're better off sticking with spaghetti."

Dale sighed. "You may be right. Besides, they like whatever Cooper makes better than anything I slave over."

"Really? Is he a good cook?" She reached out and picked up a book on cooking for singles, and then, embarrassed, slid it back before Dale could see it.

"No," he said with a laugh. "That's the thing. He's a terrible cook. So all he makes are things he can throw in the air fryer—chicken nuggets and fries, hash browns, crispy broccoli—"

"Wait. He makes broccoli in the air fryer?"

"And the kids love it." Dale shook his head. "I don't get it. Mom makes amazing food, and the kids turn their noses up at it."

Amanda laughed. "Kids are typically partial to chicken nuggets."

"I guess." He shrugged and looked around. "This place is amazing."

"It really is. I've never seen anything like it."

"It's like being in a different world."

"Like Middle Earth or Neverland," Amanda said, pointing out the vines and the paintings—or were they decals?—she hadn't noticed until just then. Mermaids, sea creatures, planets, jungle beasts, anything that graced the pages of a beloved book.

"Or Willie Wonka's Bookstore," Dale said. "My kids can never come in here."

"Afraid they'll never leave?"

"Exactly." He looked at his watch. "I guess I better get back to the station. Take care, Amanda."

"You, too, Dale."

She smiled as she watched him leave. Why hadn't anyone snatched him up yet? It had been almost three years since he lost Ruth. If her mother were here, she'd be saying, *Amanda, why haven't you thought about dating him?* To which she'd laugh and say, *And when would I find time for that?*

***

"I'm here to see Dr. Joe Blake." The stunning raven-haired woman looked around the reception area.

"Do you have an appointment?" Kallie, their newest receptionist, asked.

"No, I don't," the woman answered in a distinct Southern accent. "I'm not here as a patient."

Amanda watched the back and forth and knew she should let Kallie handle this, but she didn't want to embarrass the young woman.

"Serena Blake?" Amanda said from the doorway to the hall.

Serena turned and looked at Amanda. "Why, Amanda, I mean, Dr. Pierce." Serena walked over to Amanda and offered her hand. "I'm so pleased to finally meet you. I recognize you, but I don't think we met at the wedding. Joe and Helena have such nice things to say about you."

"Kallie, this is Dr. Blake's sister. I'll take her up to his office." She motioned for Serena to follow her up the stairs. "Kallie recently started here. You may know

Dotty, our office manager, but we've gotten so busy, we needed someone to manage the desk so Dotty could manage the rest."

"That's lovely. I know Joe is so pleased the clinic is thriving."

"I don't think Joe was expecting you yet," Amanda said. "He thought you'd arrive later tonight."

"Well, I got an early start yesterday and just kept right on driving. I stopped in Texarkana for the night, and it didn't take me any time to get here after that." A shadow crossed Serena's face, and her smile slipped for just a second before she regained her composure. Amanda felt that something was left unsaid. She knew it was better to mind her own business.

"I know Joe and Helena are anxious to see you. They'll be thrilled you arrived early. Joe should be just finishing up with a patient, so I'll take you to his office and let him know you're here."

"How about the powder room first?" Serena asked.

"Oh, of course. Joe and I have a bathroom up here next to our offices. It's that door at the end of the hall."

Amanda pointed Serena's way to the bathroom and turned as Joe came up the stairs.

"Your sister's here," she said with a smile.

"Already?" Joe asked, but his own smile was wide. "Where is she?"

Amanda motioned toward the closed door. "She'll be out in a minute."

Joe looked like a puppy waiting on his owner to greet him at the door, and Amanda laughed. "You're excited."

"I am. We haven't seen each other since the wedding, and I'm really looking forward to spending time with her. You know, there's eight years between us, so we never really got to know each other until after we were both adults." His smiled faltered. "And then after we lost Jeremy, we grew really close."

"Of course. You lost your twin, and she lost a big brother. It's natural for you to have gravitated toward each other."

"Except he up and left almost right away, and I had nobody to lean on," Serena said from the bathroom doorway. Despite her words, she beamed with affection.

"Come here, Serena. You know I'm always there for you."

Amanda watched them hug but felt like a third wheel. "Well, it's nice meeting you, Serena. I'd better go check with Kallie to see who my next patient is."

She left them alone but heard snippets of their conversation as she walked down the stairs. She smiled and thought of her own siblings back home.

Speaking of siblings, she thought as she looked out the front window in time to see Cooper Mackenzie walking down the sidewalk with Suzy and Jamie.

She hadn't thought about him lately. She'd heard he was involved in a couple daring rescues during and after the flood, and she wondered what he did when he wasn't working or watching his niece and nephew. Other than seeing him out with his brother now and then, he pretty much kept to himself.

"Okay, I'll see you at the house later," Serena called

to Joe as she walked down to the reception area. "I'm on my way to see Helena," she told Amanda. "It was so nice to meet you. I'm sure I'll see a lot of you while I'm in town."

"I hope so," Amanda told her, and she meant it.

They bade each other goodbye, and Amanda watched Serena heading in the same direction as Cooper and the kids.

"Your next patient is ready in room three, Dr. Pierce," Kallie called.

Amanda turned and thanked Kallie before heading toward the exam room. She was looking forward to spending more time with Serena and had a feeling Joe's sister was going to spice up things in Buffalo Springs.

***

"Yes, ma'am, Miss Suzy. I've got the book you requested right here," Helena said from behind the desk.

Cooper watched her retrieve the book and hand it to Suzy.

"I can check that out for you whenever you're ready, sweetie."

"What do you say, Bean?"

"Thank you, Miss Helena. Can I look around for a minute?"

"Of course. Take all the time you need." Helena looked at Cooper. "Anything I can interest you in, Coop?"

"Helena, you helped me write all my book reports in

school. I think you know the answer to that question."

Helena laughed. "Cooper, have you ever read anything by C.J. Box?"

"I can't say that I have."

A voice came from behind him. "Then you are missing out on a great read."

Helena sucked in her breath and ran from behind the desk. She and the woman embraced, and Helena bit her lips. "I'm trying to hold back a genuine squeal, but I'm so excited you're here. And you're early! Does Joe know?"

"I just left there," the woman said. She looked vaguely familiar, but Cooper couldn't place her.

"Oh, how rude of me," Helena said when she saw him looking. "Coop, this is Joe's sister, Serena. Serena, this is one of my oldest and dearest friends, Cooper Mackenzie. His brother, Dale, was in the wedding."

"Oh, yes. I recognize you. How could I forget?" Serena batted her eyes at Cooper, and there was a strong tug in his gut. He was wondering the same thing. How could he have forgotten her?

She was stunning in a cobalt blue pantsuit and high heels, a giant blue gem hanging from a chain around her neck. Her hair was halfway down her back, the front pulled back and held with a large clip.

"It's nice to see you again, Serena." He reached for her hand, and she took it, never looking away from his gaze.

"It's real nice to see you, Cooper."

"Did you need anything else, Coop?" Helena asked.

"One of those books I mentioned?"

"You know, Helena, now that you mention it, I think I'd like to try one of those Box books."

"C.J. Box," she said with a smile. "Stay right here, and I'll get the first one in the Joe Pickett series. You're going to love it."

"She's right," Serena said when Amanda walked away. "Joe loves those books, and I've read several myself."

"Uncle Coop, I'm ready to check out my books." He looked down at Suzy and smiled. He'd forgotten why he was there and whom he was with.

"Oh, okay, Bean. As soon as Miss Helena comes back, we can check them out."

"I can help," Sarah called from behind the desk. She looked hastily toward the stacks and whispered, "Helena's not supposed to be on her feet, but, well, you know Helena." She shrugged before returning her focus to her young patron. "What did you find today, Suzy?"

Cooper watched as Suzy handed Sarah her stack of books and began chatting about her finds. He looked around for Jamie and saw him sitting at a table with a girl who looked about his age. Cooper smiled at the way Jamie's eyes danced as he talked to her.

"Uncle Coop?" Serena asked. "Is that Dale's little girl?"

Cooper looked back as Serena. "Yes, Ma'am, and that's her brother, Jamie." He motioned to his nephew.

"Such a tragedy what happened to their mama. I know how close she and Helena's sister were."

Cooper nodded. "Yeah, everyone loved Ruth. She was pretty special."

"So I've heard."

"Here you go, Coop." Helena handed him a book. "Ready to check out?"

"I sure am," he said, though he wondered if he even had his library card. He wasn't sure he'd used it since high school, but he didn't want to admit that in front of Serena. "I'll get Sarah to check it out so you can visit with Serena."

"Thanks, Coop." Helena turned to her sister-in-law and linked their arms together. "Let me point the way to the house, and you can get yourself freshened up before dinner."

"Hmph," Cooper grunted. He didn't think Serena could look any fresher than she already did.

"Coop? Ready?"

He handed Sarah his book and told her he'd lost his card. By the time he was tucking his new card into his pocket, Helena was back in her office, and Serena was gone.

✳✳✳

That evening, Serena watched out the window while Helena made them both cups of herbal tea. She carried a tray into the living room and set it on the coffee table. Serena took one more glance up and down the street before fixing a smile on her face and turning to Helena.

"I can't tell you how excited I am to be here." She

picked up the teacup and took a sip of the flowery tea.

"Oh, same here," Helena said. "I've been looking forward to your visit for weeks. And it seems to have come at just the right time." Helena put down her tea and tilted her head slightly to the side, gazing at Serena sympathetically.

"Did Joe tell you?" Serena asked.

"Well, yes, and I do run a library, so I see the magazines and newspapers. You poor thing. I know what they're saying, but what really happened?"

Serena heaved a long, heavy sigh. She knew she'd have to talk about it at some point. "It was awful. Everything that could go wrong, did go wrong. And none of it was within my control. Honestly, I did the best I could to keep everything running smoothly, but everything I tried, backfired."

"The news reports said you failed to watch the weather, but come on. Everyone knew a hurricane was heading that way. Why was that on you?"

"That's not the only thing they reported," Serena said with a roll of her eyes. "It was apparently my fault that the bride got drunk and danced too close to the lanterns. Lanterns, which I said should not be moved inside because there wasn't as much room, and the lanterns were meant to provide ambience for the outdoor reception."

"Oh my gosh, and then the failed escape to the honeymoon!" Helena held her face in her hands and laughed. "How was that your fault?"

"I didn't make sure her passport was in her purse.

She changed purses!" Serena threw up her hands. "She didn't tell me she'd decided to take a different one. How was I supposed to know?"

"Why was the responsibility for the bride's passport on the wedding planner?"

"Oh, Helena, I have to hold up their dresses and wipe their behinds while they use the bathroom, for Heaven's sake. You wouldn't believe it." She took a drink of tea and reached for a pastry. "These look divine."

"My sister made them, of course. Cherry turnovers."

"Oooh, mmm." Serena wiped her mouth with her napkin and licked her lips. "A bite of heaven."

"I hate to ask," Helena said with hesitation.

"Is it true that I lost three other weddings of the century because of all the bad press?" Serena released a breath. "Yes, and the press still won't leave me alone. I'm so happy to be out of the city."

"Do you have another wedding you're currently working on?"

"Not one. I had those three booked and was working with four other brides to set dates and begin planning, and none are returning my calls."

"Over this one wedding for a female rock star and her shirt-ripping, football Fabio, fiancé? Seriously?"

Serena laughed. "It's the chance you take when you work with celebrities." She finished her tea and looked at Helena. "You know, when I first got into the business, I was all about giving women the wedding of their dreams, no matter what they could pay or what their backgrounds were. I wanted every little girl to grow up to be a beautiful bride with the perfect wedding. I never aspired to be *the* wedding planner of the stars."

"So, who says you need to be? I mean, it's your business. You can choose the clients."

"Oh, I wish that was true. Once it happens, it's just what's expected."

"But it doesn't have to be. You're in charge. You can decide whose wedding you do."

Serena thought about that for a moment. "Hmm. I guess once I started doing celebrity weddings, nobody else sought me out. I mean, I was just handed off from one star to another, and I no longer had the need to advertise. Most people probably think I'm too expensive for them, but as you know, the cost is in the wedding."

"Well, you have some time to think about what kinds of weddings you want to take on in the future. Maybe you need to start reassessing the brides and the kinds of affairs you take on."

"Maybe I do, Helena. Maybe I do."

***

"Run, Bean, run!" Cooper shouted as loudly as he could, his heart racing as Suzy tried to outrun her pursuer. Suzy started to look behind her, and Cooper almost lost it. "Don't look back, Suzy! Just run! Run, run, run!"

A cheer went up as Suzy touched the bag at home plate.

"Yes!" Cooper yelled, pumping his fist in the air. "That's my girl!" Scout let out a bark.

It was the first homerun of the season and Suzy's first foray into softball. Cooper felt himself puff up like a peacock as the other parents patted him on the back.

"You should be proud of your daughter," the dad of one of the other team's players said.

Cooper beamed at him. "My niece, but yes, Sir. I'm real proud of her."

After the game, he took Suzy and Jamie out for ice cream.

"Wait until your dad hears about your game. You're a natural! Just like your mama was."

Suzy's grin reached from ear to ear. "It was so much fun, Uncle Coop! I can't wait for the next one."

"What can I get you?"

Cooper looked at the young woman behind the counter. He recalled Paige telling him about the two sisters who opened the ice cream parlor. He smiled and told the kids to order what they wanted. He was polite and wished her good luck with the shop, but what was Paige thinking? They had to be close to ten years younger than he was. That would be like Dale dating Serena Blake. The thought made him wince, for more than one reason.

They ordered, and Cooper welcomed the sisters to the town, wishing them well with their business venture. He wasn't about to ask out anyone who wasn't born in the same decade he was, or at least close to it.

One of the girls gave Scout a doggie ice cream bar,

and they all laughed as she gobbled it down.

Cooper walked down the street with Suzy and Jamie, each licking their own ice cream cone. He was happy to have a Saturday with no plans other than being with the kids. As they neared the house, he heard his name called and stopped.

"It is Cooper, right?"

He turned and saw Serena walking toward him. He let a slow smile spread across his face.

"It is. Nice to see you again, Serena."

"And you've got Dale's children with you again. They're so much bigger than I remember from the wedding. Suzy, we didn't have a chance to talk the other day. Do you remember me?"

Suzy smiled shyly. "You helped me learn to throw the petals."

Serena beamed. "I sure did, and you were very good at it! You were the highlight of my brother's wedding. And you are…" She tapped her lip with a long-nailed finger, and Cooper found himself staring at her mouth. "Jamie. Right?"

"Yes, Ma'am. You're Uncle Joe's sister."

"Good memory, Jamie." She looked up at Cooper.

"And who is this beautiful creature?" She bent down to pet Scout. Cooper had never realized before how often people automatically started petting Scout without even asking if it was okay. No wonder there were always police calls about dog bites.

"Are you getting settled in our little town?" he asked Serena. "I know it's a far cry from Houston."

Serena laughed, stood, and clapped the fur from her hands. "That it is, and I love it. What are y'all doing on this beautiful spring day?"

"Suzy just scored a homerun in her softball game, and we got ice cream to celebrate." He held his up so she could see it and felt his face grow hot. Why was he acting like he was Suzy's age? He continued to smile, embarrassed but unsure what to do next.

"How lovely." She bent toward Suzy. "Next time, let me know when you're playing, and I'll come watch, too." She raised her eyes back to Cooper, and he swallowed hard.

"Okay," Suzy said, not taking her eyes off her dripping ice cream as she licked it from the side of the cone.

Cooper felt his throat constrict. "We'll be sure to let you know," he managed, though he didn't know how.

What was it about this woman that made him act like a pubescent teenager? After five years of not even noticing any women, why was he so tongue-tied around Serena Blake?

Serena gave him a bright smile. "Well, it was nice running into y'all. I'm going to take a stroll around your little town. I feel like I never had a chance when I was here for the wedding, and Joe says it has grown so much since then."

Neither child spoke, both concentrating heavily on their treats.

"Enjoy your stroll," Cooper said, wanting to kick himself. What a stupid response. He couldn't come up with anything better to say other than parrot her words? "Come on, kids, let's get home."

He was in a hurry to leave and save face, but he felt Serena watching him the whole way back to the house, and it took everything in him not to turn around and look like the fool she must think him to be.

***

Amanda spent her day off trying to catch up on chores. She vacuumed, dusted, and even mopped the floor. She opened all the windows and let the house air out, aware that her seasonal allergies would not be forgiving but enjoying the spring breeze and fresh air anyway. She continued her spring cleaning in her closet and carried a trash bag of clothes and shoes to her car to take to the church thrift shop. After lunch, she went outside to assess the pathetic gardens she had.

Amanda's parents had exquisite gardens, and she always wanted to have a home surrounded by colorful blossoms that bloomed from early spring to late fall. Instead, what she saw as she looked around were a few empty oak leaf hydrangeas, a row of irises along the porch that were just beginning to poke from the ground, and some daffodils and tulips just waking to spring. Frustrated, she reminded herself that her parents had a gardening staff to take care of their flowers.

Amanda went right to work on the bushes, trimming the woody stalks she hoped would produce vibrant flowers by June. She hauled away fallen sticks and branches from nearby trees and tried to determine if she needed new mulch this year.

"Hi Amanda."

She turned to see Serena watching her from the sidewalk. "Doing some spring gardening?"

Amanda gave a short snort. "I wish I could call it that. I'm not sure I'm good enough to call myself a gardener, but I'm trying. I did some research over the winter on what flowering plants grow well here, and I ordered seeds that I've got propagating inside and plan to plant tomorrow." She looked up at the sky. "It's supposed to rain again on Monday, so I've got my fingers crossed it's not too much and not too little."

"I know what you mean about not being a gardener. I always thought I could save so much money on flowers if I grew them myself, but I just don't have time for that."

"Too bad you won't be here later in the season to see Dale's gardens. I don't know how he does it. He and Ruth loved gardening together, and they put in the most magnificent gardens all over their front and back yards. He's never stopped caring for them, and it pays off. He and Mrs. Nelson seem to have a friendly competition each year to see whose gardens are the best."

Serena was silent for a moment, her expression one of deep thought before she smiled. "I didn't know that about Dale. How sweet that he still does that in his wife's memory. Joe says he's never stopped loving her."

"He's right." Amanda frowned. "It's a shame he hasn't found someone to make him want to date again.

He and those kids deserve a wife and mother who will love them as fiercely as Ruth did."

"Do you think that's possible?" Serena asked. "For someone to love like that again?"

Amanda tilted her head and pondered the question. "I honestly don't know. From what I've heard, they had a perfect love. But you know what they say, those who loved perfectly once can love even more the second time, or something like that." She laughed with a shrug.

"You know, I don't think I've ever truly loved like that, but I can see what you mean. When one has that great a capacity for love, it's only a matter of time until he loves again."

Amanda found herself thinking about Cooper and wondered why he'd never fallen in love. Or had someone broken his heart and caused him to cut himself off to another relationship?

"Well, I'm heading back to the house after a long walk, but it was real nice talking to you, Amanda. Enjoy planning your garden. I'm sure it will be magnificent." Serena waved and headed down the sidewalk toward Joe and Helena's house.

Amanda waved goodbye and turned back to her garden. Everything in it had grown, flowered, and flourished all summer, then laid dormant through the hard, cold winter. Now, there were signs of life again, signs of resilience and growth. Was it true that love was like a rose, a flower that returned each year, ready to bloom again even after shutting down all that time? Was Dale's heart meant to find true love again?

She blinked and gave a quick shake of her head. Why were her thoughts going to the Mackenzie brothers, first Cooper and then Dale? It wasn't like either had ever paid more than a moment's attention to her. Then she recalled how thoughtful Cooper had been the night they'd come upon each other in the rain. She'd been surprised at the things he said to her and, as much as she didn't want to admit it, found herself thinking about him more than once since then.

***

"Busy month for you," Sheriff Wilson said to Cooper as he filled out his paperwork.

"I like busy," Cooper said.

"I like busy, too, but this spring has been crazy. I hope the weather stabilizes. No more flooding or swelling rivers or anything of the like." She sat down across from Cooper and placed two cups of coffee on his desk.

Cooper reached for one, took a sip, and thanked her. "I have a feeling this isn't a friendly, how's it going conversation." He put down his pen and sat back.

"Sure, it is," Beverly said. "It's a friendly, how's it going, I need to check on you conversation."

He didn't like the sound of that. "Check on me?"

"I didn't say anything about your reaction during the landslide because it all worked out okay. But it's been on my mind, as well as the car rescue and the boys in the river. You seem to be jumping into all the most dangerous operations without hesitation."

"Isn't that what you pay me to do?" He tried to keep his voice level, but his temper was a live wire ready to spark.

"We do, and you're the best SAR coordinator in ten counties, but that doesn't mean you have to be the one to do the rescues every time."

"I have a good team, and we work well under my command and leadership. And I've got the dog." He gestured toward Scout, asleep on her doggie bed.

"I don't disagree." She paused. "But over the past five years, you've done a lot more rescuing the victims and a lot less leading the team."

"I would argue that leading the rescue is leading the team." He tried to remain respectful, but it wasn't easy. What was she getting at?

Sheriff Wilson looked at him for a long time before she nodded. "Like I said, you're the best there is. But you've got baggage. I know all about baggage. Try being a black, female sheriff in the South. You always feel like you have to prove yourself to everyone, but Cooper, it has to stop at some point. You pull another stunt like you did at the landslide, and you're on leave without pay until a shrink says you're good to go. You understand?"

"Yes, Ma'am" he said before something occurred to him. "Sheriff Wilson?"

She was starting to stand but eased back down. "Yes, Officer?"

"That rescue was weeks ago. Why are you just coming to me now? Has there been a complaint?"

"Not exactly," she said. "But word recently reached me that you went to see Jessie after that. I wanted to make sure everything is okay."

"It's all good," he said without hesitation.

"Glad to hear it. Don't do anything to risk that. We need you in the right head space and not in danger of being hurt. You got that?"

"Yes, Ma'am."

He watched her walk away before reaching for the coffee she'd brought him. He downed the cup and crushed it before tossing it into the trash.

He knew what she was getting at and why she was concerned, but Cooper was in the process of letting it go, letting the guilt and the anger go. He knew he wasn't as ready as Dale wanted him to be to look for love again, but he wasn't going to keep blaming himself for what happened, and he certainly wasn't trying to put himself in harm's way. It felt like he had something to prove for a long time, but that made him better at his job and, he thought, a better leader. Maybe he needed to take his boss's advice and rethink what that leadership was supposed to look like.

Seven

"So, you're the famous Cindy Kline," Serena said over coffee in the town café.

"I don't even know what to say to that," Cindy said. "I can't believe I'm sitting here at a table with the truly famous Serena Blake."

"I told you she'd be willing to meet you," Helena said to Cindy.

"More than willing," Serena told Cindy. "There's nothing I like more than talking about weddings." She meant it, too. Despite the debacle of the last wedding she planned, she still loved doing it. In fact, she was more excited about helping to plan a small-town, no-frills wedding than she had been about the wedding she planned for the crown prince of Denmark. There was something so, so honest and sincere about the couple, and it reminded Serena why she started planning weddings to begin with.

"Now, what kind of wedding are you planning on having?" She opened her iPad to her notebook app and turned on her digital pen. She'd already created a folder for the wedding and had all her sections set up and ready to fill in.

Cindy took a deep breath, glanced from Helena to Serena, then looked down at her hands twisting in her lap. "I know most girls spend their whole lives dreaming about their weddings, but I spent most of my life just trying to take care of my mom and me. I never had any reason to believe that a real wedding could happen for me. Even when I was with Ethan, I figured we'd just elope." She looked up and shrugged.

Serena knew Cindy's story and knew Ethan was one of the SEALs killed in the helicopter accident with her brother, Jeremy. She took a moment to let the air of sadness pass between them, two women who both lost men they loved. Serena reached across the table and patted Cindy's hand.

"I don't know if I've told you how sorry I am for your loss."

Cindy gave her a sad smile. "Thank you. I'm sorry about Jeremy. Ethan really looked up to him."

"Thank you. I'm sure Ethan is looking down on you and is happy that you found someone."

Cindy nodded. "Sometimes I think Ethan led me here, to this town and to Jackson."

"That's a nice way to think about it. I believe Joe feels the same way about Jeremy." Serena looked at Helena and smiled. "So, Cindy, now that you are able to plan a wedding, what do you have in mind?"

"I want it at the church. I never thought I'd have a church wedding, but that has become very important to me. And to Jackson. I want to wear white, and I want my dad to walk me down the aisle. I know who I want to be in it, and Jackson does, too, but we're keeping that to ourselves for now. The rest, well, I don't have any idea." She smiled and gave a little lift of her shoulders.

"Oh, Cindy, that's the best kind of wedding. We can start from the very beginning without any preconceived notions or fancy pie-in-the-sky ideas. This makes me so excited." And she was. This would be the first wedding Serena was looking forward to planning in years.

A bell jingled over the door, and all three women turned toward Cooper Mackenzie as though he was a sheet of metal and they were all magnets. He walked to the counter to place an order, and three sets of eyes followed him each step of the way.

"Now, that is one fine looking fellow," Serena said. "They're like the Hemsworth brothers. It should be illegal for there to be two lookers like that in one family."

"Do you know the Hemsworth brothers?" Cindy asked, her eyes wide.

"I've had the pleasure of meeting Chris and Liam, but I wasn't involved in their weddings. They're great guys, though, very down to earth."

"Wow," Cindy breathed, making Serena laugh.

"They're just people, Cindy, and believe me, that's the nicest thing I can say about most of the couples I've worked with. But my lips are sealed. The first thing I do when I plan a wedding is sign a confidentiality agreement."

"Oh, no need to do that with me. I'm an open book. Believe me."

"Hello, ladies."

All three magnets turned toward Cooper, who was looking better than ever in his sheriff's department uniform, lightly tussled brown hair, and a bit of scruff beginning to show on his chin. Serena nearly swooned, and she'd been around more than her fair share of handsome men. Of course, most of them were ineligible, in more ways than one.

"Hey, Coop," Helena said, standing to give him a hug before reaching down to scratch Scout behind an ear. "And hello, Scout. How's everyone's favorite search and rescue hero and his partner?"

Cooper blushed, and Serena found that endearing.

"None of that hero business, please. Just doing my job."

"I was talking about Scout," Helena said.

Cooper barked a laugh before turning to Cindy. "Hi, Cindy. You look great. Being engaged suits you." He smiled at Cindy before his gaze fell on Serena. He nodded. "Serena, I hope you're doing well."

Serena gave him her biggest, most brilliant smile. "Very well, Cooper. We're just talking wedding plans."

He held her gaze for a beat before looking back at Cindy. "That's great. Well, it was nice to see everyone. I, uh." He looked back at Serena. "I'll see y'all later."

They said goodbye, and Serena watched him leave.

"Yes, Sir. Those Mackenzie men sure are the biscuits and gravy."

"Is that good?" Cindy asked.

Serena turned to her with a wide grin. "Oh, believe me, Sugar, it's the absolute best compliment they could get."

***

Cooper was almost back to the station when a light rain began to fall. He was so tired of rain, but there wasn't much he could do about it. He turned his attention toward a sound on the other side of the road and walked right into something. Rather, someone. Taken by surprise, he was rendered speechless, and then his manners got the best of him.

"Dr. Pierce, I'm so sorry! I wasn't looking. Are you okay?"

The doctor laughed. "I'm fine. Honestly, I wasn't looking either. I guess that should teach us both a lesson, especially since bumping into each other seems to be becoming a habit."

Cooper realized his heart was beating quite fast, which was odd because he wasn't often surprised in a way that made his heart race.

"I shouldn't be surprised to run into you," she was saying.

"Why is that?"

She pointed to her umbrella. "It's raining."

"Excuse me?"

"We always seem to see each other when it's raining."

Cooper hadn't realized that, but she was right. Every time they'd run into each other in the past couple months, at work or otherwise, it was raining. He laughed.

"Well, I'll be. You're right. And I was thinking about how sick I am of rain, but you've given me a new perspective."

She looked confused. "Really? How?"

"If I get to run into you every time it rains, then that's not a bad thing at all." He held his smile while embarrassment flooded through him, and she opened her mouth in surprise. What made him say that? Would she think he was flirting with her? Was he flirting with her? Had he offended her?

"Oh. Well, that's a very nice thing to say." She looked away, and he could see she was blushing.

"I'm sorry if that was forward. I didn't mean for it to be. I like running into you. I mean, it's nice talking to you. Um…" He was digging a deeper hole and wanted to crawl into it. Dr. Pierce was practically a colleague of his, someone he saw most often when they were both on the job. He felt unprofessional at best and creepy at worst. He'd never been tongue-tied around any woman, but first, there was Serena, and now Dr. Pierce.

"Don't worry, Cooper. I understand what you meant. It's always nice to run into you, too. Though it's nicer when it's not the middle of the night and someone is or has been in danger." Whatever embarrassment she may have felt had vanished, and she slipped back into her normal demeanor. He was relieved that they seemed to agree that they were colleagues and both understood it.

"You've got me there," Cooper said. "It's nice to not be bringing you a victim of some adventure gone wrong or natural disaster." In fact, it was nice to be talking to her on a normal day, outside a catastrophe, even if it was raining.

"Are you on your way back to work?" She looked at the take-out bag in his hand.

"Yeah, just taking a short break to get some lunch. How about you?"

"On my way to pick up a sandwich." She bent down and scratched Scout's head. What was it with women and dogs? "Hi, Scout. Are you being good?"

"Don't let me keep you." Cooper said, though it felt nice to stand there and talk to her.

"Oh, you're not keeping me. Believe it or not, it's been a slow day at the clinic, which is unusual for a Monday."

"Slowest day of the week for me, typically," Cooper said. He had a brief notion to chuck his sandwich and offer to go with her to get a new one, but he quickly dismissed the thought. Again, they were colleagues. Professionals. And besides, he had someone else on his mind. Maybe.

"Well, I guess I'll see you the next time it rains, Cooper."

"Yes, Ma'am. Sounds about right, Dr. Pierce."

"Amanda," she said. "Please, just call me Amanda."

"Amanda," he repeated, enjoying the way it felt on his lips. "You have a great afternoon, and I'll look for you the next time there's a cloud in the sky."

Amanda laughed, and it had a nice ring to it. Quite nice. He gave her a little wave and found himself turning to watch her walk away. When he and Scout arrived back to the station, he realized he'd been grinning the rest of his walk through town. But the smile quickly faded.

He didn't make it through the station door before he heard the sheriff calling his name.

***

"You've got a patient in two," Kallie told Amanda, poking her head into the lunchroom.

Amanda quickly crinkled her sandwich wrapping and tossed it into the trash can. She took the time to brush her teeth and inspect her face for crumbs or sauce before glancing at the patient's chart.

"Stan, what brings you in today?" Amanda smiled at the local carpenter and washed her hands even though she'd just done that in the bathroom. It was as much habit as protocol.

Stan lifted his hand to show her the bloody gauze. "Little accident on the job."

"I see that. How little?"

Stan shrugged. "Big enough to bring me here but little enough that I hope to be back at work within the hour."

She put on gloves and unwrapped the gauze and

examined the cut.

"Saw?"

"Yeah. My hand just slipped right off the board."

"You're lucky. Another half inch—"

"I know. I wouldn't be back at work today or ever."

Amanda placed his hand on the silver tray next to the table. "It's going to need several stitches, and you're not going to be able to use it for a few days." She looked at him as she opened the door. "Going back to work isn't a good idea. Melanie," she called from the doorway. "I need your help in here, please."

"It's fine. With all the work I've taken on lately, I've got a whole crew now. I can supervise."

Amanda furrowed her brow and frowned at her patient. "Stan, since when do you only supervise?" She looked at Melanie. "Can you prep for stitches, please?"

"I can supervise. I know I need my hands. Don't worry. I won't do anything stupid." He winced as Melanie cleaned the wound.

"You're going to need pain meds. You can't operate machinery while you're on them."

"Understood. Really. I won't do anything I'm not supposed to do."

Amanda had no choice but to hope he meant it. Stan was no different than any other small business owner she treated. He wasn't going to let an injury keep him from doing his job.

With Melanie's assistance, she stitched his hand, keeping him talking to distract him.

"So, what are you working on now?"

"Renovating the old Burns house for Wade and Jackson. Cutting down the kitchen, turning the entranceway and living room into a reception area, converting the dining room into a conference room. The upstairs bedrooms will be turned into offices, like we did here, and the bathrooms need to be updated. It's gonna look real nice when we're done, and they'll be a lot happier than working out of Wade's kitchen. They've got a good plan for what they want, and they're both easy to work with. It's a good job."

"If it turns out anything like Joe's house and this building here, it's going to be beautiful." She stopped and looked at Stan. "You do really nice work, Stan. I mean that. Your work rivals any big city construction firm."

Stan blushed. "Thanks, Dr. Pierce. That means a lot. I try hard to do good work and make my clients happy."

"Well, it shows." She held out the twine for Melanie to cut. "All done. I'll write you a script for the pain meds." She stood, removed her gloves, and washed her hands while Melanie cleaned up. "I meant what I said. Be careful. I don't want to see you in here again because you didn't follow doctor's orders."

"I promise, Dr. Pierce. I'll be good."

"Good. Melanie, can you please give Stan his discharge instructions?"

She left the room thinking about the work Stan had done around town. Maybe it was time for her to update her 1970s kitchen and bathrooms. She'd have to give that some thought. She wondered if Stan was married to his job and if that's why he was still single. She knew he pined for Helena for years, but she never returned the feelings. What kind of woman could win his broken heart, and why was Amanda suddenly becoming a matchmaker? Dale, Cooper, Stan? Why should it matter to her if any of them dated?

Amanda shook her head and put on a smile as she opened the door to exam room three.

***

"Over here," the voice called.

Cooper and Lance made their way through the woods, limbs slapping them as they raced toward the river. When they emerged from the trees, they saw a man frantically waving to them from a rock overlooking the river.

"There!" the man pointed and yelled. "He was there. And he just got sucked down. Like something grabbed him and pulled him in, dude. It happened so fast. Like lightning." He banged his hands together and made a swishing noise.

Cooper and Lance looked at each other.

"Stay with him," Cooper told Lance. "Make sure he doesn't do anything stupid." He shed the clothes he had put on over his wetsuit.

"What's your name?" Cooper asked the man.

"Kurt. That's Chris. You gotta save him, man." Kurt broke down in tears, swatting at the air around him, and yelling at Cooper to hurry.

"Calm down, Kurt. Has he come up at all?"

"No, dude. He's been down there for a long time. Could he have been taken downstream? Maybe he's farther down. Or maybe something got him."

Cooper and Lance exchanged another look.

"Where's Lucy when we need her?" Lance said. "This guy needs something."

"Just stay with him, but not too close unless he blacks out."

"Lots of limbs and branches jutting out over there," Lance observed, pointing to the river.

"Yeah. I see that."

"What does that mean? What happened to him?" Kurt yelled.

Cooper leaned closer to the agitated man and took several quick breaths through his nose. "Sir, have you been drinking or taking drugs?"

"Maybe. A little. I mean, earlier."

"Before you got in your kayaks?"

The man swallowed. "Yeah, but we were cool. I mean, we didn't do that much."

"Your friend, too?"

"Yeah, but he was okay, man. I know he was."

"He may have been, but even sober, he'd have a hard time if he hit a strainer. He might've gotten out and made it downstream. Under the influence, though, I don't know."

"What's a strainer?"

"Kind of like a whirlpool. You stay here, okay?" Cooper told Kurt as he clipped a heavy rope around his waist. The other end, Lance harnessed to a tree. "You ready?" Cooper asked Lance.

"Yeah. You start, and I'll go in if you get tired and haven't found—" he looked at Kurt. "If you need to switch."

"Here goes," Cooper said before diving into the water. He swam with confidence toward the strainer, feeling the pull as he got closer. He was almost to the site when he stopped and raised his head out of the water. Before he could get his breath, there was a sudden gush nearby, and a kayak was pushed up out of the water just past the strainer. Cooper dove out of the way as the kayak crashed down beside him.

"Coop!" Lance yelled, pulling on the rope.

Cooper popped up and signaled that he was okay. He could hear the man screaming from the riverbank as Cooper swam over to the battered kayak. As he suspected, there was nobody inside, nobody caught in the lining rope that ran around the cockpit. Cooper took a deep breath and dove under the water. He held onto anything he could grasp to keep from being pulled into the strainer. He went down several times but saw nothing. He swam away from the tidal force and emerged, shaking his head.

"I don't see him," he called.

"Let me have a go," Lance said.

Cooper's instinct told him no, but the words from the sheriff came back to him, and he made his way to shore.

"It's not a rescue mission anymore," he told Lance

as they switched off with the rope. "We should call it in."

"You want to radio in while I make my way over."

"Let me call it in first. If you don't see anything, I'll get Scout to work the riverbank, but I'm not hopeful."

He radioed the news, and Sheriff Wilson informed him that an ambulance was already on its way. He signed off and made sure the rope was secure before he gave the okay for Lance to go in.

Chris wasn't located, though the search continued for several hours. Scout did her best with no luck.

Kurt was arrested and charged with boating under the influence of drugs and alcohol. Cooper knew, at some point, the man's body would turn up, but with the cold temperatures in the river, it could be weeks. Since the body was nowhere near the scene, Chris most likely didn't drown right away and was carried downstream, hitting rocks and limbs along the way. It was a gruesome death, and one Cooper didn't like to think about. Some days, the best job in the world turned out to be the worst.

***

Once again, Amanda hadn't thought about dinner before leaving for work and was too exhausted to make anything. Her slow morning was the calm before the storm of a hectic afternoon. She tried not to get carry-out too often, but she was picking up her ready-made dinners more and more. At least once a week, she went to Rick's. That night was when she treated herself to a Bogart burger, mushroom and Swiss on sourdough bread.

Amanda walked into Rick's and stopped. Instead of walking to the register to order, she did something out of character. She sidled up to a man at the bar.

"Hey, there. Rough afternoon?"

Cooper turned and looked at her, his hand wrapped around a bottle of beer, and his eyes glazed over in what she now knew was not an alcohol-induced haze but a battle to keep his emotions in check.

"You could say that."

"Bad rescue?"

"No rescue. Too late for that."

Her heart lurched. "Oh, gosh, Cooper. I'm so sorry." She instinctively laid her hand on his arm, and he jerked away. Amanda jumped, pulling her hand back as if he was a coiling snake ready to attack.

Cooper winced. "I'm sorry. Reflex. On days like this…"

She imagined a thousand endings to that sentence, and her heart went out to him.

"Anything I can do to help?"

He shook his head and took another swig. "Nope, but thanks. I'm going to finish my beer and then do the only thing I know to do in times like this."

She understood, thinking back to the night she'd run into him outside the church.

"Want company?" she asked, having had no intentions of doing so. "I mean, I guess that's a private thing, but if you don't want to go alone, I could go with you. For support." She didn't know why she kept talking.

She should get up and leave.

Cooper's silence was ear-splitting. What an idiot she was for trespassing on his ritual, for acting like her presence could make everything better.

"Thanks for the offer. Really. It's kind of you, but I'm good. I've got company." He gestured to Scout and tipped the bottle back, letting the rest of the beer slide down his throat. A beautiful throat, smooth and tanned, a kissable throat.

Amanda jolted like she'd been pinched. What was she thinking?

"You okay?" he asked, his brow raised and his mouth resembling a sideways question mark.

"Yes, fine. Thanks. I, uh, didn't prepare anything for dinner, so I just stopped by to pick up a burger. Better put my order in." She stood to leave but felt his hand on her arm. She looked at his hand, calloused like Stan's hand that she'd stitched. Her gaze moved up to his green eyes, eyes like a cat's, the color of the old-fashioned marbles she'd played with at her grandmother's house when she was a kid.

"Thanks again for the offer of your company. I appreciate it."

She swallowed, lost in those beautiful round marbles. "You're welcome," she said breathlessly before turning to go, feeling his hand slowly drop from her arm.

"Hey, Amanda," he called when she was halfway to the register. She turned. "You got an umbrella with you tonight?"

"An umbrella?" she asked, feeling slightly off-kilter.

"Yeah, you know, in case it's raining out there." A slow, sexy grin spread across his face, and Amanda stood there like a fool, transfixed by everything about him, until she understood what he meant. She managed a smile.

"Not tonight, Cooper. Do you think there's been a change in the weather?"

There had been. She'd felt it. Only, maybe it was just her. Maybe he felt nothing at all.

He just looked at her and smiled before he stood and tossed a handful of bills on the bar. "See you next time it rains," he said before sauntering across the room and out the door, leaving her with a racing heart and jumbled thoughts.

***

Cooper lit a candle and knelt in an empty pew. Scout lay quietly on the carpeted aisle. It was understood by everyone in town, including his elderly priest, that Scout and Cooper were a team, necessitating them being together at almost all times.

Cooper knew the drowned man was an idiot and did the dumbest thing ever by getting in that kayak, but people did things all the time that were stupid. That didn't mean they deserved to die. Cooper said a few prayers for the man and his family before sitting back in the pew and gazing at the tabernacle.

"Good evening, Cooper." Father Michael slid into the pew beside him as he sometimes did when Cooper showed up on days like this. "Another loss?"

Cooper blew out a long breath. "Yes, Father. A man in his early thirties, wife and kids at home. Kayaking under the influence, drugs and alcohol." He shook his head and sighed. "I just don't get it. Why do something like that? Why take that kind of risk?"

"Often, we can't explain the actions of others."

For several moments, they sat in silence watching the flickering candles.

"How are you doing, Cooper?"

Cooper smiled. "You talked to Mom."

"She may have stopped by a week or two ago."

"She stops by all the time. I know my mother. I guess she told you about my trip to see Jessie."

"She did. She also told me you were going to, as she put it, start living. How's that going?"

"Not so great. I mean, I'm having fun with the kids, really throwing myself into enjoying my time with them instead of just going through the motions."

"That's good. That's a good start."

"I met someone. She's…interesting. Beautiful, smart, successful."

"Cooper," Father Michael said with a smile, his voice rising an octave. "Good for you. Someone local?"

"No. She's…" He was about to say she was just visiting, but his words caught in his throat. He thought he was telling Father about Serena, but in his mind, he was picturing someone else, someone unexpected, and he pushed the thoughts of both women away, confused and unsure. "You know, Father, I don't know."

"You don't know if she's local?"

"I don't know if she's the one I'm, well, I just don't know."

"Sounds like you have some more praying to do. I'll leave you to it." The priest stood but Cooper stopped him.

"Father, can I ask you a question?"

"Sure, Cooper. What is it?" He sat back down.

"My mother told me God has a plan for me and all I need to do is listen for him and follow the path he's laid out. But I don't hear him. Ever. Not even when I sit in here and listen for him. How do I know which path is the right one when I don't hear him telling me which way to go?"

Father Michael smiled. "Cooper, that's the biggest question we all have. I can't tell you how many times in my almost-fifty years as a priest I've been asked that."

"And?"

"And the answer is different for everyone. God doesn't speak to any two people in the same way. For some, he speaks through the language of nature. For others, his words come from the mouths of friends and loved ones, even complete strangers. We often miss what he says because we're listening to the wrong voices or looking for him in the wrong places."

"But I'm here. I'm always looking for him in here. Shouldn't this be where I find him?"

"Of course, he's here. He's always here waiting for you Cooper. But the truth is, most people spend their time in church talking to him rather than listening for him. So he waits for them in places they least expect, when they're open to their surroundings and their circumstances, and he can approach them right there and then when they're ready to hear what he has to say. Like Elijah in the cave or Moses on the mountain."

"How do I know when it's his voice I'm hearing and not my own thoughts?"

"You will know, Cooper. I promise you that when the Lord truly speaks to you, you will know. Now, my son, how about a blessing?"

Cooper bowed his head while the priest prayed over him and blessed him with the Sign of the Cross. When he raised his head to thank him, Father was already standing. He gave Scout a blessing, too, before leaving. Cooper was alone in the silent church, the only faint sounds, those of a closing door and distant fading footsteps.

Eight

There was indeed a change in the weather. Instead of rain every other day, the first of May brought the shining sun and rising temperatures. Amanda felt sweat running down her back even though it was barely morning as she ran along the backstreets and country roads in and around town. She loved her morning runs, but they were becoming tedious. A car sped by, its force almost pushing Amanda off the road, and she decided she needed a change of scenery.

She was off this coming weekend, completely off, not even on call, and she was thinking of trading her run for a good, long hike in the national park. Joe often talked about running with his friends on the trail that wound through the park, but Amanda was looking for something more. She'd lived in Buffalo Springs for over three years and had never taken the time to hike through the forest. She knew there were beautiful waterfalls and breath-taking mountain views, and she thought it was time she discovered those for herself.

As she re-entered town, she caught sight of the visitor's center. She'd been told it was one of the first places Andi and Wade created when they started rebuilding the town. Amanda went there once, when she moved to Buffalo Springs, collected a few brochures, and never went back. The brochures now served as nothing more than drawer liners in the hutch in her kitchen. Maybe it was time to pull them out and see if she had a trail map of the park.

By the time Amanda went home, showered, dressed, and arrived at work, she was daydreaming about waterfalls and spectacular views. There was a definite change in the air, and Amanda was going to take advantage of it.

***

"I'm home!" Cooper called when he walked into the empty house. "Anyone here?"

Dale's car wasn't in the driveway though he was supposed to be home. And it wasn't his mother's car sitting at the curb. It was a red convertible with Texas plates. Why would Serena be at Dale's house?

"Hello?"

The house was silent, and Cooper began to worry. Where was everyone?

He put his keys in the basket they kept by the door—a holdover from Ruth's teacher tidiness—and walked from the entryway into the open-space living room. He peeked into the kitchen, but he didn't see a soul. As he walked to the back door to look out into the yard, he heard a giggle from behind the chair in the corner.

Cooper smiled. "Where is everyone, Scout? Did they go somewhere without me? Did they forget about me?" He stood with his back to the chair and let out a long, contemplative sigh. "Where could they have gone? Maybe I should command you to find them and lick them until they squeal."

"I'm here, Uncle Coop!" Suzy shouted as she jumped out from behind the chair.

Jamie climbed out from behind the television, and Serena slowly made her way around the chair where Suzy had been. Cooper laughed at all of them, but especially at Serena. He didn't think this was her typical way of spending an evening.

"You all sure surprised me." He didn't take his eyes off Serena as he spoke, and she smiled at his amusement at her expense.

"It was Suzy's idea," Serena said. "She said you'd think it was funny."

"You could say that," he said with a laugh. "What are you doing here?"

"Dale was at the clinic, dropping off something to Joe, when he had an emergency call. I was with Helena, picking out nursery furniture on the Internet, when Joe called her and asked if they could help, so I volunteered."

"That was nice," he said, wondering what made her jump in and help. Had she known he would be home eventually? His gut did a somersault at the thought.

"What was the emergency?" Cooper asked, taking off his boots before grabbing a Coke from the fridge.

"I'm not sure. He said he wouldn't be late."

"Well, I appreciate you helping." He took a long sip of his soda.

"I love being with Suzy and Jamie. They're great. And Dale needed the help, so it was a win-win."

No mention of Cooper.

"What's for dinner?" he asked, trying not to sound disappointed that he wasn't part of her reason for being there. "Did Mama drop anything by?" He opened the refrigerator again and looked inside.

"We ordered pizza," Jamie said. "Aunt Serena said she doesn't cook."

She shrugged and gave him a look that clearly conveyed, *What can I say? I'm a busy woman.* Cooper laughed.

"Pizza it is. I'm going to change out of my uniform. I'll be right back. Be nice to *Aunt* Serena."

As he changed, he heard them talking and was surprised by how at-ease she sounded. He never pictured her as the maternal type, but maybe she was the favorite aunt type. He liked the idea of her being the aunt to his being the uncle.

In a t-shirt and jeans, Cooper descended the stairs to the sound of the doorbell.

"I've got it," Serena called.

Cooper watched her answer the door and hand the delivery boy way too much money without asking for change. That didn't surprise him. He assumed she made a lot of money working with celebrities and politicians.

"So, did you get Cindy's wedding all planned?" he asked as she laid the pizza on the counter. He fed Scout then reached for the paper plates in one of the cabinets.

"We're getting there. She wants it pretty simple, but she deserves elegance. She's had a rough life, and I'd like this to be one day where she's treated like a queen."

"I'm sure all your clients are treated like queens on their wedding day."

"I try, but most of them are used to that. Cindy isn't, and I'd like her day to be more than perfect. But we've got plenty of time to plan. She doesn't want to get married until next spring, so we'll keep meeting and fine-tuning until everything is just right."

Cooper watched Serena pour iced tea in their glasses and place them on the table. She laid out napkins and then took the plates from Cooper after he added a slice of pizza to each one.

"Do you want a knife and fork," he asked. "Or do you want to eat with your fingers like the rest of us unrefined beasts?"

Serena laughed. "Pizza, like barbecue, is meant to be eaten with one's fingers." There was an emphasized twang in her voice that made him smile.

Dale still wasn't home by the time the kitchen was clean, homework finished and packed away, and the kids were sound asleep. Cooper cleaned while Serena tucked them in, returning downstairs after reading four books to Suzy.

"You got off easy," Cooper told her, but she said she

didn't mind and would've read more if Suzy wasn't already falling asleep.

Instead of sitting next to Cooper on the couch, where he left plenty of room for her, Serena curled up in the armchair and asked about his job. He told her a few of his most daring and exciting rescues, and she seemed to hang on every word, but she stayed in the chair, and he made himself more comfortable on the couch until Dale walked in.

After thanking her, Dale walked Serena to the door, and Cooper watched them say goodbye. Serena hadn't flirted with Cooper or sat next to him all evening, but she never took her eyes off Dale. While she had hung on Cooper's every word, she was riveted by Dale's account of his evening escapade breaking up a bar fight and waiting at the station for the wives to pick up their husbands. One wife had to be convinced to pick up her husband instead of forcing him to stay in the cell overnight. Stories like this always made Cooper think of his brother as Andy Taylor taking care of the citizens of Mayberry, but Serena didn't act like she thought they were just a bunch of hicks in a small, Southern town.

As Cooper lay in bed that night thinking about the evening, he wondered what Serena thought about Buffalo Springs, about Dale, and about himself. When she talked about Cindy's wedding, she made it sound like she'd be around for a while, or at least would be back often. He wondered what it was about this town that could possibly interest a woman like her. He had hoped it was him, but now, he wasn't so sure.

***

"Forty-eight hours?" Cooper verified.

"Yes. Family is worried. Should've been home yesterday. This is his first backcountry overnight, so he's not experienced. Maybe got lost. Could be hurt." Sheriff Wilson shook her head. "I guess everyone has to have a first time, but still."

"Did Chin leave an itinerary with anyone?"

"Not much of one. He said he was hiking Hemmed-in-Hollow and camping one night. Not much to go on."

"We'll find him," Cooper said, picking up his radio and calling his team together as he walked to his truck.

Steven Chin's car was at the trailhead, but it showed no signs that he'd returned to it at any point. No camping gear was visible, but they didn't have access to the trunk. They had to assume he had set up camp somewhere.

"It's a long trail and a steep one. It's not for a first timer." Cooper looked around the area, taking in their surroundings. Some of the leaves looked heavy with moisture, and there were some small, shallow puddles here and there. He looked doubtfully at Scout. "Plus, this area has had some rain since Chin went missing."

"They didn't say it was his first time hiking, just his first time doing a backcountry overnight," Lance offered. "Hopefully, he's got enough experience to make the hike without getting hurt."

"We'll all be taking the same trail from the trailhead,"

Cooper explained. "But we'll be splitting up wherever it looks like someone has gone off the trail. There are only four of us today, and it's a long trail, so we have no choice but to split. Keep in touch constantly. I want to know where you are at all times. You leave the trail, radio in. You take the right split at a Y, you radio it in. Clear?"

"Yes, Sir," they answered.

"Look for footprints, broken branches, debris, anything that shows signs that someone was there. Cell phones will be sketchy back there, so keep your radio turned up. Scout's not going to do us much good, especially if it did rain. Unless we can find Chin's camp site or anything else helpful, this isn't going to be easy."

He wasn't telling them anything they didn't know about their search plan and their chances, but it was always good to be reminded. Every rescue was different, and Cooper never knew what was going to make the difference between rescue and recovery.

"With all the rain we've had and whatever rain came through in the last forty-eight hours, there could be washouts, landslides, and eroded trails. The waterfall should be at its peak, and that can cause issues, too, if he didn't know how to maneuver around it. Any questions?"

When nobody raised a hand, Cooper gave the orders to get started. Each time they saw a place where someone may have gone off-trail, he sent someone to investigate. Before long, he and Scout were alone and at a crossroads. The main trail went to the east, but an alternate trail went to the west. It wasn't a marked trail, but the broken limbs and flattened grass let Cooper know it had been hiked by a fair number of people that day. He radioed his location and started down the unmarked trail.

Though spring was still in its early days, the sun was hot, and Cooper was drenched with sweat when he spotted the first cause for alarm.

A tent had been erected off the trail, but nobody was around. There was a food bag tied high up in a tree, and it looked full. Whoever was camping never had a chance to eat whatever they brought with them. The tent was wet as was the fire circle. There was no way to tell when the last fire had been made, but Cooper didn't think anyone had stayed there the night before.

There was a duffle bag inside the tent containing a few clothes, but they were all clean and neatly folded, albeit damp. They'd probably been washed after they were last worn, and the dampness didn't help. Scout might be able to catch a scent, but she probably wouldn't.

He called her over to the bag and told her to smell it. She did as told and walked around the site, but nothing seemed to excite her. The wag of her tail changed, and Cooper could see she was becoming anxious, so he assured her that it was okay and told her she did a good job.

Cooper had the tracking skills of a panther, so he went old-school and relied on his instincts. He crouched down by the fire and looked in all directions, examining every dirt surface and each blade of grass. After several moments, he spotted what he'd been looking for, a barely visible footprint, almost washed away, heading toward one section of the woods. He called Scout over and had her sniff along the trail. She made it several dozen yards before losing the scent. Cooper radioed what he'd found to the team and headed into the trees, hoping Scout would find something that would help her track the missing camper.

"Steven," Cooper called. "Steven, search and rescue. Call out if you can hear me."

He followed a series of broken limbs and crushed plants until the trail ended at the edge of a drop off. He could hear the waterfall in the distance. He continued to call and listen for a response, but there was none.

Cooper carefully walked to the drop off and looked down. What he saw sent his heart racing. There were bloody skid marks on the rock face where someone or something had gone down. Without putting himself or Scout in danger, Cooper peered over the ledge as best he could. There were no signs of anyone below, but with a drop like that, there was no way to know for certain. He radioed the team to head to the lower district, and to hurry.

He raced back toward the trail, aware that he needed to be careful and avoid injury but knowing there was little time to waste. Scout kept up, seeming to sense the urgency. Someone, presumably Steven Chin, slid down the rock-face and was most likely hurt, if not worse.

"I'm almost to the bottom," Lance's voice came over the radio. "No sign of anyone yet."

"I'm not far," Lucy chimed in.

Cooper hurried to catch up, but there was a lot of ground to cover. They were deep in the woods, and Chin could be anywhere. Or maybe he was still at the foot of the cliff, unconscious or... Cooper picked up his pace, calling on St. Bernard's intercession once again.

***

Amanda tried her cell phone again, but she still had no signal. She looked at the man she'd found some distance off the trail. She'd heard a cry of pain and then a crash and pushed her way through the brush to find him lying on the ground, nearly unconscious. His lips were parched with dehydration, his skin red and blistered from the sun, and he was hurt, based on the way he collapsed when she'd attempted to help him get back on the trail. He could barely open his mouth to take a sip of water from her bottle. He hadn't shaved in several days, and his clothes were dirty and torn. It was impossible to determine his age. He could be seventeen or fifty.

"I've got you. Can you drink some water?"

He didn't answer and gave no indication of hearing her.

Amanda switched on her phone's flashlight and pulled back the underpart of his eyes. She looked at his pupils then felt around his head for an injury. The pupils don't lie. The back of his head was covered with dried blood, and he had several knots. He'd fallen, from someplace high from the looks of him, and took quite a beating. She examined his abdomen to feel for internal bleeding.

"Can you tell me your name? How long you've been out here?"

This time, he tried to speak, but his throat was too dry.

"Did you fall?"

He nodded slightly. Amanda untied her sweatshirt from around her waist, balled it up, and laid it under his head. She didn't bandage his head since the bleeding had stopped, and she didn't have proper cleaning supplies.

She'd been enjoying her hike along Centerpoint Trail through the Ponca Wilderness, an old wagon road that descended to the Buffalo River. Her destination wasn't the river but the view at Big Bluff, off Goat Trail, where she'd been told she would be rewarded with the most iconic panoramic view of the Ozark Mountains. She hadn't made it.

"Okay," Amanda said to the man. "Let's see what I can do to get some water in you."

She pulled open her backpack and rummaged through what limited hiking gear she had. She pulled out a package of electrolytes and dumped the powder into her water bottle. She shook the bottle until everything dissolved then dug through the pack again until she found a tin of hiker's balm.

"I'm going to rub some of this on your lips to give them some moisture," she told the man who was only half-conscious and fading fast. She worked quickly, rubbing the balm on his lips, then carefully inserting the straw of her bottle into his mouth. She knew he wouldn't be able to suck, so she tilted the bottle and squeezed the straw. She wasn't sure how effective that was, but the man began to cough, and a few drops dribbled down his chin.

"Good, good. You had to get something in there. Let's try again."

Little by little, she got him to drink. When she held up the bottle, it looked like it was down by maybe a quarter cup, but that was better than nothing.

She sat the bottle down and looked at his ankle.

"I told you I'm a doctor. I'd like to get a better look at that ankle. Is that okay?"

The man didn't answer, but Amanda thought she detected a small movement of his head and took that as agreement. She gingerly rolled up his hiking pants and tried to remove his hiking boot. Though still not fully cognizant, he gasped and recoiled in pain.

"I'm so sorry. I'll try to be as gentle as I can."

She loosened the ties as much as possible and ever so carefully slid the short boot from his foot. He gasped again but didn't move. When she pulled back his sock, she was the one to gasp. The ankle was most likely broken based on the swelling and the black coloring.

"I think it's broken, but I don't want to move it. I'm going to make you a splint." She gently laid his foot down on the dirt and stood. "I'll be right back"

Amanda looked around for a stick that would be the right size and thickness. Once she found one that would work, she folded the man's sock in half and used it for padding. Lining up the stick with the sock, she used his boot laces to secure them in place, but she didn't feel like it was enough. She reached into her hair and pulled out the bandana she had tied around her ponytail. It was one she'd had most of her life and was covered with green trefoils. She smiled.

"Once a Girl Scout, always a Girl Scout," she said aloud as she wrapped the bandana around the makeshift splint.

The man was almost fully unconscious, so she forced more water and electrolytes into his mouth. He didn't cough or gag, so she gave him more every few minutes. She looked at her phone again, but no matter how much she tried to will it, no bars appeared on the screen.

"I've got to get help," she said, amazed that no other hikers had gone by on such a beautiful, spring Saturday. Then again, they weren't exactly on the trail and probably weren't visible to anyone passing by. And Amanda was concentrating so hard on the man, she hadn't been listening for sounds of people.

She stood and tried to remember from which direction she came. The last thing she needed was for both of them to be lost and stranded in the woods. Recalling the wilderness badge she earned all those years ago, she looked at the brush and determined the right direction. She retraced her steps and looked up and down the trail for any signs of life.

From off in the distance, she thought she heard

someone calling out.

"Hello! Can anyone hear me?" She didn't want to move from where she stood. The woods all looked the same, and she was afraid she wouldn't be able to find her way back to the man.

"Hello!" she called again. "We need help here!" She nearly whispered, "please," aware that her calls in the thick forest wouldn't carry far.

"Hello! Search and Rescue. Call back if you hear me."

Amanda's heart began pumping like she was running a marathon. "Help! Help! Over here! Please help us!"

They called back and forth for several minutes before another woman came running down the trail.

"I'm here. What do you need?"

"A man. I found a man. I heard him cry out, and I followed the sound." By now, Amanda and the woman—Lucy, if she remembered correctly—were both clawing their way back through the foliage. When they reached the man, the woman fell to her knees beside him and removed her radio from its holster.

"Cooper, I found him." She looked up at Amanda. "Well, I didn't find him, but I'm with him, and he's in bad shape."

"Copy. Where are you?"

She looked around and then at Amanda who had joined her on the ground. "We've been walking for days. I'm not even sure where we are anymore."

"Off Goat Trail, on the way to Big Bluff. The main trail is Centerpoint."

She repeated that to Cooper, and Amanda was so happy to hear his voice, she could have cried with relief.

Lucy went right to work pulling medical equipment from her bag. She checked his pulse, listened to his chest, and yanked up his sleeve. She began prepping his arm for an IV.

"He's badly dehydrated," Amanda said. "No internal bleeding from what I could tell, but a large occipital wound. Clotted around several hematomas. I left it alone because I didn't have anything sanitary to clean it with. He has multiple cuts and contusions. A badly broken ankle, which I splinted."

Lucy looked down at the ankle and nodded. "Good job on that. Doctor, nurse, or medic?"

"Doctor. Dr. Amanda Pierce."

Lucy looked at Amanda, leaning in and squinting for a better view. "Dr. Pierce? I didn't recognize you. It's Lucy from SAR."

"Yes, you've brought patients in with Cooper. I recognized you."

Lucy inserted the needle and ran a line to a bag of fluids.

"What can I do to help?"

"Can you clean and assess his head wound while I continue monitoring vitals?"

"Sure. What have you got?"

Lucy handed her the cleanser and bandages.

The man moaned when Amanda squirted his head with antiseptic. She carefully cleaned his wounds and began padding and wrapping his head with gauze.

"Steven, can you hear me?" Lucy grasped his hand. "Squeeze my hand if you can hear and understand."

Amanda continued wrapping his head as Cooper lightly squeeze Lucy's hand.

"Good job, Steven. You are Steven Chin, right?"

Another squeeze.

"Great. We'll let your family know you're okay."

"How long have you been out here?" Amanda asked Lucy.

"Three days. He's been missing for five."

Amanda looked down at the man she was bandaging. Five days. And it was pure luck Amanda came by when she did and heard him.

"Wow," she said. "Does this happen a lot?"

"Define a lot," Lucy said, continuing to monitor his vitals. "Once seems like more than enough, but yes, a few times a year."

"Lucy!"

"In here, Coop!"

Amanda watched as Cooper and Scout made their way through the trees. Cooper had as much scruff as Steven did, along with some cuts on his hands and face. He looked dirty and tired but still, Amanda admitted, strikingly handsome. Scout immediately sat as though she was merely an onlooker.

Cooper knelt beside them and began assessing Steven much the same way Amanda and Lucy had.

"How is he?"

"Better than expected, thanks to Dr. Pierce."

Cooper looked up, his expression of confusion

turning to shock. "Amanda?"

"Hi Coop," she managed, feeling as disconcerted as he probably was to find her there with a strange man's head in her lap in the middle of the woods.

"What? How?"

She briefly recounted what happened and her assessment of the patient. By the time she finished, Lance was there with the Stokes basket, and she was helping them load the man into it. The sound of a helicopter broke the quiet of the forest as they made their way out of the trees to another SAR responder who helped guide the basket into the air.

They watched as Steven disappeared into the chopper, and Amanda suddenly felt the weight of all that had happened. She grabbed Cooper's sleeve and wobbled into his arms.

"Hey, Amanda. It's over. It's all good."

"Get her to the ground." Lucy said. "She's coming down from the adrenaline high. She'll be okay, but she needs to sit and breathe for a few minutes."

"I've got her," Cooper told Lucy. "You need to get up there."

"Are you sure?" Lucy asked.

"I'm sure," Cooper said. "Chin needs you in that chopper, and Amanda's a friend. I'll take care of her."

Amanda heard what they were saying, but it all felt like a dream. Her vision began to blur, and she was overcome with wooziness. Before she could register what was happening, the world went black.

***

"Hey there."

She blinked once, twice, three times then looked up at him, trying to focus. Cooper smiled and felt his insides go warm. He'd been watching her sleep, knowing she was all right, and just waiting for her to come to. He had lots of time to take in what she wore and make assumptions—workout capris and a dry-weave t-shirt, ankle socks, and running shoes. She had walking poles, the kind they sold in the visitor's center in town. She shouldn't have been out there alone any more than Steven Chin.

"You're awake."

She tried to sit up but instantly fell back.

"Whoa, slow down. Take it easy."

"Did I faint?" she asked, clearly confused and distressed.

"Yes and no. Reflex syncope. It's normal after a high-adrenaline event."

"Yep, I fainted." She closed her eyes and exhaled.

"If you want to call it that, sure."

"That's never happened before, and I have adrenaline rushes all the time. Every day."

"Probably not like this one. Our jobs are very similar yet very different."

She nodded, her eyes still closed, then sat up and looked around. Scout's head popped over the seat in front of them. "Where are we?"

"Still at the park. In my truck."

"How did I get here?"

"The guys helped me carry you out."

"And Steven?"

"He's okay. He'll be in the hospital for a few days and will need surgery on his ankle, but he's going to be fine."

"How did he get out there to begin with?"

"He slid off a sloping cliff, broke his ankle, wandered around the forest for three days until the pain was too much to keep going. He decided he needed to get out of the sun, at which point, he got lost in the woods. It happens. Not often, but often enough."

"And I found him. I didn't know you were looking for him. I was afraid we'd both be lost out there." She locked eyes with his, and his stomach rolled like the rapids. "I've never been so afraid."

"Afraid?" Cooper said quietly, his heart tugging at his chest. "Lucy said she'd never met anyone so brave. She said you had already saved him before she even got there. He's alive because you found him and wouldn't let him die. He's alive because you stabilized him and then called for help."

Amanda looked down at her lap without speaking, and Cooper wished he could read her mind. He dealt with these rescues all the time, and he knew she did, too, to an extent, but this was an extreme case. The clinic handled plenty of their extreme cases, but he knew this one was different. Amanda was there from the start, part of the extraction, and that left an impression on someone.

When Amanda finally looked up, she had tears in her eyes.

"I wasn't sure he would make it, and it was up to me to keep him alive. It's never been like that before. Until Lucy arrived, I was all alone." She paused. "I didn't know if I could do it. Plus, there were brief moments when I wondered if I…" She shook her head. "I knew I couldn't leave him, and I caught myself wondering what would happen if nobody came."

"Hey, you did save him, and we came. You did everything right, and you know that. Your training, your instincts kicked in, just like they're supposed to."

"Have you ever had doubts? I mean, did you ever think you might lose someone out here, away from technology and medical expertise and other people to assist? I know you have your team, but—"

"Of course," he stopped her. "We've all felt like that at some point. First, we're not doctors, and only Lucy is a medic. Second, we're out in nature where anything can and does happen. What you did without your staff, equipment, and meds, that was heroic."

Amanda let out a breath. "I just did what had to be done."

"Exactly what we do. Whatever needs to be done."

"And he's really going to be okay?"

"He is."

Cooper understood how she was feeling. He'd been there many times. It didn't surprise him that now, when it was all over, she burst into tears.

"I don't know why I'm crying," she said. "I'm just so

overwhelmed."

Cooper did what needed to be done. He pulled her into his arms and held her until her tears stopped.

***

Amanda pulled into her driveway feeling more tired than she ever had in her life. She sat in the car, unable, to move, until she looked in the rearview mirror and saw Cooper's truck idling by the curb. Summoning her strength, Amanda turned off her car and opened the door. She walked slowly to the front door, unlocked it, and turned, giving Cooper a wave to let him know she was fine.

As he pulled away, she wondered, again, what kind of man he was. A good man, obviously. A kind and caring man. A man who took care of his brother's children and spent his life rescuing people, saving lives. Yet he lived an existence where he was closed off from the rest of the world. Even his job took place in the wilderness, on top of mountains, at the bottom of ravines, remote places where most people never ventured. Was that a coincidence, or had he chosen a career that allowed him to help people without having any real attachments to others?

She drew a bath, grateful for the large, antique, clawfoot tub, while rethinking her assessment of Cooper. He had attachments to his crew. It was obvious they trusted each other with their lives. You couldn't close yourself off to people and still have their complete trust, could you?

Every muscle in her body hurt as she slowly undressed, and thought about the lack of pain she felt when Cooper held her in his arms. Even as she cried and felt more mentally and physically exhausted than she knew possible, all warmth, goodness, and security filled her.

Amanda eased herself into the hot water and laid her head back on the cold, hard porcelain tub. She might have fallen asleep there if her phone hadn't buzzed. She dried her hand on the towel she'd laid nearby and reached for the phone that rested on the closed toilet lid.

"Hello?"

"Are you okay?"

It took her moment to recognize Andi's voice.

"I'm okay. How did you—?"

"Dale heard it on the police scanner. You saved some guy's life in the national park? That's amazing. I mean, I know you and Joe save people all the time, but this is different. I mean, this is emotionally different. Are you sure you're okay?"

Andi would know. She might be the only person other than the SAR responders who could possibly understand. How many lives had she saved as a Navy SEAL?

"I'm…" She didn't know how to answer. "I'm exhausted and relieved and still can't believe it all happened."

"I get it. Do you need anything? Can I bring you food? Wine? Whiskey?"

Amanda laughed. "Thanks, but no thanks. I'm too tired to even think about food. I'm actually in the tub in the hall bathroom. Standing in my shower seemed impossible. After this, I'm going to bed."

"Okay. Call me if you need anything. I mean it."

"I know you do. Thanks, Andi."

They said goodbye, and Amanda disconnected the phone. She didn't have the energy to move again, so she tossed it on the floor. When she woke up, it was dark outside, the water was cold, and she was shivering and starving. After she dried off and wrapped herself in a heavy terrycloth robe, she picked up her phone and saw that she had a message.

There's food outside your front door. You're going to be hungry when you wake up. Thanks again for all you did today. Eat, get some sleep, and take it easy tomorrow. Coop

How had he gotten her number? She was sure they'd never texted before, not even after he dropped off a patient. He must've asked Joe.

Amanda threw on a pair of comfortable pajamas and went to the front door. Inside the bag was a Bogart burger from Rick's, with sweet potato fries, coleslaw, and two pickles. She smiled as she headed to the kitchen to heat up the meal.

It had never tasted so good.

Nine

The church was full on Sunday morning, forcing Cooper to sit in the back by himself instead of joining his family several pews ahead. He sat after Father Michael read the Gospel and focused on his priest and friend.

"Three times, Peter denied, and three times, the Lord asked, 'Do you love me?' First, 'Do you love me like a brother?' Phila. Second, 'Do you love me like my Father loves you?' Agape. Third, 'Do you love me like a brother?' The original Greek translation shows us what the modern translation does not. Jesus met Peter where he was, asking of him only what he could handle."

Cooper listened intently to Father Michael. This was a teaching he'd never heard before, or had never listened to or understood. Different kinds of love?

"Peter wasn't ready. He wasn't ready to give up his life for Jesus, to love with the kind of love Jesus demonstrated on the cross, and Jesus knew that, and he accepted it. He told Peter that the day would come when Peter was ready, when he would let someone lead him to his death, the same death as Christ. Peter would go willingly to the cross. But at that moment, there on the shores of Galilee, Peter wasn't ready to give up his life for Christ.

"Sometimes, I think there was a reason Peter wasn't ready, a bigger reason than his own human weakness to accept his cross. Let's go back to the night of the denials, when the cock crowed after the third denial. I always imagine Peter's head going up, his eyes searching, and his gaze meeting the Lord's. At that moment, Jesus, bloodied and bruised, gives Peter a look, a look that says, I warned you, but I still love you, and I forgive you. Yet here we are, after the passion, after the death and resurrection, and Peter is still grappling with his guilt, his inability to forgive himself. Jesus offers him three chances to make up for the three denials. All Peter has to do is tell the Lord how much he loves him, and Peter falls short."

Cooper swallowed as he listened to the priest. He always felt like he was falling short, not living as the man the Lord expected him to be.

"But instead of chastising him, instead of pushing him, and most importantly, instead of disowning, disinheriting, or dismissing him, Christ tells Peter it's okay. He accepts him for whom and where he is, and tells him that he will grow in his love for Christ and the Church. This is the God of love and forgiveness, the God who wants to sit with you and talk to you and tell you that you are forgiven. He wants to meet you where you are and help you find the strength you need to grow into the person he knows you can be. But there's something you need to do first before you can become that person. You need to tell God you love him, and you need to allow him to forgive you, but most importantly, you need to forgive yourself."

Cooper sat up straighter, listening to the words, wondering if they were meant for him.

"Until you allow yourself forgiveness, you won't be able to fully love God, yourself, or others. The Lord knows the great things he has in store for you, but you need to go to him as you are and let him meet you there, accepting his forgiveness and allowing yourself to forgive in return. Until you do, you will never understand or be able to accomplish all the Lord has in mind for you."

The church was silent after Father took his seat beside the altar. Cooper closed his eyes. That was the one thing he'd been unable to do. He found the courage to visit Jessie. He listened to her father tell him to live, and he took it to heart. He'd gone over in his mind the advice of his mother and his priest to listen for the voice of God. But he'd blocked out the voice telling him it wasn't his fault, and even if it was, nobody was holding it against him but himself.

Maybe it was time to let it go, to allow himself to heal, to tell himself he didn't have to live his life as penance for what happened to Jessie. Maybe it was okay for him to move on and find happiness, to open his heart to love. He'd said as much to Dale, but he hadn't really believed it.

As they stood to recite the Creed, Cooper looked up at the stained-glass window depicting St. Peter holding the keys to Heaven. What if the key to Heaven wasn't an actual thing but a metaphor? What if the real key, the thing that opened doors to the future and the Promised Land was what Peter learned from the Lord? Maybe the key to Heaven is learning to forgive, not just others who hurt you, but the person who can hurt you the most—yourself. It was all Cooper could do not to cry as he told himself, *I forgive you.*

***

Amanda wasn't a regular churchgoer. Her family attended when it was convenient, and she'd fallen into the same habit. Once she moved to Buffalo Springs, she found herself attending more often, but it still wasn't part of her routine. That Sunday morning, however, she was compelled to be there, to thank God and all the saints and angels for the strength and courage they gave her the previous day. She knew she hadn't done it alone. Even all the training she had and the instincts that kicked in weren't enough. And she didn't believe in luck. A force larger than herself got her through it, and the least she could do was show up to say thank you.

When she walked out after the service ended, she was surprised to see Cooper near the parking lot. The sun was out, but a light rain fell, the kind that dappled the sidewalk and left tiny droplets on the car but didn't feel wet to the skin.

"Hi, Cooper," Amanda said with a smile. She held out her hand, palm up. "Did you bring the rain?"

Cooper laughed. "Not on purpose. I wanted to check on you. How are you feeling?"

"Okay. Tired, relieved. Oh, and I fell asleep in the tub and woke up starving. Thank you."

"You're welcome. It was the least I could do."

"I have a whole new appreciation for what you do. I don't think I could go through that on a regular basis."

"That's fair. I don't think I could work at the clinic on a regular basis. Not enough action," he said with a grin.

"I think I'll take the lack of action," Amanda told him, smiling back and noticing how his marble-green eyes danced in the sun.

"I, uh, noticed you had on running shoes the other day. You don't hike regularly, I take it."

She shook her head. "Nope. I'm a runner, but it's been so nice the past few days, and I got bored running through town, so I thought I'd change things up. I was hoping to make it out to Big Bluff." She shrugged. "I guess God had other plans."

"I guess he did," Cooper replied, and she could tell he wanted to say more.

"What?"

"You were on Goat Trail, so I assumed you had experience, but then I saw your shoes."

"And? I'm not sure what you mean."

"It's a pretty dangerous trail. It's narrow and steep and not someplace you should hike alone. In fact, it's the number one SAR location in the entire area."

"Really?" She had no idea. She'd just picked up the trail map and thought it looked like a good hike. Then again, what did she know about hiking? She thought back to the young woman Cooper had brought to the clinic weeks before and how shocked she was that the woman was alone. Yet she went on the hike alone anyway, knowing but not calculating the risks. Her face grew warm. "I didn't know that," she said quietly.

"Not that you couldn't have handled it," he said, waving his hands as though he was trying to clear the air. "I mean, you're in great shape and all, but a few weeks back, I rescued a young woman who was out there alone, and she was really hurt. When I found her, she'd fallen off a ledge and had a bone sticking right out of her leg."

Her face grew hotter. "Yes, the one who ended up needing surgery."

"Yeah, that's the one."

"You know, I remember asking Joe why she thought it was a good idea to go hiking alone. I didn't even think about it when I went. How stupid of me."

"I'm not going to argue, but in the end, it's good that you were there. Like you said, and my mama would agree, it was God's plan."

He was letting her off easy, and she appreciated it. Amanda looked up at the sky. "I think it's slowing down."

He nodded. "It was just a passing spring shower. A

blip on the map. Hey, I was wondering—"

"Amanda," Joe's voice rang out. She turned to see him, Helena, and Serena approaching. "We heard you had quite the adventure. How are you doing?"

She turned to them and told them briefly about the ordeal, only sharing the bare minimum. She was afraid she would be expected to tell the story over again in the next few days.

"Honestly, I don't know how much longer I could've found the strength to keep going. Thank Heaven Cooper and his team showed up." She turned around to bring Cooper into the conversation, letting him share in the moment, but he had disappeared. Amanda looked around but didn't see him anywhere. Her smile subsided as she realized how sorry she was to find him gone.

***

Monday brought sunny skies and warm temperatures, but Serena suppressed a shiver as she turned off her phone. She couldn't read one more message or decline one more call from another reporter. It was bad enough that all her clients had cancelled on her. She hadn't done anything to ruin that wedding, but all the blame was falling on her, and she would look worse if she responded. Trying to explain everything that happened would look like she was throwing the blame elsewhere and not taking responsibility for herself and her business. But would not responding make it look worse? Like she was hiding and unwilling to accept responsibility and apologize? She didn't know what was worse. And there was one anonymous person whose texts—

"Everything okay?" Helena asked. They were sitting in the sunroom, enjoying the May morning over coffee—decaf for Helena—and scones from Andi.

"Everything is fine," Serena replied with a smile and forced cheerfulness. "I think I'll take a walk after breakfast if you think you'll be okay."

Helena waved her off. "I'm fine. A little bored, but fine."

"Do you want to come?" Serena asked, already knowing the answer and feeling a little guilty for abandoning her sister-in-law.

"No, thanks. Doctor's orders to rest and keep my feet up, you know."

"Okay. I won't be long."

"Take your time. Joe said to let the paint dry before I hang up anything, so we can tackle the nursery this afternoon, if that's okay with you."

"That sounds delightful," Serena said, and she meant it. She loved helping Helena and Joe get the nursery ready for the baby. She was happy for them and enjoyed watching them nesting and preparing. "I'll be back soon," she promised.

Serena found solace in strolling the streets of the sleepy, little town. Buffalo Springs wasn't anything like Houston, but she didn't experience an ounce of homesickness as she waved hello to the townspeople she'd met. She inhaled deeply as she passed Andi's bakery, stopped to admire the dresses in the recently opened boutique, and picked through the sidewalk display of treasures outside the antique store. For the third time in the past week, she turned down a side street and made her way toward the other main road in town. Like both times before, she stopped and looked at the empty building next to Rick's.

It was a two-story, white with blue trim and blue shutters. It had a front porch and reminded Serena of the house from the old movie, *To Kill a Mockingbird,* with Gregory Peck, that she'd watched in her high school American Lit class. Unlike the one in the movie, this house had boards on the windows and broken glass over the front door. On the other side of the building was the candy store, adorned to look like a gingerbread house, and Serena could picture Hansel and Gretel delighting in the décor.

She didn't know how long she stood and stared at the empty house. The windows were full-length, the kind you find on some turn-of-the-century homes, that would have been opened wide on warm nights to let the breeze in. She could picture them without the wooden rails and stiles, just glass panes that would allow a full-window display. A mannequin in a wedding gown could go in one window and a bridesmaid or groom in the other.

She frowned. Or a bride and groom together in one and a bridesmaid and maid of honor in the other? Or something to display a mock reception. She tilted her head and cupped her elbow in one hand, her chin in her other hand, as she pictured the possibilities.

"What has you so enthralled?"

Serena jumped and sucked in her breath.

"Sorry, I didn't mean to scare you." Dale reached out to steady her.

"No, it's okay. I was lost in thought." She smiled at the chief of police. "I was thinking about what a nice bridal shop this would make."

"Bridal shop? Does Buffalo Springs need a bridal shop?"

"Does Buffalo Spring have brides?"

Dale laughed. "I guess we do. There does always seem to be somebody getting married around here. Why?"

She shrugged. "Just a thought. I like this house. There's something about it that really draws me in."

"This house has quite the story," Dale said as he joined her in gazing at the façade. "One you'd appreciate."

"Really?" She turned and looked at him. He was every bit as handsome as his brother. Cleaner cut with shorter hair rather than the longer front and sides that framed Cooper's face. Dale's close-cropped hair showed off his forehead, just the right size—not too high or too low—and his adorable ears. She blushed at the thought and looked back toward the house.

"Tell me the story," she asked.

"The house was built after the Civil War by a Confederate soldier for his sweetheart. He wanted to forget about his part in the war and escape to the

Rockies, but he didn't have the money to get there from Little Rock, so he made his way to the Ozarks. It's one of the original houses in town but was renovated and updated in the early 2000s just before the big recession and housing crisis in 2007.

"But back to the story. The soldier built the house by hand himself, working in the mines, writing to his sweetheart each month to update her on the progress. It took years for him to finish, but she was faithful to him throughout. When it was finished, he sent a letter asking her to come join him. Her father, an Arkansas statesman, found the letter just as the young bride was climbing into the stagecoach. He forbade her from marrying the man he believed turned his back on the Confederacy by denouncing the war. He'd never supported the cause, but he joined up anyway, like all good Southern boys of the time. He did his part, fought until the end, and came home destitute, broken, and injured. The only thing that saved him was this house and the love of his life."

Dale took a deep breath and sighed as they stood on the sidewalk. Serena waited patiently, for a time.

"And?" she asked when he didn't continue. "Did she come?"

He smiled, and she thought he was holding back on purpose to tease her.

"She came. Her father disinherited her, but she didn't care. She arrived on the stagecoach, and he was there to meet her. Only there was no priest in town, no preacher of any kind, not even a church at that point. The miners had a saloon." He motioned to Rick's. "And a jail." He pointed behind them in the direction of the jail on the other side of town which was now the visitor's center. "There was a bank and a general store." He pointed toward those. "The original main street ran perpendicular to the current one."

"So, what did they do?"

"Well, turns out the young woman was of Scottish heritage, so they handfasted."

Serena swooned. "Just like Roger and Brianna."

"Who?" Dale asked.

"Never mind," she said. "You've obviously not read the *Outlander* books."

Dale smiled. "No, but Ruth read them all. Well, all the ones that were printed… Anyway, they handfasted right here inside the house. Even without a priest, it was considered the first marriage in town. They lived here their entire lives and raised six kids in that house."

"Do they have relatives who still live here?"

Dale grinned. "Well, the man's last name was Montgomery."

"Montgomery. That sounds familiar."

"Wade's the former mayor. His family has been here for almost 150 years."

"Helena's brother-in-law."

"Yep."

"Wow. What a rich and beautiful history this house has. And it was really where the first wedding in town took place?"

"It was," Dale told her. After a few moments, he asked, "So, a bridal shop?"

"I think it was meant to be," she told him, her heart bursting with certainty.

Dale turned and met her gaze, and her heart skipped a beat.

***

I hear the weather will be perfect for hiking this weekend. Still want to see Big Bluff? I'd rather you not hike it alone.

Amanda read the text a second time. She still didn't know how he'd gotten her number, but she was intrigued by his question.

What did you have in mind?

She waited as the dots blinked on the screen.

I thought we could hike on Saturday. If I don't get any calls.

Amanda thought about it. She was on call, so that might be an issue.

I'll have to check. I'll get back to you.

She pocketed the phone then headed to see her next patient.

"Good news," Joe told her as they passed in the hallway. "Shelly Olsen has accepted our offer. She can start in two weeks."

"Really? That's great!" It was more than great. It was the best news Amanda had heard in a long time, not counting the news that Steven Chin was going to recover.

"It is. I'm so relieved. Helena is due any day now,

and I was worried about being able to cover the clinic and be there for her and the baby."

Why didn't I see that? I should have known that his sudden acquiescence to hire a physician's assistant was because of Helena. I should have offered to take on more hours. But when? We're both stretched as far as we can go.

"I'm so happy for y'all. This is going to be perfect. I really liked Shelly."

"Me, too. And she's from here, so she comes with a trust factor that neither of us has."

"It's like the plot of a Hallmark movie or a Netflix series."

"Sure, with crazy exes and corrupt politicians and bank robbers. Netflix, for sure."

Amanda laughed. "It's been quiet for two years. No bad guys roaming around or anything."

"Don't jinx it," Joe said before looking at his iPad outside exam room one. He gestured toward room two. "Now, don't you have a patient to see in there?"

"Aye, aye, captain." She saluted and consulted her own device. Even if the hike didn't work out for this weekend, she would finally have more time to do the things she'd been wanting to do. And more time to spend with…others.

***

"Something wrong?" Sheriff Wilson asked.

Cooper tucked his phone back into his pocket, disappointed Amanda hadn't answered him back. "No.

Just something I was trying to set up. Looks like it may not work."

"Something important?"

"Nah, just something I thought of doing this weekend. No big deal."

And it wasn't. Amanda was great, but Cooper still wasn't certain he wanted to go down that road. Forgiving himself was one thing. Jumping right into dating was another.

"I need you to investigate something for me. It's not exactly the kind of job you're used to, and it's probably nothing, but I'd like to be sure. If I'm wrong, it could be a job for your team anyway."

Cooper was intrigued. "Sure. What is it?"

An hour later, Cooper found himself in the National Wilderness checking out a possible abandoned campsite. Nobody had been reported missing, and no distress calls had been called in, but the rangers found the site several days before and never saw anyone coming or going. It just sat empty, and that concerned them.

Cooper rummaged through the things left at the site—a one-person tent and ratty sleeping bag, a poorly constructed campfire, a stick that looked like it had been used to cook something over the fire, but bugs had eaten whatever residue may have been on it. There were no signs that a bear had been by and no tracks leading into the woods. Though rare, attacks did happen every now and then. There were, however, tire tracks where somebody had pulled off the road to make camp.

Why set up camp, eat something, then leave without

breaking down the tent? Why abandon it?

Sheriff Wilson was right. Something was off.

Cooper looked around, tried to figure out what he was missing. No signs they were coming back except the tent and sleeping bag. No clothes or food or personal items. He went back to the tent and lifted the sleeping bag, looking for anything left behind.

He was about to give up when something caught his eye from the far side of the tent. He crawled inside, pushing the sleeping bag out of the way. The thought of touching it more than necessary grossed him out. He reached for the shiny, colorful object that glinted in the sun streaming from the open doorway. It was a magazine.

He expected *Outdoor Magazine*, *Game & Fish*, or perhaps *Backcountry*. What he found sent a chill down his back. The cover photo on the sleezy tabloid showed a celebrity couple in wedding clothes. The bride—easily recognizable from all the news stories and record covers—was in tears. The groom—not as familiar out of his football jersey—looked ready to punch someone. Photoshopped behind them was a stunning brunette looking like a deer caught in the headlights. The headline read, *America's Favorite Couple Blames Wedding Woes on Wedding Planner.*

Two hours later, Scout had found no trail and nobody they came across knew anything about the campsite. Whoever was staying there, or had stayed there, went from the tent to their car and nowhere else. The reason was as elusive as a cloud at the top of the bluff. There was no pinning it down.

***

"I'm not sure how much business you'll have," Jackson told her. "I mean, other than Cindy and me, I can't think of anyone local who's planning a wedding."

Serena nodded. "I know it's a small town, but that's part of the draw. Why go with a generic planner or a warehouse dress supplier in the city when you could have specialized attention, one-of-a-kind dresses, and expert help in a down-home atmosphere?"

"And who's going to supply the one-of-a-kind dress and expert, specialized attention?"

"Who do you think?"

"You? But you live in Houston." Jackson sighed. "How could you possibly make this work?"

"By not living in Houston," she said with a smile.

Jackson's mouth dropped open.

"Wait. You'd move here? To Buffalo Springs?" He shook his head. "Cindy says you're some celebrity wedding planner for the stars. I know you haven't been here long, but have you noticed there aren't too many stars lurking around town? Celebrities usually move *away* from places like this once they hit it big. Our whole state doesn't have a concert venue that holds more than four-thousand people. We don't even have a professional football team."

"Thank Heaven for that," Serena said under her breath. "Look, I know your job is to make sure the buildings are sold to solid businesses with big investors, but I can foot this. What I can get for my home alone would pay for twice what the building is selling for."

"Then why did you come see us? You could've just called the agent and bought the house yourself."

"Yes, I can, and I will. But I need you and Wade to back me, to help me grow the business here and convince brides from the other towns throughout Northwest Arkansas to come to my shop instead of others, especially the big box ones. I need some local muscle and local money behind me, or all my talk about it being a small-town business means nothing. I don't want this to be a Houston-based or even Houston-like business. I don't want to attract celebrities. I want to attract young women like Cindy who have a dream that I can make come true without the fake lighting and props and flashing cameras of the paparazzi. I want to do what I started out doing before any celebrity ever knew my name."

Jackson stared at her for so long, she wondered if she had food in her teeth or a horn growing from her forehead.

"Are you serious about this?"

"As serious as the business end of a Colt 45."

Jackson chuckled. "All right, let me talk to Wade, see what we can come up with. You have the name, and apparently the talent, to draw people, but you're right that we need to give them bigger incentive to come all the way out to Buffalo Springs. If Wade's good with this, we can make it happen, but we might have to pull in a politician or two to really make it work. Will that be okay with you?"

Serena rolled her lips and held them between her teeth. That's exactly how things started in Houston. Right after that first big wedding for a politician's daughter, the calls began rolling in, and her entire business exploded, in ways good and bad.

"How high-level a politician are we talking?"

"A local one, from a nearby town or city, daughter, granddaughter, maybe a relative of a state legislator. Wade knows everyone at every level."

"I get to have the final say on who that person is."

Jackson nodded. "Okay. Let me see what we can do."

Serena stood and held out her hand. "Thank you, Mr. Nelson. It was a pleasure doing business with you."

"Serena, are you really going to buy that old house and turn it into a wedding shop?"

"You can hang your hat on it, darlin'."

***

"You want me to do what?" Dale's look of disbelief was just what Cooper expected.

"Have someone watch her. Just like you did for Cindy a couple years ago when she was being followed."

"Cindy and Helena's house was broken into. Nothing has happened to warrant this. I don't have the manpower to—"

"To protect your kids the next time she volunteers

to babysit?"

That shut him up. Dale's face paled, and his mouth gaped.

"And she's living with your best friend and his pregnant wife. What if something happens there? To one of them?"

"And just what do you think is going to happen? Some crazy bridezilla is going to show up in town and try to take her out?"

"It's happened before," Cooper said, thinking of Joe's ex-fiancé who tried to poison Helena and maim Joe a few years back

Dale shook his head. "This is ridiculous. Why would anyone want to hurt Serena over some botched wedding?"

"People go nuts over weddings. Mothers and daughters stop speaking. Best friends turn into enemies." He shrugged. "You know it's true."

"Coop, those are not things that call for police protection." Dale squinted his eyes at his brother. "Is there something going on between you and Serena? Are you two seeing each other? Is this why you want her followed? To see if she's being faithful?"

Cooper rolled his eyes and exhaled. Should he even dignify that with an answer? "No, we're not seeing each other." He didn't confess that the thought had crossed his mind more than once. "But she's Joe's sister, and I think someone followed her here. Wouldn't be the first time for that either. Or did you forget Cindy's father and the guy looking for the money he stole?"

"That was different. Cindy's father had just been released from federal prison for his part in a bank robbery turned murder. What did Serena do? Set a bride's dress on fire? It was an accident, according to Joe."

"So, you do know about the 'Wedding Woes'." Cooper pointed to the magazine sitting on Dale's desk.

"Yes, I know about it, and I hardly think the biggest popstar in the world hired a hitman to take out her wedding planner."

Cooper blew out another breath. "Fine. Don't assign someone to watch her. Do it yourself."

"What? I don't have time for that."

"Just do some drive-bys, drop in to check on her and Helena, let her know you're around if she needs anything."

"I'll think about it."

"You do that."

***

"Can I be honest with y'all? This drink is terrible. I'd just as soon eat a bug than drink this."

Everyone laughed raucously at Serena's statement and her face. Amanda wanted to give her a high-five.

"What? Y'all know I'm right? It's absolutely disgusting." She slammed her glass down on the table, and they all started laughing again.

"She's right, you know. It's just awful," Amanda said, following Serena's lead and slamming down her glass.

"But it's our signature drink," Andi protested. "We've been drinking Southern Comfort and lemonade since we were in high school."

"And there's your problem," Serena said. "It's a drink for teenagers who don't know any better." She motioned to the waitress and gestured to Amanda and herself. "Sugar, we'll have two of your best glasses of red wine."

"We only have merlot and cab."

Serena made a face that sent everyone into a fit of laughter again. "What about whiskey? You do have decent whiskey, don't you?"

"Yes, Ma'am, a whole shelf of good whiskeys."

"Then bring us each a shot of your best one."

"Oh, no," Amanda protested. "I'm not a whiskey drinker, and I don't do shots."

Serena sighed. "How about Margaritas? Can your bartender make a good Margarita?"

"The best in three towns," the waitress said, lifting her chin.

"Then two of those, please."

"We're supposed to be celebrating and toasting our newest member and citizen, and you're already insulting us," Andi said, laughter in her voice and eyes. "Are you sure you're ready to say goodbye to the big city and move all the way out here where our drinks aren't sophisticated enough for you?"

Serena looked around the table, and Amanda wondered what she thought about their small town.

"I'm more than ready. I want to live in a small town. I want friends and neighbors who don't stay closed up in their big, fancy houses all the time. I want to work with young women who are looking for their dream wedding, not the cover of *People Magazine*."

"You won't regret it," Cindy said. "I don't ever want to go back to Southern California. How about you, Amanda?"

Amanda was listening, but only half-heartedly. She was too busy watching the family who walked in the door.

"I'm sorry, Cindy. What did you say?"

Every woman at the table followed her gaze to the front of the restaurant.

"Something got your attention?" Helena asked with a smile. "Or someone?"

"What? No," Amanda said with mock indignation. She took a gulp of her margarita.

"Had any more texts lately?" Andi asked Amanda with a sly smile.

"Texts?" Helena asked. "What kind of texts?"

Amanda, who was trying not to look at Andi, noticed Serena hastily grab her own phone and turn it over. What was that about?

"Amanda?" Andi asked.

"Texts? I don't know what you're talking about," Amanda answered, shooting her friend a look she hoped said, *Drop it, Andi.*

"Guess Dale and Cooper didn't feel like cooking tonight," Serena said, changing the subject. Amanda gave her a grateful smile.

"We need a family restaurant in town," Cindy said. "Something other than La Forna. It's good, but you can't do pasta every night."

"You can't?" Helena asked, rubbing her stomach. "It's just about all I want these days."

Amanda casually slid her gaze to the table across the room where she was met with a sexy grin from a handsome man with marble-green eyes. She blushed and looked away.

"Speaking of food, we'd better order," Andi said. "I have to be up early tomorrow."

They all agreed and looked at their menus, though they had it memorized.

"Evening, ladies."

The women turned to say hello to the chief of police.

"Hey, Dale," Andi said. "Night out?"

"Yeah. The kids had ball practice after school, and I had to work late. Coop was on the job all afternoon, and it's Mom's bridge night."

"Aunt Serena!" Suzy yelled as she barreled herself into Serena. "Why haven't you come back to the house? We didn't get to play with my dollhouse yet."

"You're right, Sugar. We'll do that real soon."

"Hi, Miss Helena," Suzy said, putting her hands around Helena's stomach. She buried her face in Helena's dress and whispered, "Hello, baby."

Amanda thought her heart would melt. She glanced over at Serena and saw the most endearing look on her face as she watched Suzy. Then Amanda looked up and saw a strange look on Dale's face as he watched Serena, like he was assessing a crime scene. What was that about?

Amanda felt Andi's gaze on her and looked up to meet her closest friend's eyes. Andi's brow was raised in surprise, and she gave Amanda a questioning look. Amanda gave a small shrug. She didn't know if Andi had noticed Dale's questioning gaze or her own lingering gaze on Cooper.

"We don't want to interrupt," Dale said, gently extricating Suzy from Helena's stomach. "Just thought I'd say hello."

"You're not interrupting," Andi and Serena said at the same time. Amanda saw the blush rise in Serena's face, but Dale didn't seem to notice as he turned to Andi.

"Tell Wade I said hello." He turned to Helena. "And Joe. Come on, Suzy."

Suzy turned to Serena and gave her one last hug. "You'll come back and play with me soon, right?"

"Sugar, I can't wait."

"He needs a wife," Helena said as he walked away.

"Don't meddle," Andi told her sister. "When the time is right, it will happen."

Amanda noticed Serena was silent, paying close attention to the Margarita glass in front of her.

***

"Uncle Coop, why does Aunt Serena call me Sugar?" Suzy asked after Cooper finished reading to her.

"I think that's just the way they talk in Texas. You

know, like when Grandma calls you Honeypie."

She wrinkled her nose. "Why do people call each other food stuff?"

Cooper laughed. "That's a good question, Suze. Maybe because people like food, and sweet foods like sugar and pie make people feel good. And if the person is sweet, then calling them something sweet fits."

"Fits?"

"Makes sense. Like, me calling you Bean because you're as hyper as a jumping bean. It fits."

"What is a jumping bean anyway?"

Cooper laughed. "You know what, Bean? I have no idea." He kissed her on the top of her head and stood. "Good night, Suzy."

"Uncle Coop?"

Cooper knew better than to indulge in another question, but he did anyway.

"Yes, Bean?"

"Mommy called me Pumpkin. But I don't look like a pumpkin."

"No, honey. It's another one of those food names that make people feel good." He sat back down on the edge of the bed. "Pumpkins come out in the fall when people are starting to think about the holidays and being together. When do we eat Miss Andi's pumpkin pie?"

"Thanksgiving?"

"Right, and that's when families all get together to thank God for all the blessings he's given them. Pumpkins make people happy, and you made your mom happy."

"Uncle Coop?"

The smallness of her voice and the moisture in her eyes let Cooper know what was coming. It was the question Suzy asked more than any other.

"Yes, Bean?"

"Why did Mommy have to die? Why couldn't she stay with us?"

"I've told you before. God needed her in Heaven. We don't know why, but there must've been a very special reason."

"And I'll see her someday when God needs me?"

"You bet. Now, time for bed, okay?"

"Okay." She sighed with resignation. Cooper knew the answer wasn't enough, but no answer would be.

As he turned off the lamp and closed the door, his thoughts drifted to Jessie. Why was she in a perpetual coma? What purpose did that serve? And why did he have to wait until he got to Heaven to find out?

There were just some questions that had no good answers.

Ten

Serena smelled smoke. And dust. And…wait. Smoke? Her eyes flew open, and she tried to lift her head, but the pain pushed her back. The throbbing in her head, neck, chest, and various other parts of her body caused dazzling bright lights to swim through her vision. She clamped her eyes shut again.

Where was she? Why did she feel strapped down, unable to move?

Slowly, she opened her eyes and lifted her head. Though her vision was blurry, she could make out a headrest in front of her. Not her white leather headrest. It was tan. She was in the backseat of a car. She squinted to see through the bright light. Joe's car. Joe had driven them to the restaurant. She'd been in back, and he and Helena had been in front.

Her eyes snapped all the way open. Joe and Helena!

She tried to see them, but she couldn't move. She

looked down and realized the seatbelt had become a straitjacket. Her fingers fumbled as she worked to unhook it. Everything ached, but her head and chest were the worst. The seatbelt had done its job but also caused some kind of injury, she thought. Bruised ribs? Broken maybe? She groaned as she forced herself to look over the front seat.

The bright white airbags were blinding as the light of the full moon illuminated them like giant, glowing orbs even though they had already deflated. Joe's head was angled back, and blood ran from his mouth. Serena reached her hand out to touch his throat. He had a pulse, but she thought it was weak. Then again, what did she know? She didn't even know First Aid.

She tried to tamp down her panic and turned toward Helena whose head lolled to the other side. She also had a pulse, but it was racing. Helena groaned.

"Helena, are you all right? Can you answer me?" Serena heard the desperation in her own voice. "Helena, please answer me."

"What…what happened?"

"I don't know. I don't remember. Are you okay?"

"I…I think…I think I peed myself."

Helena sounded calm, too calm, and that, more than anything, sent Serena into a panic. She had a bride once whose mother had a heart attack at the wedding. The bride was overly calm just before she went into shock. What would that mean for Helena? For the baby? And was the car slowly filling with smoke? That was bad. Really bad.

"Joe!" Serena started to yell. "Joe, wake up!" She pushed and pulled at her brother, yelling his name, trying everything to get him to open his eyes, even slapping what she could reach of his face.

"The deer," Helena said as if dreaming. "Did we hit it?"

"A deer? Was there a deer?" Serena now recalled looking at her phone, feeling a sense of dread as she read the texts. She wasn't paying attention to what was happening, but then she heard Helena scream, felt the car swerve and leave the road before going over… Was it a cliff? Had they gone over a cliff?

She recalled Helena's pleas to drive into the national park to see the sunset on their way home from dinner. Joe hadn't wanted to, but Helena begged. The sky was perfect, she said, for the most stunning sunset. They had watched the sun drop behind the mountains, and Helena had been right. It was spectacular. Then they started their way out of the park.

"Oooh," Helena moaned. "Oooooh." The moans increased. "It hurts, it hurts. Ooooh. Help me, Joe. Help me. It hurts."

"What hurts?" Serena asked.

"My…the…ooooh." Helena clutched her stomach, and Serena knew the awful truth. Helena hadn't peed. Her water had broken. The baby was coming.

Serena fumbled in the backseat for her phone. Where was it? She must have dropped it in the accident. She scoured the floor, her fingers frantically roaming over the car mats and under the seats, pain searing her chest where she determined her ribs were bruised but not broken, she hoped. Finally, her hand closed over the phone. Who should she call? Logically, it should be 911, but they'd gone off the road. She was sure of it. They were at the bottom of a cliff. And cell service was spotty out here. Would they even be able to locate them? Serena had no idea where they were.

She opened the door and hurried from the car as she dialed the number anyway.

"911, what…emergency?"

"We've been in an accident." She ran around the car and opened Helena's door.

"I'm sorry…you…that? …breaking up." The call was going digital on her, but she tried again.

"We've. Been. In. An. Accident!" she yelled into the phone. "Help us!" She looked at Helena and tried to figure out how to get her from the car to a safe place.

"Did…say accident?"

"Yes! Yes!"

"Where…you?"

"I don't know! I don't know where we are. Can you triangulate us or whatever it is you do to find cell phones?"

"…sorry… repeat…"

Frustrated, Serena hung up the phone. She took several breaths, trying to come up with a plan. Helena continued to moan from inside the car. Serena ran to the other side and reached through the broken window. She yelped when the jagged glass sliced through her upper arm.

"Joe!" Serena yelled, this time pounding on her brother's arm, shoulder, whatever she could reach. She spotted his phone plugged into the dashboard and ran back to the other side. She managed to crawl over Helena enough to yank the phone from the charger. She knew Joe's passcode and punched it in. It took three tries to hit the right numbers. Her hands were shaking.

"Hello, hello. Can you hear me?" She almost cried in relief. "Please help."

***

Cooper heard the buzzing and swatted at the giant mosquito disrupting his search. He was in the national forest, and there was smoke everywhere. Why was there a mosquito? The smoke should've deterred it. Where was Jessie? He had to find her. But that darn mosquito.

Suddenly, his eyes flew open, and he grabbed his vibrating phone. It was his night off from the sheriff's office, but that meant nothing when there was a SAR event. Who was calling him? He stared at the screen for a moment before answering.

"Joe? It's the middle of the night. Everything okay?"

"Hello, hello. Can you hear me?"

"Helena?"

There was a strangled cry. "Please help."

"Helena? What's wrong?" He was out of the bed in a flash, pulling on his jeans as he raced down the hall toward Dale's room. He didn't bother knocking, and Dale sat up with a start when Cooper barged through the door.

"It's Serena. Can…hear me?"

"Serena? Yeah, I hear you. What's wrong?"

"Accident…park…a cliff."

Cooper's heart began racing, the kind of racing he was used to, the racing that propelled him into action. He was no longer thinking about his brother's best friend, or the friend's sister, or any particular person. He was only thinking about the rescue.

"Where are you?"

"National…sunset…there was a deer…Joe…cliff… he's hurt."

"What?" Dale was asking, already dressed.

"I'm on my way, Serena. I'll find you."

"Wait!"

"What?"

"Helena…water broke…coming."

Cooper's eyes widened, and he sent his brother a look of panic as he swallowed the lump in his throat. This was something he'd never dealt with before.

"It's okay. We're on our way. Keep her calm. And Serena, try not to let her have the baby."

"What?" Dale asked again, his voice loud and frantic.

Cooper disconnected the call. "It was Serena on Joe's phone. The connection was bad, but I'm pretty sure they've been in an accident somewhere in the national forest. And Helena's water broke. The baby's coming."

"I'll call Mom."

"I'm not waiting. I'm calling Bud and Lucy first, then

the rest of the team. I'll let you know where they are when we find them."

"I'll let EMS know we're going to need a bus."

"Or two," Cooper said. "I think Joe may be hurt."

Cooper called his team as he headed to his truck but made a stop partway through town. He didn't take the time to call. He hopped out of the running truck and raced up the walkway. He banged on the door. He banged harder. He began shouting. Finally, the door flew open.

"I need you. I'll tell you on the way. Get dressed and grab whatever medical stuff you have. Hurry." He took a deep breath. "Please. It's Joe and Helena. And the baby."

His phone rang, and he turned away to answer it without waiting for a reaction. By the time he answered all the sheriff's questions, Amanda was at his side, racing toward his truck.

***

"Ever been in a chopper?" Cooper asked, shouting above the noise.

Amanda shook her head and took the headset he was holding out to her.

"Put these on so you can hear." He motioned to his ear as he spoke.

She wasn't hearing every word, but she knew what he was telling her. She put on the headset and listened to Cooper's instructions to the pilot. Before she finished snapping in her seatbelt, she felt them leave the ground. Cooper turned his attention back to her.

"Lucy will take care of Joe, you take care of Helena. I have no idea if Serena is hurt, so we'll have to assess and address when we get there. I'll do whatever you two tell me to do."

Amanda nodded. Her heart was galloping at a breakneck speed. She'd never done anything like this. Never flown into an accident scene. Never delivered a baby in distress. Never delivered a baby outside of a hospital. Or outside period.

Cooper was no longer talking. He and Lucy peered into the trees below, scanning for any signs of life, signs of a car or an accident. Amanda wasn't sure what to look for. Downed trees? People standing in the road waving? This wasn't TV. How would they find them?

"There!" shouted the pilot. "I see lights."

"I see them," Cooper said. He relayed the information into his radio, sharing what the pilot was telling him—coordinates, maybe? Highway numbers? As soon as he finished, Cooper began unbuckling. Lucy did the same. Amanda was frozen. What were they doing? Were they going to leave her? Jump out of the helicopter?

Cooper stopped and looked at Amanda. "Undo your seatbelt, and put this on."

He handed her a harness of some sort. She unbuckled with shaking hands and held up the harness. She had no idea how to put it on. Did they expect her to parachute out of this thing? Her heart was beating so hard against her chest wall, Amanda thought it would burst through her ribs and skin and go flying across the helicopter.

"Like this," Lucy said, and Amanda realized she was talking to her. She observed Lucy and tried to mirror her actions as she slipped the harness between her legs and over her hips. Finally, Cooper reached over and helped her fasten it around her waist and over her chest.

"You okay?"

Amanda didn't answer. Her entire body trembled with fear.

"Amanda, look at me." She looked up into those marble eyes and felt something shift. Her breathing began to normalize. Her head cleared. "You're going to go down with me on a cable, okay? It's going to be hooked to the chopper and to both of us. We can't fall. We're perfectly safe. You understand?"

A calming sensation overtook her as she stared into those hypnotic eyes. She nodded, feeling her heartbeat begin to slow. Until Cooper opened the door, and the force of the air blew her hair and caused her to lose her balance. But his steadying hands were back on her, holding her upright, gently pulling her toward him, and then clipping the cable to her harness.

"Ready?"

Before she could answer, they were flying through the sky. Well, not flying. More like dropping at an easy pace. She'd never felt anything like it. Fear, anxiety, but also breathtaking awe as they approached the treetops, saw the car getting bigger, felt Cooper's arms around her. It was like nothing she'd ever experienced. In mere minutes, their feet were on the ground, and Cooper was unhooking the cable and shaking out of his harness.

"That was amazing," Amanda breathed. And despite the harrowing situation they were in, Amanda heard him laugh just before he headed for the car.

***

Serena ran to them and threw her arms around Cooper. The force almost knocked him off his feet, and he grabbed hold of her to steady himself. One arm was covered with blood, but she'd had enough wits about her to tie off a tourniquet above it.

"Thank God, you're here. I didn't think he was listening." She turned to Amanda who was pulling her hair into a knot behind her head. "She's been asking for Joe. She's more alert now, and she's scared."

"How soon are the contractions?"

A scream ripped through the dark night, and Amanda ran to the car without waiting for a response.

"Where is she?"

"There was smoke coming in. I moved her. Is that okay? Did I do the right thing?"

"Exactly the right thing," Cooper assured her.

"She's over here." Serena led them to a trail opening about twenty yards from the car.

Amanda knelt beside her friend. "Helena, I'm here." She laid her hand on Helena's forehead. "She's clammy and cool, pulse rapid." Amanda looked into her eyes and nodded. "In labor, yes, but also in shock." She went right to work assessing the rest of Helena's vitals.

"I can't get the door open," Lucy called from the car. "Dr. Blake is trapped, and there's smoke coming from the engine."

"We can't stay here," Cooper said to Serena. "We need to get away from the car." But he couldn't help her find a way. He needed to get to Joe. He handed Serena his flashlight. "See if the trail bends away from this area." She nodded and disappeared into the trees.

Breaking branches and rustling trees caught his attention, and he turned to see Lance and Danny rappelling down the bank. Headlamps shone from their helmets.

"Fire trucks are almost here," Lance said. "Mike and Rob are with them. What do you need?"

"Smoke's coming from the engine. We're going to need hoses. And Joe's door won't open. We need to get him out."

"I've got this." Danny held up a crowbar. Cooper grabbed the crowbar, and Danny moved closer, shining his light on the door.

Cooper wedged the crowbar into the space by the door and heaved it as hard as he could. The door opened some, but it took Danny, Lance, and Cooper to pull it off. Joe's body slumped into the opening, straining the seatbelt even more. Cooper pulled out a utility knife and cut through the seatbelt. Then the three men lifted Joe out of the car.

"Is he okay?" Serena pleaded.

"I don't feel a pulse," Lucy said. She looked around. "Coop, we need to get them out of this area, but I've got to shock him. Fast."

"We can go down the trail. It bends and keeps going," Serena told them.

Cooper nodded. He could hear Helena screaming but didn't see her. He didn't know how Amanda had managed to move her farther down the trail. Maybe Serena had helped. The full moon gave them a good deal of light, but it would be dark further in the trees.

"Let's get him onto that trail. Lucy, you get the AED ready while we move him." He looked at Lance and Danny. "Keep your headlamps on. We're going to need the light. Ready?"

They carried Joe onto the trail and kept moving until they were well away from the car. Helena and Amanda were a little way ahead. Cooper could see the reflection from a mylar blanket that Helena was lying on. Another one was draped over her, and it looked like Amanda was taking her blood pressure, but they were shadowed by the trees.

"How is she?" Cooper asked, sitting beside Amanda while Lucy and Lance took care of Joe.

"She needs a hospital. BP is 150 over 95. Waters are broken, and the contractions are three to four minutes apart."

"I've got rhythm!" Lucy called.

Cooper heard Serena begin to cry, and then the cliff above them was bathed in flashing red lights.

"Cooper! You down there?"

"We're down here."

There was a sudden whooshing noise, and Cooper instinctively shouted, "The car's going to blow, take cover!"

Without thinking, he leaped over Amanda and Helena and covered them with as much of his body as he could. The explosion shook the night. Leaves, limbs, metal, and fire rained from the sky. Crackling and hissing took over the silence.

"Are you okay?" Cooper asked Amanda as a large piece of metal slammed into the ground next to them.

Amanda nodded and turned back to Helena who let out a blood-curdling scream.

"Serena!" Amanda yelled. "I need you!" She looked at Cooper. "Go. Save Joe. Put out the fire. Whatever you need to do to get us all out of here."

Cooper didn't waste a minute. He was on his feet, grabbing the end of the hose that was lowered from above. He pulled it toward the car and the inferno that was once a tranquil forest. He was quickly joined by a team of firefighters and relinquished the hose to them. He went back to his team who were strapping Joe to the Stokes basket. The chopper had put down in a clearing a few miles away to wait for orders, but it was back and dropped a cable down to Lance who grabbed it and hooked it to the basket.

They watched as Joe was lifted out of the ravine and carried to the waiting ambulance above them.

"I'm going to have Bud send down a cable," Danny told Cooper. "I'll take Serena up so she can ride with him. She should be checked out, too. I can tell she's in pain."

"Good call," Cooper said.

He swung around as another scream came, and watched in amazement as Amanda, calm as Edwards Lake on a summer day, reached under the blanket and give Helena instructions. Serena held Helena's head in her lap and stroked her forehead, whispering things Cooper couldn't hear. Seconds later, Amanda pulled the baby out from the blanket. He rushed to their side.

"Serena, go with Danny. You can ride with Joe." He looked toward the others and shouted, "Lucy, come help Amanda." Then he turned to the doctor. "What can I do?"

"Take off your shirt," She commanded.

Cooper looked down and, without asking why, unbuttoned and removed his shirt. His undershirt was soaked with sweat and stuck to his chest. He laid his shirt out wide, inside out, on the dirt between them, reading Amanda's thoughts.

"Got him," Lucy said, kneeling beside Cooper and taking the baby from Amanda. She swiped a finger between the baby's lips and tilted his head back. He let out a scream that rivaled his mother's.

"Is that him? Or her?" Helena asked through tears, trying to turn toward the cry. "Is the baby okay?"

"He's perfect," Lucy said as she cut the umbilical cord. She enfolded the baby in Cooper's shirt and handed him to his mother. "Here you go, Mama."

"It's a boy?" Helena asked. "Really?"

"It's a boy," Lucy told her. "I need to get his vitals but from what I see, he looks healthy as a horse."

"Helena, you're not done yet. I need you to give me one last big push, okay?" Helena did as told, and Cooper saw Amanda moving behind the blanket. "Almost done here," she said before looking up and catching his eye. She smiled tentatively and nodded.

"Coop," Lance nudged him from behind, and Cooper looked up at him. "Basket's ready. Is she okay to go?"

Cooper looked at Amanda. "The ambulance is waiting for them. Can she be lifted out?"

"One second," Amanda said from behind the blanket. "Okay, she's good." Amanda pulled the blanket down over Helena's lower body and looked at the new mother. "You and your son are going to get a ride to the top, Helena. Are you ready?"

"Where's Joe?" she asked, as if suddenly realizing he wasn't there. "Where is he?"

Cooper rushed to lay his hand on her arm. "Joe's on his way to Mountain Home. He's stable, but he's hurt. Serena's with him. The sooner we get you out of these woods, the sooner you and this little one can go see Daddy."

"Then get us out of here," Helena said, and Cooper patted her arm.

"Take 'em away guys."

Another basket dropped, and Lance, Danny, and Lucy loaded Helena and baby inside and stood back as they were lifted into the sky. Cooper handed Amanda a bottle of water, and she poured it over her hands and arms, cleaning them as best she could.

"We need to clear out," Cooper said as he began to cough. There was so much going on, he hadn't realized the woods were filling with smoke. Suddenly, his throat and lungs rebelled, and he was choking.

"I've got the climbing gear rigged," Lance said. "But it's back that way." He pointed toward the fire.

Cooper looked around. "We need to hike out." He coughed again, this time feeling the burn of the smoke. "Now. Hurry."

They didn't have any of the gear they needed to survive a fire, and Cooper knew they'd already inhaled too much smoke when the adrenaline of the baby's birth kept them focused on Helena and not the fire.

"Man down!"

Everyone stopped and turned back.

"I've got it," Lucy said. "You get Dr. Pierce out of here."

Cooper looked from Amanda to the chaos behind them.

"Go," Amanda said. "I won't be alone. I'll be okay."

Cooper felt dizzy. Amanda's words mingled with the same words he'd heard long ago. He couldn't let that happen again. A hand gripped his arm, and he looked down. He followed the hand up to the face of his friend and teammate.

"Coop, we've got this," Lance told him. "Go with her. Make sure she's okay."

Without another thought about the fire or being a

hero or trying to show how good he was at his job, Cooper took Amanda's hand and ran with her through the forest.

***

"Cooper, stop." Amanda doubled over and began coughing uncontrollably. "I can't," she huffed. "I'm winded. The smoke." She coughed some more.

"We have to keep going. We can't stay here."

"I can't keep running. My lungs are screaming." She knew they couldn't stop, but she could barely breathe. Her lungs felt like one of those old-fashioned things you squeezed to blow air on a fire, only it was stuck on compression, so air was only going out and not in.

Suddenly, Cooper picked her up and threw her over his shoulder.

"Cooper! What are you doing? Put me down!"

"No way," he yelled.

She thought about pounding on his back, but she was more stunned by his speed than by his caveman instincts. Even with her added weight, he flew through the forest, hurdling over fallen limbs and careening around bends. He didn't stop until they were far from the smoke. He set Amanda gently down on her own two feet. He didn't even seem to be out of breath.

"Better? I think we're away from the thick of it."

"That was amazing," Amanda said.

"What was?"

"The way you did that?" She gestured behind them.

"I mean, I never thought some guy would throw me over his shoulders and run off with me, but the way you ran out of there. You don't even look winded. That was amazing."

"Yeah, well, unless you want me to do it again, we need to keep going."

It was then that she heard the catch in his voice, the way his words were a bit forced. He wasn't a superhero after all, but in her mind, he would always be Superman. She smiled at the thought as they hurried down the trail. It fit. He was always flying off to rescue those in need, doing daring stunts to save the day, even leaping off tall cliffs and dropping from the air.

Amanda had never once in her life thought of herself as a damsel in distress or someone who needed saving. Today, however, she realized everyone needs saving at some point in their lives. Nobody can go it alone forever. At the very least, everyone needs someone they can call in an emergency, someone they know will be there in any situation to carry them when they aren't able to find a way out.

***

A running Polaris ATV was waiting for them when they reached the trailhead.

"Hop in," Dale said with a wave of his arm.

Cooper gestured for Amanda to climb in front with Dale, and he took one of the backseats.

"How's it going?"

"Almost contained. Thankfully, they were ahead of it since you were already at the scene before the fire started."

Cooper was relieved to hear that. "And Joe?" He was afraid to ask but hoped for good news.

"No word. He was still unconscious when the bus took him. Lucy was great. She probably saved his life."

"Was Serena able to go with him?"

"Yeah. Wade and Andi showed up, so Andi rode with Helena. Plus, Serena needs stitches and a chest x-ray. Once Joe was in the bus, she realized how much pain she was in."

"I'm glad they all got out without a problem. Amanda was amazing."

"I was just doing my job."

Dale shook his head. "Don't brush off what you just did. Delivering a baby in that situation was high-risk, and you know it. Mother and baby are both doing well, and that's thanks to you."

"Thank you. Both of you." She turned to look at Cooper, and he resisted the urge to reach up and wipe the soot and smears of blood from her face.

They pulled up behind Dale's cruiser and climbed from the ATV. Sheriff Wilson rushed over to them.

"Good job, Officer Mackenzie." She turned to Amanda. "And Dr. Pierce. You two and the rest of your crew saved lives today. I know that's the norm for you," she said to Cooper, "and probably for you, too, Dr. Pierce, but this was no ordinary rescue or ordinary delivery. They're all lucky you got to them when you did."

"That was Serena," Cooper said. "She was able to get just enough information to me that we could find them."

"I listened to the 911 call," the sheriff said. "There wasn't much to go by, and what could be heard was covered with static. I'm glad you were able to decipher what she was saying."

"Coop!"

He turned to see Lance, Danny, and Lucy heading in their direction. They all hugged, gave high fives, and shared praise with each other.

"Dr. Pierce," Lucy said. "I couldn't have done all that without you. Thank you."

"Don't thank me. Cooper's the one who showed up at my place and told me he needed help."

"That's the second time you've aided our team in saving lives," Lance said. "Maybe you should consider a change of careers. We're always looking for good people."

Amanda laughed. "I think the clinic provides enough excitement in my life."

Cooper knew Lance was kidding, but his stomach still churned at the thought. He swallowed the bile that rose to his throat. When he hoisted Amanda over his shoulder and started running through the forest, he knew it was Amanda he was carrying, but somehow, it seemed like he was living five years in the past, doing now what he couldn't do then. Just the thought of losing Amanda the way he'd lost Jessie was more than terrifying.

But what made him think she was his to lose?

He looked at her now as she talked and joked with his crew. The hair she had pulled back had come loose, releasing soft waves that swayed around her face. Ash, soot, and blood were smeared with sweat across her nose and cheeks, and though she smiled, there was fatigue in her eyes. She was class and spunk and bravery all wrapped in one.

His eyes caught hers as she laughed at something Lucy said, and a twinge ran from his gut to his heart. Had she felt it, too? What exactly was happening between them? And was he ready to take the chance of getting his heart broken all over again?

No, he couldn't go there. He thought he could try, but tonight proved him wrong. He'd brought Amanda out there, and yes, she'd saved lives, but she could've lost hers. And it would've been on him. Again. Then he'd be right back where he started—knowing that he was the reason someone he cared about was gone. How many times could he forgive himself for hurting someone he cared about?

He pushed away the thought, the one that told him to give her a chance, give them a chance. Cooper just wasn't ready despite the voice coming, not from his head, but from his heart.

Eleven

"Oh, my gosh. He's beautiful," Amanda gushed over Jeremy Joshua Blake. "After Joe's brother and your father?"

Helena nodded. "It only seemed right to name him after the man who brought us together from Heaven."

Amanda agreed. "Well, you look wonderful."

Helena laughed. "I hardly think so, but if I do, it's thanks to you."

"Any news about Joe?" Amanda asked, biting her lips together.

Helena's eyes welled with tears. "I don't know. He has internal bleeding and several broken ribs. The airbag saved him, but it did a lot of damage. The driver's side took a beating on the way down, and he absorbed the brunt of it. They tell me he'll be in surgery for hours, but the doctors are hopeful. Father Michael made it here just in time to see him before they started."

"Is there anything I can do?" Amanda asked.

"Pray. Please pray. They say, if the surgery is successful, he can go back to work and live a normal life, but they have to get through surgery first. And they hope they don't find anything unexpected while they're in there."

Amanda understood. Joe wasn't out of the woods, but the doctors were hoping for the best.

"Well, wait until he sees this little one. He's going to recover in no time just so he can hold him and spoil him the way he already does his niece."

Helena's smile didn't reach her eyes. "Thanks. I hope you're right."

"Hey, sis. I brought you a real coffee." Andi slid in next to Amanda. She set the coffee on the rolling table and leaned down to give Helena a hug and kiss. "I talked to Mom and Dad. They'll be here soon. And Jackson and Cindy."

"Thank you. Did Wade go home?"

"Yeah. We left Alicia with Mom and Dad last night, so he picked her up so they can come here. He'll come back as soon as the nanny arrives."

"Did everyone else go home?" Amanda asked.

"Yeah, most of them. They were all exhausted. Once they found out Helena and the baby are okay, and Joe would be in surgery, they went home to get some sleep."

"You said most of them."

Andi nodded. "Dale's still here with Cooper, and Serena, of course. They're waiting for Joe to come out of surgery." She looked at Helena. "Serena's anxious to come see you, but she wants to hear from the doctor first."

"Is Serena okay?" Amanda asked.

"A bunch of stitches in her arm and one fractured rib, but it could've been a lot worse."

"I wish I could be down there with them. They won't let me leave the room until all the tests come back," Helena said, her voice cracking with emotion.

"As soon as they give you the go-ahead, I'll get you down there," Andi told her.

"Do you mind if I go down and sit with the others?" Amanda asked. "If you need anything, I'm happy to get it for you." She wanted to hear what the doctor had to say after surgery.

"Of course, you go," Helena said. "If the doctor has an update, I'd like you to be there."

Amanda nodded. "I'll see if I can find out anything in the meantime."

"Thank you, Amanda," Helena said as a tear fell from her eyes. "It means a lot to me. And to Joe."

"You bet." Amanda hugged Helena and turned to leave. Andi grabbed her by the sleeve once they left the room and leaned in to hug her.

"Thank you. For everything."

"Of course," Amanda told her.

"And if it means anything, it says a lot that Cooper took you out there. He trusts you."

Amanda nodded. "I'm glad he trusted me enough to help. We hardly know each other after all."

"Well enough for him to get you out of bed at night and take you on a rescue mission."

"I guess after the incident with Steven the hiker, he knows I can handle an emergency out in the wild."

Andi shot her friend a look, but Amanda put an end to the conversation. "How about we go check on Joe?"

Without waiting for an answer, she hurried down the hall, her heart thumping against her rib cage. She and Cooper were friends and colleagues. Nothing more. She knew she had a bit of a thing for him, but it was just what therapists would call a trauma bond. They were tied by their experiences. They knew they could trust each other in a high-stress situation. He had her back, and she had his. That was all.

***

Cooper watched Dale pace the waiting room. If he drank one more cup of coffee, Cooper would be able to tie a tail to him and sail him up to the sky. Just the opposite was Serena. She sat in a chair, her back stiff and her face pale. She didn't get up or walk about or even look around her. The only sign of her worry was the way she fingered her Rosary beads—at such a harried pace, he thought it was more a way to occupy her hands than an actual prayer. Each of them was in their own world of pain and grief.

One glance out the window at the pink glow off the mountain tops told him dawn wouldn't be long in coming. It had been a long night, and he felt it in every inch of his body, but he couldn't go home. Joe and Wade were his brother's best friends. And Serena was Joe's sister and had nobody else nearby except Helena. Cooper didn't know what was happening inside the OR, but he was going to be there when they received news.

"I need more coffee," Dale said, coming to an abrupt stop in front of Cooper.

"I'm not sure your body can handle more coffee," Cooper told him. "I can get you a bottle of water." He started to stand.

"Coffee. I need coffee," Dale said as though the words were staccato beats from a snare drum.

"Fine," Cooper said, lifting himself from the barely cushioned, wooden-armed hospital chair. "I'll get you more coffee, but Joe would be the first to tell you to give your heart a break. It's working overtime just to keep up with the caffeine you're feeding it. You might as well be on an IV."

"Who needs an IV?"

Cooper turned to see Amanda walking their way. Her auburn hair had been pulled back into a ponytail, no loose strands lingered along her cheekbones. She had washed her face, but she couldn't hide the hollows of exhaustion or the weariness in her eyes.

"Serena Blake?" Came a voice that splintered the walls they'd each erected. Dale spun on his heels. Serena shot up from her chair like a canon, wincing in pain, and Cooper found his mind echoing a silent prayer.

"Yes, I'm here," Serena said, hurrying toward the doctor.

"Joe's doing well." Dr. Robbins assured her. "He came through surgery like a champ. He has several broken ribs which pierced his lung and liver. He suffered respiratory failure and tension pneumothorax due to the lung collapse which affected his cardiac function. That's why his heart stopped at the scene. It doesn't appear there was anything wrong with his heart previously nor was it permanently damaged. We relieved the pressure in his chest, but he'll need surgery on the liver tomorrow. Another doctor will take over there. Of all the organs that could have been perforated, he picked the right one. They should be able to successfully repair that. He'll be here for a few days and will need a lot of rest once he's released, but I expect him to make a full recovery."

Amanda began asking a few more questions, but they were lost on the others.

"Thank Heaven," Serena breathed as she staggered back to the chair. Cooper helped her ease into the chair while Dale collapsed next to her and buried his face in his hands.

Cooper stood and went to Amanda after the doctor returned to the OR. "What do you think? It sounds good. Anything else we should know?"

"Well, I'm not a surgeon, and I don't have any expertise in heart, lungs, or liver, but he said Joe got here in time to prevent any further problems. At least, he hopes so. He'll need surgery on the liver tomorrow, but the doctor said they don't expect any problems or surprises."

"Hey," Andi said, joining them and addressing Cooper. "Sorry. My parents arrived as I was heading down, so I stayed with them and Helena for a bit. You get news?"

"We did, and it sounds good. He's got a long road to recovery, but he will recover." She filled Andi in on the rest.

"Guess you guys hired that PA just in time," Andi said to Amanda.

"Yeah, I guess so."

Cooper frowned, and Andi left them to go check on Dale and Serena.

"So, the new PA. Won't he or she be a help while Joe is out of commission? You sounded unsure."

Amanda offered a tentative smile. "Yeah, sorry. It definitely helps to have another hand."

Cooper saw her weariness deepen and thought about some of the things she'd told him and what he knew about the clinic.

"I guess it won't help you get any of that extra sleep you've been craving."

Amanda gave him a grateful look. "It won't, but it's selfish of me to go there. I should be focusing on Joe and his recovery, not on my lost sleep."

Cooper reached up and plucked a piece of a leaf from her hair that he hadn't noticed before. Amanda watched it glide to the floor, but Cooper kept his eyes on her face. The gesture felt intimate, and he blinked, trying to keep his mind off carrying her out of there so she could go home and get the rest she so desperately needed. He knew it wouldn't be a fireman's carry this time, and the thought threw him off balance.

"Is everything okay?" Amanda asked, looking into

his eyes again.

"Yeah, everything's good. How's Helena?"

Amanda smiled. "Worried about Joe, but otherwise, she's fine. The baby is healthy and at thirty-eight weeks, is considered full-term. They should be out of here in a day or two."

"That's good."

"I need to go see her, actually. I'm sure Dr. Robbins will get up to see her at some point and give her the good news, but I told her I'd let her know what he said."

"Let me go with you," Cooper offered. "I'm sure you're as beat as I am. You can tell her what the doctor said, and then I can take you home."

"Oh, you don't have to do that. I'm sure I can ride with Dale or someone."

"Amanda, I brought you into all this. The least I can do is see that you get home."

She hesitated for a moment, and he wondered why, but she smiled and nodded. "You're right, and Serena might need Dale to stay with her a little longer."

Cooper cast his gaze behind Amanda and saw Dale, his arms around Serena, as she cried what he assumed were tears of relief. He didn't see Andi, just Dale and Serena, and the scene felt as intimate as when he'd plucked the leaf from Amanda's hair. His gut gave a twinge. Amanda turned and followed his gaze.

"Do you think…?" he began to ask but stopped, unsure whether to voice what he was thinking.

"I'm not sure," Amanda said. "but for tonight, they need each other."

Cooper realized his initial attraction to Serena had transformed into admiration and fondness, but there was no desire there. He turned back to Amanda and felt his stomach spin. That voice spoke up again, telling him to touch her, take her hand, pull her into a hug, anything that brought her body closer to his. He realized he was fighting with fire, but he didn't know how to put it out. Every time he was near her, he was just fanning the flames.

***

"Hey, Amanda." The soft whisper penetrated her dream, causing her to stir and blink lazily, his face coming into focus.

"Cooper," she whispered. Was she still dreaming? They were the same eyes that gazed at her in sleep.

"Come on, Doc, time to get you inside."

Amanda opened her eyes and recognized the dashboard of Cooper's truck. Memories of the last twelve hours swirled through her brain, and in an instant, she went from terror to shock to relief all over again.

"Let me help you," Cooper said, reaching over to undo her seatbelt. "You can lean on me. You were out of it for the entire hour-ride home."

"I'm so tired," she said, her brain filled with the fog of exhaustion. The sunlight filtered through the fog, and she realized it was well into the daytime. "What time is it?"

"After nine," he told her as he guided her to the

front door. "Are your keys in your purse?"

Amanda thought about that. Did she have her purse? She must have. Didn't she have it at the hospital? No, she only had her phone. She must have left the house without it the night before.

"Under the flowerpot," she told him.

Cooper chuckled. "Original." He must have found it because in a matter of seconds, they were inside, and he was asking her where her bedroom was.

Without any real thoughts playing in her mind, she directed him up the stairs. By the time he laid her on the bed and covered her with an afghan, she was already drifting back to sleep.

***

Cooper was used to catching sleep when he could, so he wasn't surprised to find himself wide awake by one in the afternoon. He laid in bed and stared at the ceiling. It had been quite a night, and he realized he was sore from head to toe. His aches and pains, from wrenching open the car door, running through the woods, carrying Amanda, not to mention sitting up all night in that awful chair, made him feel ten years older than he was. He groaned as he climbed out of bed and made his way to the bathroom.

The house was quiet with the kids at school and Dale at work—or maybe sleeping or even still at the hospital. Cooper didn't like the quiet. It made him think. It made him go too deep inside himself.

He looked in the bathroom mirror and wondered who the man was staring back at him. He used to be the life of the party, the Romeo to every Juliet in school, even the class clown as well as the star athlete. If there was a superlative to be had, Cooper was branded with it. Now, he was a thirty-two-year-old man with a five o'clock shadow and sunken eyes who spent his days waiting for a call to take him on a perilous adventure and many nights going from sitting on a barstool listening to Rick complain about life to sitting in an empty church listening for the voice of God.

Was it worth it? Worth the risks, the lack of sleep, the crazy hours, the adrenaline highs and crushing lows? He'd never stopped to ask himself that question before, but it was always there, looming in the back of his mind. He did what he did to save lives, but was there more to it than that? Was it a way to avoid saving his own life? Was it a way to avoid a normal job, a wife and kids? After all, how could any wife put up with what he did?

And then, as always happened when he wasn't sure about his life choices, he thought about the flipside. What if he hadn't been there last night? What if he hadn't been the one who got the call from Serena because she hadn't known who to call? What if he didn't have the crew he'd practically hand-picked, trained, and knew could be counted on? What if he hadn't made the snap decision to take Amanda along?

Amanda.

He'd carried her because he couldn't leave her. He couldn't risk losing someone else on his team, even if she wasn't officially one of them. He couldn't risk another life which had been entrusted to him.

Or was that it at all? Perhaps it was his own life he was risking, his own losses he didn't want to face. Maybe all these years brooding over what his mistake or lapse in judgment had cost Jessie, the real thing he was brooding over was the loss of trust in himself. The loss of his own heart.

He turned on the shower and let the water heat to one degree below scalding. Throwing a towel over the curtain rod, he stepped in and allowed the water to warm his aching muscles and joints while it washed his thoughts away. He watched the water as it circled the drain, a mini whirlpool amidst the storms of his life, dark clouds that always gathered and never went away. He knew what he did mattered, that the lives he saved mattered. He also knew that, whether at work or in life, he was always one incident away from ripping open those clouds and his own pain all over again.

The question was, should he do it anyway? He didn't know if his question referred to his career or his heart.

***

Storm clouds gathered over the town, and Amanda thought she could smell rain in the air. For a brief moment, she thought of him and wondered if the rain would bring him to her once again. She shook her head and took a long drink of the hot coffee she held in her hands, the third one of the afternoon. She'd be lucky if she was able to close her eyes that night.

"Dr. Pierce, I can't find the suture kit."

Amanda turned to look at the young PA. She was fresh off her residency, so young and unexperienced, and Amanda recalled her own first days on the job at the hospital in Nashville.

"They tend to get shuffled around in the cabinet. Melanie would be the best person to ask."

"Thank you," Shelly said with a smile. "Any more word on Dr. Blake?"

"He's doing well. Awake. Driving the doctors crazy asking how soon he can be released even though he's been out of his second surgery less than thirty-six hours."

"That's good, right?"

"It is good. And he's been able to spend time with Helena and his son."

"I'm so glad. He and Helena deserve to be happy. I have such fond memories of growing up in the library. It was a second home to me, long before Helena took over. And she just made it even better."

"I'm sure she'd appreciate hearing that." Amanda took one last sip of coffee and slipped the cup into the dishwasher that had been in the little kitchen long before the house became a clinic. It had somehow survived the fire a few years back, as resilient as Joe was.

Amanda smiled at Shelly. "Now, you've got a patient waiting for stitches, and I've got a consult to get to."

"Yes, Ma'am. But Dr. Pierce?"

"Yes, Shelly?"

"Thank you for hiring me. For you and Dr. Blake hiring me. I know most kids my age wouldn't want to move back to their little hometown to work, but it was all I wanted."

"We're happy to have you. As long as you're working," she said with a smile and a nod toward the door.

"Yes, Ma'am. On it."

Amanda watched her go and smiled. She lifted her hand to knock on the door where her patient waited, but her eyes drifted to the window at the end of the hall. Droplets of rain slid down the panes, and Amanda allowed her thoughts to drift to him again.

All afternoon, she found herself wondering what he was doing. Was he saving another life? Was he doing homework with his niece and nephew? Was he wondering about her?

By the time she dashed through the rain to her car, Amanda was scolding herself for her lack of attention at work that day. She blamed it on their busy schedule— they thought they'd have three sets of hands when they filled all the available appointments for the day. She chucked some of her brain fog up to thoughts about Joe and Helena. But as she tossed the umbrella into her car, she knew she was fooling herself.

She told herself that it was transference, hero worship even. They'd shared some extremely intense and intimate moments. This was a normal reaction. She was projecting, seeing him as someone he wasn't, seeing them as people they weren't. For the three years she'd been at the clinic, he'd shown no interest in her, no interest in anyone. He made it clear that he didn't do commitments, and that was fine. She didn't want a commitment. She didn't even date. She worked all the time, and when she wasn't working, she liked the time to herself. Time to visit the new bookstore—which even Helena was enchanted with—time to catch a quick bite with Andi or a drink with the girls, time to decompress with a good book and a nice glass of wine. She didn't need some green-eyed, handsome, sexy—there, she admitted it, he was sexy—man taking over her life.

She reached for the ignition button on her car but was startled by a knock on the passenger-side window. She motioned, and the door opened, a wet, sexy man entered with a grin, but not the one she'd been thinking about.

"Thought I'd find you here."

"Well, I do work here," she said, wondering what he was doing here, looking for her, sitting in her car.

Dale nodded. "I need a favor."

"Okay." She had no idea where this was going. She and Dale were friends, but what kind of favor could he possibly want from her?

His answer came in one long, rushed sentence. "Joe told me today that Serena's birthday is in a few days, and he wants to get her something, but he's stuck in the hospital and doesn't know for how long, and even though Helena and the baby come home tomorrow, she's not exactly able to go gift shopping."

Amanda felt out of breath listening to him even as

she realized he still hadn't told her what he wanted.

"Okay, and?" Amanda prompted.

"He asked me to get her something. I have no clue what to get. I barely know her. I've spent like five minutes with her."

"Did Joe give you any ideas?"

Dale shook his head. "Nothing. He said she's hard to buy for. Which doesn't make it easier for me."

Amanda laughed. "No, it doesn't. But I'm not sure I would be much help. I don't know her that well either."

"Well, I thought maybe we could go into Harrison, visit a few shops, and toss some ideas back and forth. I'll buy you dinner to thank you. It's the only night I'm able to go."

The last thing Amanda wanted to do was go shopping. She hated shopping. She especially hated shopping when she didn't even know what she was buying. But she was still hyped from all the caffeine, and she had no food in the house.

"Okay, but I'm not a big shopper. Let's brainstorm on the way so we don't waste time once we get there."

"Sounds good," Dale said. "Why don't I drive? I'd hate for you to spend the gas on my errand."

The rain was coming down harder, and Amanda didn't like driving in the rain.

"Fine by me. Let's go."

✳✳✳

"Three hikers, either out of water or having trouble

with a water crossing. Situation unclear due to cell communication. Might be the rain swelled the river again. Might be something else."

"Got it. On my way," Cooper replied, pulling back on the clothes he'd recently discarded for the night. He punched a button on his phone. "Mama, sorry, I need your help."

He found the kids in the living room, homework done, watching a show on Disney+.

"Guys, I've got to go to work. Grandma will be here soon. Your dad is running some kind of errand, but he said he won't be too late. Do you need anything?"

Neither turned away from the television. Suzy shook her head, and Jamie gave him a thumb's up. Cooper rolled his eyes and began pulling on his boots.

Once his team was gathered at the COE, he relayed what he knew.

"Several calls have come in from family members who received text messages. We still aren't sure what the problem is, but we know they weren't planning on staying the night in the park, so they don't have camping gear or food. Still unsure what the messages about water mean. They could be out and unable to collect more, or they could be trapped by water somewhere."

"You think they had water bottles to collect the rain?" Danny asked.

"Depends. If they were prepared, they may have good, wide-mouthed bottles. If not, they could be stuck with plastic bottles from Walmart. Or they could be using water bladders with no way to fill them."

"Do we know where they were headed?" Lance asked.

"We've located their trail check-in, and it looks like they were attempting to hike the loop."

The team groaned. "That's a beast," Lucy said. "It's not long, but with all this rain… And they weren't staying overnight?"

Cooper shook his head. "Not the plan, so we have no idea what kind of shape they're in." He looked at his watch. "Time's wasting. Let's get a move on. Lance, Danny, take the ATVs. Rob, Kevin, take the upper district hiking trails. Lucy, we'll take Scout and go on foot in the lower district."

After an hour of searching, Cooper's radio sounded.

"Coop, nothing so far," Lance relayed. "Talked to some campers who said they haven't seen anyone else."

"Copy. We're still looking. Not much for us or Scout to go on. Keep up the search. If we don't find them by daylight, we go to Plan B."

He could hear the smile in Lance's voice. "Copy. You know how much I love Plan B."

"Boys and their toys," Lucy mumbled. "At least it's helped a couple times."

Cooper looked around at the trees. "Not for much longer. In another month, we won't be able to see anything from the air."

"Maybe sooner if we keep getting rain." Lucy pulled her hood lower onto her forehead as they continued up the trail. "I'm so tired of rain."

"Haven't had anything substantial for a few weeks,

just a shower here and there. We needed it."

"Still tired of it."

Cooper laughed. "I know. Never makes our job easier."

The rain slowed down enough for them to speed up, for their flashlights to be more effective, but Cooper was worried.

"Let's take this trail toward the water. Might be they tried to cross and couldn't. Maybe someone slipped on rocks and is hurt."

"Would explain why they didn't double back."

They trudged through the woods, but Cooper was growing weary. The rain washed away any footprints, and typical signs of hikers—snagged clothing, broken or bent branches, even fresh urine or feces—were harder to spot.

"Nothing," Lucy said when they reached the river. "It's not even swelling."

Cooper shook his head and looked at his messages from the dispatcher. "We've got to keep looking. The few texts they've managed to send in the last hour seem to indicate they're in need of water. So, no more veering off to check possible crossings."

He looked up, cursing the clouds and crescent moon that played peek-a-boo with them. They had no idea how long the group had been without water. They weren't in danger yet, but that would come if they couldn't be found in a day or two.

By dawn, there was still no sign of the campers. Cooper gave the okay for Lance to search by drone. He and Lucy took a break and waited for word.

"So, have you seen or talked to Amanda since the accident?"

Cooper looked at Lucy with a wrinkled brow. "No. Why do you ask?"

"No reason. You two just seem to work well together, like you read each other's thoughts. It's pretty impressive how in-tune with each other you both are."

Cooper straightened a bit and looked off into the distance. "What makes you say that?" he asked as he turned his gaze back on her.

Lucy looked at him with curious eyes. "I've seen you two together twice now. You seem to communicate without words. Like when she asked you to take off your shirt, and you didn't even question why. You knew just what she wanted."

There was a stir in his gut. In different circumstances… He cleared his throat. "Yeah, well, that was just instinct. I mean, what else would she have wanted with it?"

Lucy nodded slowly, never taking her gaze from him. "If you say so, but if you want my opinion—"

"Which I don't," he said hastily.

"I think she's good for you. She's intelligent, friendly, well-liked and respected, and she's beautiful."

Cooper arched his brow.

"Women do recognize when other women are beautiful, you know. It's what makes our claws come out."

He snorted.

"Seriously, you should think about it," she told him.

"Coop? We've got something."

He grabbed his radio and asked what they saw.

"There's a tent set up by the river, close to Jones Cemetery."

"Copy. On our way there."

They made their way to the campsite and let Scout poke around a bit. Before they had a chance to follow her scent, the three campers burst through the trees.

"Oh, my gosh," a young woman cried out in relief. "You found us."

After Lucy checked them all out and gave them plenty to drink, the trio began to tell their story, each talking over one another as the details spilled like water from a bottle.

"The hike was taking a lot longer than we thought it would."

"We ran out of water before we were halfway, and we didn't have any way to get more."

"We were afraid to drink from the river because of contaminants and stuff."

"And then we got lost, and it was getting dark, so we set up camp."

"Which wasn't even planned. We made fun of Tim for even bringing the tent, but we were happy to have it by then because our phones wouldn't work, and they were almost out of juice."

"We were so thirsty, it was hard to go to sleep, but we were also exhausted."

"It was so cold, but in that tiny tent, we had no

choice but to sleep close together, so we managed to keep each other from freezing."

Cooper's head was spinning by the time they finished their story, but he was glad everyone was safe. This wasn't the first time he'd dealt with clueless, unprepared hikers who'd veered off the trail. And it wouldn't be the last.

Twelve

"Dale, thank you so much for this," Serena said after he scooted in her chair and took a seat across from her.

"I figured you could use an evening out. You came here thinking you'd be helping Helena and the baby. You didn't know you'd be nursing Joe, too. And with your parents here, I'm sure you don't have a minute to yourself."

"Oh, I don't mind. I'm just happy they're both finally home. Besides, it's what families do, and..." She looked away, her heart heavy with emotion.

"What?" he asked gently.

She turned her gaze back to him and tried to smile. "I don't know what I'd do if I lost him, too."

"After Jeremy," Dale said quietly.

Serena nodded. "Mama and Daddy took it so hard, and Joe was his twin, and I know he felt like part of him died, too. Sometimes, I felt like I couldn't grieve, that I had to stay strong for all of them."

"That's a lot to put on yourself. Your business was probably just taking off, and there you were, trying to hold your family together."

She took a deep breath and let it out. "Yes, but in some ways, I think that's why the business took off. I was young and just getting started, and I didn't want to fall apart, so whenever I wasn't doing whatever I needed to do for the family, I was throwing myself into work. I think Joe was doing the same thing. He worked the craziest hours at the hospital, not coming home for days on end. And Mama was volunteering more than ever even though she still worked full time." She paused and took a drink of water. "You know, I think we were all just trying to do what we could to get by."

The waitress appeared and took their drink order, asking Dale about his family and if Suzy was ready for the big spelling bee. Their daughters were in the same class, he explained to Serena after making introductions.

Serena listened to their exchange and thought about her own family. She knew her parents would be fine when she told them she was moving—something she knew all too well she had to do before they went back home—but she would miss them.

They took a few minutes to look over the menu and both ended up ordering one of the night's specials. When it was time for dessert, Serena was surprised when all the wait staff at Al Forna made a ring around their table and sang happy birthday. She blushed and thanked them, then turned to Dale after they'd left.

"How did you know my birthday was yesterday?"

Dale shrugged. "Joe told me."

"Of course. He gave me the sweetest gift. In fact, I'm wearing it right now." She lifted the pendant from just below her neck. "It's a knot because I help tie the knot for so many happy couples. Considering what I've been through lately, I'm glad somebody still thinks that."

Dale leaned closer and looked at the pendant. "It's really nice. Joe has good taste."

"You know, I think Helena must have ordered from somewhere. Joe isn't very good at gift buying, and I know he hasn't been anywhere since the accident."

Dale didn't meet her eyes but started fiddling with his silverware as he said, "Yep, you're probably right."

Serena was as intuitive as they came. She had to be in her line of business.

"Dale, do you know something about my birthday present?"

Dale looked up in surprise. "No, of course not. I mean, why would I?"

Serena smiled and reached for her wine. Dale was in the right line of business himself. He was a terrible liar.

***

"Yes, Mama. I know I haven't been home in a while, and I know you and Daddy want me to visit. I just can't leave while Joe's still recovering."

Amanda held in a sigh by taking a long swig of her coffee. She paced the kitchen while listening to her mother tell her how disappointed everyone in the family was that she hadn't made it home for her niece's First Communion.

"I can send the jet to pick you up and a whole team of medical personnel to—"

"Mama, stop right there. I'm staying because Joe needs me, not your medical team, me. I have responsibilities here."

"Yes, I understand, but if you ever want to come home and can't get a flight, you just let me know. We all miss you."

"I know, and you know how much I wanted to be there for Jordan, but Joe has done so much for me, trusting me to become his partner with only a few years' experience, giving me a share in the business, listening to my views and opinions and taking them to heart. Not all females in my profession, or any profession, are that lucky, and right now, he needs me, he and Helena both."

"Well, when will you be home, sweetie? We'd like to see you."

"I know, Mama. I'd like to see you, too," she said truthfully. "I do miss y'all. Buffalo Springs is such a family-oriented town, and everyone has a houseful of siblings and cousins down the road, and it makes me miss y'all even more. I promise, I'll get home soon. Joe's already been home for a week, and he's stronger every day." She went on to gush about baby Jeremy, whom they called JJ, and managed somehow to avoid her mother's favorite question, *Are you seeing anyone?*

When they said their goodbyes, Amanda scrolled

through her phone to her calendar. If Joe continued recovering at this pace, she should be able to see her parents for the long holiday weekend in June. She wouldn't say anything to her mother until she was certain, but she thought that would work.

Amanda had just picked up her gardening gloves when the doorbell rang. It wasn't Andi. She would've just walked in. Amanda checked the time. Not quite nine o'clock. Who would be dropping by so early on a Saturday morning?

She opened the door to find Cooper standing on her front porch.

"Cooper!" she said in surprise. "I didn't expect you."

"I know, and I get that this is last minute, but I'm off today, Dale and Wade are fishing, and Mama took the kids out for the day, so I thought maybe we could finally get that hike in that I promised you. If you still want to."

Amanda remembered Cooper offering to go with her to hike Big Bluff, but she was so busy, and then the accident happened...

"If this is a bad time, I under—"

"No, no it's not a bad time at all. Is it too late to start though? How long will it take us?"

"We'll be fine if you think you can leave right away. It's about a six hour walk for beginners and four hours for people with experience. What do you consider yourself?"

Amanda clicked her tongue in the back of her mouth as she gave it a thought. "Honestly?" She asked, scrunching her nose. "Probably more on the less experienced side."

Cooper laughed. "Yeah, I thought so."

Amanda felt a flash of annoyance. "Oh, yeah? Why is that?"

"Your shoes."

"My shoes?" She looked down at the tennis shoes on her feet, ones she only wore in the yard.

"The shoes you had on the day you found the hiker, Steven Chin. They were running shoes, not hiking shoes. You told me you were a runner but didn't have a lot of hiking experience."

"Oh," she said in surprise. *He remembered that?* "No, I haven't done a lot of hiking, and you were right when you said I shouldn't have been on the trail alone. I guess I was almost one of your victims."

He winced, and Amanda knew she hit a nerve, but he recovered quickly.

"Anyway," Cooper said. "I remembered you saying you didn't have hiking shoes, which is why I brought these." He removed his hand from behind his back and held out a pair of hiking shoes. "Helena said you're the same size, and she won't need these any time soon, so…" He shrugged, and Amanda's heart did a small flip.

"Cooper, that's so thoughtful of you. How can I say no after you've gone to so much trouble?"

"It's no trouble, Amanda. Honestly." He smiled as he gazed into her eyes.

Her breath caught in her chest as they stood there looking at each other. She swallowed, heat building in her middle.

"Well," he said, clearing his throat. "Is that a yes?"

"Oh! Yes, um, let me go change. I'll be quick."

He took in her yoga pants and Ashley McBryde t-shirt, and her face grew hot.

"Why change? You look great. I mean, you're dressed just fine for hiking."

"Are you sure?" She felt dressed down, right for gardening but not at all what she'd choose to spend the day hiking with Cooper.

"Amanda, I think you look perfect," he said as though he could read her thoughts.

She swallowed again, wanting to do this but knowing she was on the verge of opening herself up to something she didn't know if she was ready for.

"It's just a hike, right? I mean, we're not going out to dinner."

She breathed a sigh of relief. He was right. They were going hiking, hardly anything romantic. She had nothing to worry about.

***

"We're walking on an old wagon road," Cooper told Amanda as they made their way down the trail. "It's one of the most popular trails with backcountry hikers, but you can still go for hours without seeing another soul. There are a lot of side trails, and of course, it's not an easy hike."

"It's so beautiful though," Amanda said, stopping to

take in one of the many panoramic views of the Buffalo River below.

"It is." Cooper stopped beside her and resisted the urge to gaze at her the way she was gazing at the view. "We should keep going, though. There are dozens of views like this along the way, and we got a little bit of a late start."

"I thought you said we had plenty of time," Amanda said as they started walking again.

"We should, but I'd like to get to the bluff by early afternoon just to be safe."

When they got to Goat Trail, Cooper took the lead, marveling that Amanda had been able to hike this far on her own without any experience or proper shoes.

"We're almost to where I found Steven, aren't we?" she asked, reading his mind.

"We are. Good thing, too."

"Why?" she asked from behind.

Cooper stopped and turned back, reaching his hand out to help her over a large boulder on the narrow path.

"Because you might not have made it much farther. I'm glad he was where he was and that you heard him. Just wait, you'll see."

She took his hand, and he pulled her up to him. She landed close enough that their bodies were almost touching. Her breathing was shallow, as was his own.

"You okay?"

"Yeah. Just a little out of breath."

Her jaw tensed, and his eyes were drawn to the hollow of her neck. He looked back up and was struck by the gold flecks in her eyes.

"I thought your eyes were brown," he said, hearing the catch in his voice.

"They are," she breathed.

"With gold in them, sun-kissed like the dew."

She shivered, and he realized he was still holding her hand. He couldn't stop looking into her eyes, taking in the way the gold flecks danced as she looked back at him. She blinked slowly, and he leaned toward her.

Amanda jerked, and he grabbed her.

"Sorry," she said hastily. "I lost my footing."

He smiled. "Come on. We've got a ways to go."

He helped her climb down to the other side of the boulder but kept a hold of her hand. He told himself it was safer for her if he was holding onto her, but he suddenly realized he was the one who needed holding onto. Had needed that for a very long time.

***

"I've never seen anything like this," Amanda breathed as she looked out over the bluff.

The river ran far below, and there were mountains as far as she could see. They sat on a ledge jutting out from the rock that formed the bluff, away from the edge, but close enough to see all the way to the bottom. The sun's rays glinted off a mountain peak, and Amanda raised her hand to shield her eyes.

"Worth the hike?"

She turned toward him. "Well worth the hike." She

smiled at him before turning back to the view.

Cooper reached into his backpack and pulled out a bag of trail mix.

"Here, have some. Your muscles need the protein and complex carbs."

Amanda reached into the bag and took out a handful, and Cooper did the same.

"Now I know why people love hiking. It's so beautiful and peaceful. I could stay here for hours."

"Unfortunately, that's not allowed. No camping here, and we need to be heading back in time to be off Goat Trail before dark."

"We certainly don't want to repeat Steven's mistake."

"We don't," he agreed, taking another handful of trail mix for himself. They both washed down the mixture of nuts, raisins, and chocolate chips with water from their water bottles.

"How often do you get up here?" Amanda asked.

"Not often enough, and usually not when I can enjoy the view."

"That must be hard, doing so many rescues in a place where you'd want to be able to stop and enjoy everything around you."

"It's not that hard. I hike a few times a season, and rescuing people gives me a great sense of satisfaction. It's not exactly enjoyment, but in a way, it comes close."

Amanda nodded. "I get that. I don't want any of my patients to be hurt or in pain, but that rush I get when I've helped someone or performed some medical act that may save a life, that's a feeling that can't be beat."

"What would you do if you couldn't be a doctor?"

Amanda looked at him, trying to figure out how to answer. "I'm not sure. It's all I've ever wanted to do. What about you?"

Cooper looked at the rocky ground they sat on and let out a long breath. "I don't know. Like you, it's all I've ever wanted to do, but lately…"

She let him sit with his thoughts for a minute before asking, "Lately, you've been thinking of a change?"

He sighed and sat back against the rock wall behind them. "I don't know. I look at Dale, and Wade and Andi, and now Joe and Helena, and I can't help but wonder, is this the life I want?"

Amanda wasn't sure what to say. She hadn't expected this. She hadn't wanted most of what she was experiencing today. He showed up unexpectedly. He said things to her that made her feel seen for the first time in her life. The way her body reacted when he touched her, took her hand, those moments on that boulder miles beneath them, stirred feelings she'd never felt before. Now, he was talking to her about such intimate thoughts.

"What is the life you want?" she heard herself ask him.

Cooper turned to Amanda, his eyes locking on hers. "I'm not so sure anymore. I don't know if it's worth the risk."

She didn't know if he was talking about the job or something else.

"I don't know either. I guess there's no way to know unless you give it a try."

Her pulse quickened as they sat, looking into each other's eyes, close enough that she could feel his warm breath on her cheek and wondered if it was her heart she felt pounding, or his. He leaned toward her, and she leaned toward him, closing her eyes, dabbing her lips with her tongue.

"Hey, there!"

Amanda and Cooper both jumped.

"Beautiful view, isn't it?"

Two other hikers stood nearby taking in the vista.

"It sure is," Cooper said, his gaze swinging back to Amanda. "Most beautiful view I've ever seen."

Her insides went soft and warm like the center of her mama's famous molten lava cake.

"We're gonna take a rest and have some sandwiches. You two care for anything?" the young woman asked. "I always make extra."

"She makes the best sandwiches," the young man said, tossing his backpack aside and sitting on the red sand and rock ledge. Amanda judged them to be in their early- to mid-twenties.

Cooper looked at Amanda and smiled, taking her hand and pulling her from the ledge.

"We're going to start heading back. You two might want to eat quickly and head down yourselves. The walk back is just as treacherous as the walk up, and I don't want to have to come back up here to rescue you later."

"Huh?" the guy asked.

"SAR. If you're up here too long and don't make it out by dark, chances are, I'll be called to come get you. Just be careful, and get back while it's still light."

"Uh, okay. Sure. Thanks."

Amanda suppressed a giggle as they made their way down from the rocky top and back onto the trail.

"You scared that poor kid to death."

"He deserved it," she heard Cooper mutter under his breath, and she couldn't help but silently agree.

***

There were no calls that night about any lost or stranded hikers, but a call came in not long after Cooper fell asleep.

"We've got a dog who fell down an embankment. The owner estimates she's about seventy-five feet down."

Cooper looked at Scout and couldn't imagine the fear of the dog or the owner. He immediately began pulling together some of his team—he let the others sleep in for once—and told Scout she had to stay behind. He didn't need two stranded dogs to deal with in the dark wilderness.

When Cooper and the others arrived, two park rangers stood beside the dog's owner, shining lights down into the embankment. He shook hands with the rangers and introduced himself and his team to Manuel who explained what happened.

"He's such a good dog. There wasn't anyone else

around, so I thought it would be okay if I took him off leash, just for a few minutes." He shook his head. "I think he saw something move in the trees, a squirrel or rabbit, I don't know. He just took off over that rock wall and ran to the ledge. The next thing I knew, he was gone." He wiped his eyes with the back of his hand and looked down at his feet.

"We tried to find a way to get to him, but it's too steep and slippery. We figured we should call you," one of the rangers told Cooper.

"You did the right thing. One bad move, and we might be rescuing you, too." He gave orders, and they went into action.

"You ready?" he asked Lance once they were both harnessed and secured.

"Ready, Coop."

"Let's go," Cooper said, pushing off and over the side.

They rappelled to the ground below, a small parcel of land between the walls of two mountains that completely enclosed the area. They approached the German Shepherd tentatively. The dog's whole body shook, and his eyes were dilated with fear.

"It's okay, Benito. Good boy, good boy," Manuel yelled from above.

"I'd feel better if he wasn't snarling at us," Lance said.

"He's scared. Stand back, and let me try." Cooper moved slowly toward the dog, talking in a low, gentle voice. "Come here, Benito. Want to smell me? I've got a dog, too. A beautiful girl, she is. You'd like her." He took one of Scout's treats from his pocket. He'd grabbed them just in case they needed to convince the dog they were friends.

Benito sniffed the treat then sniffed Cooper's hand. He eyed both men before gingerly taking the treat and swallowing it after two quick chews. He looked at Cooper's hand before moving his gaze to his face. Cooper chuckled.

"Want another one? Here you go, boy." He handed the dog another treat then took a step back.

After two more doggie treats were happily consumed, Benito was close enough to the men to let them check him over for injuries.

"He's limping on his back, left leg," he called up to Manual, "but otherwise he seems okay."

Benito let them slip the dog lift harness under his belly, and Cooper continued to praise him as they secured the harness and clipped it to a cable. After another treat, they signaled Danny to take him up. Once Benito was safe at the top and reunited with Manuel, Lance and Cooper ascended.

"...for failure to keep your dog on a leash and for bringing a pet onto a restricted trail," one of the rangers was saying to Manuel as he tore off a citation from his ledger.

Manual accepted his penance and thanked everyone for their help.

"I'll take a call like that any day," Danny said as they headed to the parking lot.

"Quick, easy, and no collateral damage," Lance agreed. "That guy's going to have some pretty hefty fines to pay."

"Yeah, but where would we be if people followed the rules?" Danny asked, laughing at the irony.

"I don't think we'll ever have to worry about finding out," Cooper assured him. "Nobody ever thinks the signs, warnings, rules are made for them."

They all agreed on that and knew that the next time, they might not have it so easy.

***

"You look tired," Amanda commented when she met Cooper after church the next morning. It was a beautiful day with bright sunshine and clear skies.

"Is that a professional opinion?" he asked with a grin as they strolled down the sidewalk.

Amanda smiled. "Yes, Mr. Mackenzie, that is an official medical observation. Late call?"

"Yeah, but not too late. A hiker decided it was a good idea to take his dog on a trail where pets aren't allowed and then decided it was an even better idea to take him off his leash."

"Oh, no. What happened?"

"The dog chased something into the woods, jumped a retaining wall, and went over a cliff into an embankment about seventy-five feet below."

"Was the dog hurt?"

Cooper lifted his shoulders. "Looks like he hurt his

leg or hip, but mostly he was just scared and trapped between rock walls."

"Why were they there at night?"

"They took an afternoon hike and were on their way out of the park when he took off. By the time he found a ranger, it was after dark. They had to locate the place where he went over, not easy by then with the lack of light and the guy not sure exactly where they were. Then the rangers had to assess the situation. I got the call around midnight."

"Could've been worse," Amanda remarked.

"The time or the rescue?"

"Both?" She said as a question, looking at him and returning his earlier shrug.

Cooper laughed. "Can't argue with you. It wasn't quite the middle of the night, and it turned out to be an easy rescue."

"Where's Scout this morning?" Amanda asked when they stopped at the corner of her street.

"I left her home. I'm technically not working today, though I never know when I'll get a call. I just thought she might like to stay home for once instead of trying to find the best way to stay out of the way in church."

She smiled. "Want to come in for a cup of coffee?" She held her breath, not sure if he would accept, less sure if she wanted him to. He was on her mind more and more these days, and after their hike—she was positive he wanted to kiss her up there on Big Bluff—she wasn't sure where they stood.

She could see his hesitation, felt his uncertainty as

much as her own.

"It's okay if you can't. It was spur of the moment."

"I'd love to," he said quickly, his voice huskier than usual. Amanda's stomach did a pirouette.

"Great. I have one of Andi's cherry pies if you're interested," she said, beginning to walk toward her house.

"I'm always interested in anything Andi bakes." He followed her up the walkway and waited for her to open the door and go inside.

Amanda tried to assess the house through his eyes. It was an older house, but not one of the oldest houses in town. Built in the mid-1950s, it had the typical front entrance that opened into a dining area where it boasted a slate-backed fireplace-turned-wood stove. A decent-sized—though not Joe-sized—kitchen, which had been updated in the seventies, was off to the side in the back of the house. Amanda had definitively decided it needed an update.

She was pretty sure the house was once cut into smaller rooms and had an actual dining room, but before she bought the house, it had been converted to an open-space design. She loved her original hardwood floors and the way they shined in the sun, and she'd bought the oak farmhouse tables and six chairs at a junk store in Harrison. Adjacent to the dining area was the family room space with a wall of glass doors opening to the small but well-tended back yard.

Cooper walked around the space while Amanda snapped a pod into the coffee machine. She retrieved the pie and watched him look out into the back yard. He turned and took in the family room with its modest grey couch and loveseat. He inspected the row of family photos on a side table behind the couch.

"Are these all your brothers?" he asked, turning to her with eyes wide and mouth slightly open.

Amanda laughed. "All five of them." She popped in the second pod and went to stand next to him.

"You're the only girl?"

"Yep, and the youngest. That one in the red." She pointed to the photo. "That's Peter. We're the closest in age and closest in general. He's the only one not married with kids."

"Do they all live in Nashville?"

She started walking back toward the kitchen. "Three of them do, Derrick, Mason, and Peter. Luke is stationed in Germany, and Paul lives in Alabama. He went to college there, met a girl, and decided to stay. He's the oldest. He and Missy have four kids, all boys so far. Mason has one of each, and Derrick has a girl." She laid two slices of pie on the counter. "How do you like your coffee?"

"Black," he said, joining her in the kitchen.

Amanda added a drop of milk with no sugar to hers before picking up the mug and a slice of pie. "Let's go out on the patio. It's such a nice day. I don't want to waste it by staying inside."

Cooper picked up his coffee and pie and followed her. When she tried to juggle her plate and her coffee to open the door, he dropped his pie on the table and said,

"Let me." He waited for her to go out before he picked up his pie and placed it on top of his mug so he could close the door.

They took seats on the wicker chairs she bought at the same junk shop as the table and chairs inside.

"This is nice," Cooper said. "I like your yard."

"It's a work in progress. The last owners did a nice job with the gardens, but they did almost all annuals, and I just don't have time for that. I'm slowly planting perennials and hoping to have beautiful flowers before I'm too old to enjoy them."

"You should get some seeds from my mom and Andi's mom."

"I should. They have the best gardens in town, besides Dale's. Andi said her mom is rooting some cuttings for me."

They sat in silence, enjoying their pie and sipping their coffee. They watched a territorial fight ensue between a Ruby-throated hummingbird and a feisty Anna's hummingbird. Rather than feeling awkward, Amanda was quite comfortable sitting on the patio, watching the birds, and not saying a word. She found that she enjoyed spending time with Cooper no matter what they were doing. Well, maybe not when she was covered with dirt or fainting or being carried out of a fire. Scratch that. She kind of liked the carrying part.

"What's the smile about?" Cooper asked, and Amanda felt the heat spread through her cheeks.

"Nothing, just thinking."

"About what?" he asked, leaning in closer to her

chair, his empty plate dangling from his hand.

"Nothing, really. Just that this is nice. I mean, not being in some kind of dangerous situation or—"

"Or standing in the rain?" he offered.

"Yeah, or that," she said. "Though I don't mind the rain."

"Neither do I," he said, sitting back in the chair and crossing one knee over his leg. "I don't like the problems it causes, but I like the sound it makes on the roof at night."

Amanda nodded her head vigorously. "Same. I love lying in bed at night, listening to the sound of the raindrops, falling asleep to its cadence, like the steady rhythm of nature's lullaby."

"I like how you put that," Cooper told her. "I'm going to remember that the next time I'm falling asleep during a rainstorm."

"I love storms, too. There's nothing like watching a bolt of lightning rip open the sky to feel how little power we have on this earth where we're always trying to be in control."

"My mama always says life goes much more smoothly when we surrender control and let God's will be done."

Amanda took a deep breath and let it out, feeling utterly content. "I think I'd like your mama."

He nodded. "You would. And she'd like you."

"She's never been to the clinic. How come?"

He shrugged. "I guess she doesn't think she needs to be seen."

"She should come in. Everyone should have an annual checkup."

"I'll tell her."

Amanda sat still, holding his gaze. She didn't think anyone had ever looked at her the way he does, and while her cheeks warmed, a tingle down her spine elicited an involuntary shiver.

"Are you cold?" he asked, his voice taking on that husky tone again.

"Not at all," she said, unable to break the lock of his gaze, this moment between them. Her heartbeat and breath quickened and before a shot of disappointment hit her when he looked away and stood.

"I'd better get going. I need to check on Scout and see if Dale needs help around the house."

Amanda stood, but her legs felt shaky, and her stomach dropped with regret. She didn't want him to leave, but she didn't have the courage to ask him to stay. And what would she say? *I'm so lonely, please don't go.* Or *I think about you all the time and really want to spend more time with you, all my time with you.* That was just pathetic.

Cooper opened the back door, and Amanda followed him into the house, making a concerted effort not to let her disappointment show. He placed the cup and plate in the sink then stood aside while she did the same. When Amanda turned toward him, a strange look crossed his face. What was it? Regret? Sadness? Uncertainty? She couldn't tell and didn't know what he was thinking.

"Thank you," he said, "for the coffee and pie. And

for…just being you."

Amanda's mouth opened slightly. She was at a loss for words, for real words, so she just said, "Thank you."

They were close enough for her to see his chest go in and out, his Adam's apple bob as he swallowed, his eyes fill with clouds. He took a step back.

"I'll see you later, Amanda."

"Yeah, see you later, Cooper," she said as he walked past her and disappeared out the front door.

She leaned back against the counter, her breath coming in waves.

What just happened? What is he thinking and feeling? What am I thinking and feeling?

She didn't know the answers to two of the three questions, but she was pretty sure she knew the answer to the third, and it scared her to death.

***

For three days, Cooper thought about little else other than his day hiking with Amanda and their shared coffee after church. No matter what he did, he couldn't get her off his mind. And it had to stop.

"What's got into you?" Dale asked him on a particularly grumpy evening.

"Nothin's got into me. What's *your* problem?"

Dale shook his head as he took the plate out of his brother's hands. "If you dry that plate any more or any harder, you're going to wear a hole right through it."

Cooper looked at the dish towel in his hand and the

empty rack on the sink. He had no idea how long ago he'd reached for the last plate or how long he'd been 'drying' it. He tossed the towel onto the counter and walked to the back door, looking out at the twilight sky.

"Talk to me," Dale said in that quiet voice of his that let Cooper know he was concerned.

"I've got nothing to say."

"Well, that's apparent. You've said nothing for days. Are you getting itchy because you haven't had a call since Saturday night?"

Cooper shook his head. "No. Just means something big is coming our way."

"I know that's not what's bothering you because you live for that. So, what is it?"

Cooper turned to his brother. "Living for that. You're right. I do live for that. I live for the thrill of the hunt, the adrenaline of the rescue, the curveballs we're thrown and the messes we clean up. I live for all of it."

Dale's forehead pinched, and his eyes narrowed. "Okay. So what? You feel bad for looking forward to other people's life-threatening shenanigans?"

"No, I don't feel bad. Not at all. I feel like I don't know who I'd be without them."

"Maybe we should sit down for this," Dale said, opening the refrigerator. "And have a drink." He poked his head into the living room. "You two okay if Uncle Coop and I sit outside for a while?"

Both brothers knew that no answer was an affirmative answer. Dale held out a beer to Cooper and opened the door to the back deck.

Once they were seated, he asked, "Come clean. Exactly what is bothering you?"

Cooper let out a long breath, took a long drink, and gazed at the rising moon for a long minute.

"Remember how it was before Daddy retired?"

"Remember how what was?"

"Life. Our family. Daddy spent most of his evenings and weekends at the station with the guys waiting for a call, and when he was home, he was always on alert, ready to jump in his truck and head to the station at a moment's notice. He and Mama were always fighting. She wanted him to be around more, and he could never get her to understand that fighting fires was more than a hobby. He hated his job at the post office and resented having to work there to make money."

"I don't understand what this has to do with now. Daddy hasn't worked a fire for years."

"Only because he started having back problems. I guarantee you, if he could, he'd still be doing it."

"Okay, you're probably right. So what?"

"It's not just something you grow out of, that you stop doing because you get married and have a family and suddenly have a change of heart."

"Maybe," Dale said. "Maybe some people do have a change of heart. Maybe some people feel that same adrenaline, get that same rush at little league games and when watching their kid ride a bike for the first time or kissing their daughter goodnight, knowing he's there to protect her from bumps in the night."

"Maybe some people do," Cooper admitted,

knowing he wasn't one of them. "But I need to stay focused. No distractions."

"Look, Coop. There comes a time in every man's life when he needs to decide what he's going to do with his life. I'm not talking about after high school or in college. I'm talking about when he meets the right woman and starts thinking about being with her and giving her all she deserves, including a good husband. Is that what we're talking about here?"

Cooper didn't know how to answer. If he said yes, he'd have to answer a million questions about who and how and when. If he said no, he'd get no answers for his own questions.

"I saw you walk Amanda home on Sunday. I also know you took her hiking the day before."

Cooper looked at him and shrugged. "Yeah?"

"We live in a town of a thousand people, Coop. Word gets around."

His face grew hot, and his body went rigid. "What's that mean? What are people saying?"

"Relax. People are saying you've been seen together outside the clinic or a rescue. And people like what they see. A lot."

He let himself exhale and loosened his fists. "It's not like that," he said.

"Your reaction just now says otherwise," Dale said, not looking at Cooper. He took a long drink and waited for Cooper to respond.

"It's not. But what if I want it to be?" Cooper asked quietly.

A slow grin spread across Dale's face. "What if?"

"I don't want to give up my job."

"Has she asked you to?"

"We're not there yet. We're not anywhere." He stood and walked to the edge of the deck. He braced his hands on the railing and stood for a few moments before turning to look at Dale. "I think I'm falling for her. Really falling. It's not even like it was with Jessie. It's…"

"Like you think about her all the time, hope you'll run into her every time you walk out the door, want to spend every second with her, and when you're actually with her, it's still not enough?"

Cooper chuckled. "Yeah, something like that. And I don't know if this has been gradually heading this way, or if it just hit me between the eyes, but suddenly, I want to touch her every time we're together but don't want to get too close because I don't want to touch her and feel the things I know I'm going to feel." He went back and sat down, looking intently at his brother. "I'm afraid if I go down that road, I won't be able to turn back, and it changes everything."

"What does it change?" Dale asked.

"It'll change the way I do my job, for one. I can't take the kind of risks I take if I've got someone waiting for me at home. And don't go thinking this is about what happened to Jessie. She put herself at risk, and I was the one left behind, but I knew the costs, and it nearly killed me. Amanda doesn't know, she could never understand what it's like to do what I do and want to keep going back again and again."

"But doesn't she?" Dale asked quietly. "First, she's a doctor at the only clinic within sixty miles. She's on call almost as much as you are. And she's experienced what you do, more than once."

"And it scared the daylights out of her. What would she go through every time I walk out the door to go do what she's seen firsthand could make me end up like Jessie? And what about the fighting, the arguments about my late-night calls and the times I'm away for days searching for someone whose gone off the trail? All that leads to distractions for me and heartache for her."

"Coop, Daddy was eighteen when he and Mama got married. Eighteen. You're thirty-two. You have so much more wisdom and experience than he had. Plus, you're already thinking about all this before you've even walked down the aisle. You're not Daddy, and Amanda isn't Mama. She doesn't expect you to give up your job, and you don't expect her to sit home all night, waiting for you with dinner on the table. As far as distractions, a wife, a family, someone to come home to, they're not distractions, not in a bad way. They're the kind of distractions, for lack of a better word, that make you better at your job. You want to help people, so their families don't go through what you went through, and you want to go home to people who love you and support you. Those aren't distractions. They're reasons to be good at what you do and reasons to come home every night and appreciate what you've got."

Cooper thought about that. He'd never considered the fact that he was older than his father was way back then. And as much as he loved his mama, she and Amanda weren't the same at all. And he was beginning to like the idea of having someone to come home to. Maybe Dale was right.

"One more thing, Coop."

He looked up at Dale. "Yeah?"

"Maybe you should take a woman out on a real date at least once before you start planning all the arguments you're going to have after you're married."

Cooper grinned and then started laughing. "You know, big brother, sometimes you aren't as dumb as you look."

Thirteen

It was early morning on Friday as Serena watched out the window and Helena fed the baby. Joe was almost feeling well enough to go back to work, but Serena still felt responsible for making sure everyone was fed and the house was clean. Ever since their parents left on Monday, she felt like she was going stir crazy inside the house. On the other hand, she was becoming more fearful of showing her face, even in Buffalo Springs.

Right on cue, her phone buzzed, and she told herself not to look, while at the same time, she opened the message.

You can't hide forever. I know where you are. Soon the world will know what kind of person you really are.

She deleted the message and blocked the caller. At first, the messages were simply annoying. Every tabloid reporter from here to the Pacific wanted a quote, a soundbite, or an interview. She turned them all down. Slowly, they turned to other news stories and began leaving her alone. Except for one. She assumed it was one. Every time she blocked the number, she thought that was the end of it, but within a couple days, she received another text from a different number with a similar message. She thought these were related to the wedding on fire story that all the others wanted to talk about, but now she wasn't so sure. These seemed more menacing even though the threats, if you could call them that, weren't really threatening anything or anyone other than her reputation, which she knew was stellar despite the recent headlines.

"Anything interesting happening out in the world?" Helena asked.

Serena almost dropped her phone. "Nope, just looking out at this beautiful day." She turned and smiled at her sister-in-law. "Do we need anything at the store?" Though she didn't want to leave the house, she needed to get out.

"Joe needs coffee, and I could probably use diapers."

"Great," Serena said without hesitation. "I'll be back in a bit." She was out the door before Helena could question her.

As she walked down the street, Serena inhaled the scents of spring—lilacs bursting into bloom, apple blossoms floating in the breeze, and the rich, musty smell of rotting leaves and tilled soil. These smells were far different from those she was used to in downtown Houston where car exhaust and cheap take-out assaulted you when you tried to take a walk.

She took her time walking to the Shop-A-Lot and

took even more time perusing the aisles, checking out things she knew they didn't need.

"Hi, Serena."

She turned toward the friendly voice and smiled. "Amanda, it's so good to see you." They hugged before Serena put the box of brownie mix back on the shelf.

"Doing some baking?" Amanda asked.

"Not really. Just needed to get out of the house for a few minutes."

Amanda asked about the patients, and Serena filled her in.

"Joe's planning on coming back to work?"

"That's what he says," Serena told her, surprised Joe hadn't talked to his partner about returning, but knowing doctors don't always do what they should. "He's doing remarkably well. He knows he has a few more weeks until he's able to return to all things normal, but I think he just wants to be at the office, feeling like he's pulling his weight."

"I'm not gonna lie," Amanda said. "Even if he's just giving shots, it helps."

"I'm sure. Now, how about you? Dale tells me you and Cooper went hiking on Saturday." She winked at Amanda "Cooper's a real sweetheart. I wouldn't let him get away if I were you."

Amanda's smile faltered. "Oh, Serena, there's nothing going on between Cooper and me. We're colleagues. That's all."

Serena gave Amanda a hard stare, pursed her lips, and exhaled through her nose. "Well, that's a darn shame. From what I can see, you two are perfect for each other. Dale thinks so, too."

"And what about you and Dale? When are you having all these private conversations about Cooper and me?"

Serena felt herself blush and turned back to the baking supplies. "He's at the house all the time visiting Joe. Sometimes, when Joe's resting, he and I talk about the goings on in the town."

"And that's all?" Amanda pressed, and Serena wished she'd kept her mouth shut about Cooper and Dale both.

"That's all, Sugar. Now, I'd better get those diapers Helena asked for and get back to the house. I'm sure I'll see you around real soon."

She hurried away before Amanda could ask any more questions. Serena thought Dale was the bee's knees, but there was no way she'd ever fit into his world or compete with the ghost of his dead wife. She was the perfect girl-next-door, wife, and mother, and Serena could never fit into her shoes. Not to mention the age difference. She was sure Dale saw her as nothing more than Joe's little sister.

***

"Hey, Sissie, how're you doing?"

"Peter, I'm great. How about you? You don't normally use your phone to make actual voice calls. Are your fingers broken?" She waited for him to laugh, but he didn't.

"Yeah, well, I need to talk to you."

Amanda sat down behind her desk. Something about his voice, his tone, was off. "What's wrong? Are you okay? Are you sick? Do you need medical advice?"

"Sissie, listen. You need to come home."

Her heart picked up speed, and she gripped the phone tighter. "Peter, you're scaring me. What's going on?"

"We didn't want to tell you over the phone. We were hoping you'd come home, but you didn't."

She heard the edge in his voice and tried to swallow, but her mouth had gone dry. "Peter, what's wrong? Whose 'we'?"

She heard him take a deep breath before he spoke again, and it seemed like her blood pressure rose with each passing minute.

"It's Dad. The cancer's back. And it's worse this time. He needs you. Not as a doctor but as a daughter."

A vice tightened around Amanda's neck, rendering her speechless. She took several short, gasping breaths as hot tears flooded her eyes. "How long?" she managed to ask with a raspy voice.

"Not long. Please, come. Don't wait. He doesn't have much time."

She tried swallowing, but the choking sensation wouldn't ease. She couldn't breathe. Her vision blurred. She was dizzy. "Yes," she whispered what was barely a breath before disconnecting the call.

Time seemed to stand still as she closed her eyes and

sat there, trying to force her breath, to stop her out of control heart. She fumbled to pick up her phone, to activate the screen and find the number.

"Joe, Joe, I need…" The tears came, hard and fast. She could hear him asking if she was okay, if she needed help. "I…need…to go home. To Nashville."

She didn't wait for an answer. She ended the call and laid her head on her desk and cried.

***

"What do you mean, she's gone?" Cooper stood in Dale's office, his mouth hanging open, his heart thumping against his chest wall.

Dale shrugged. "That's all I know. She told Joe she had to go home to Nashville. I guess we'll know more when she gets there."

Had he done or said something wrong? Or was it what he hadn't done? He'd felt that pull between them, felt his own lips tingling, longing for hers, that day on the bluff. He'd felt the static between them in her kitchen. He wanted to kiss her, to reach out and hold her, but it seemed impossible. It felt like too much to ask, too much to think that she could feel the same or accept him for who he was, for what he did, too much to risk everything to tell her how he felt about her. And now, she was gone.

Cooper began to pace. "I should've told her. I should've let her know how I…" He stopped and looked at Dale. "Joe doesn't have any idea why she left?"

Dale slowly shook his head from side to side. "Not that he's sharing."

Cooper turned and reached for the door. "I've got to go."

Dale leaped from his seat. "You aren't going to Nashville, are you?"

"No, but I know where I might get some answers."

He walked briskly and purposefully, focused on his destination, on getting answers. The bell over the door was almost jarring when he opened it. Andi took one look at him, wiped her hands on her apron, and said to Naomi, "I need a few minutes," before motioning for him to follow her to the back of the bakery.

Cooper nodded at Naomi, with whom he'd graduated from high school, and joined Andi in her office behind the kitchen. She gestured for him to sit and closed the door. She walked to her seat behind her desk and sat down.

"You heard."

"I heard about Amanda leaving town, if that's what you mean."

"She left a message for you, in case you asked. She didn't think you would, but she left one anyway."

He didn't know if it made him feel better or worse that she wanted to tell him something. He prepared himself for a punch to the gut.

"Her father has cancer and doesn't have much time left. She didn't know. They wanted to tell her when she was home for her niece's First Communion a couple weeks ago, but there was the accident, and she didn't go.

Her brother called her yesterday."

"Peter?"

Andi looked surprised, either that he knew the name or that it would've been Peter who called her, or both.

"Yeah, they're close."

"The closest."

Again, Andi looked surprised.

"That's all I know, Coop. I wish I knew more."

"Is she coming back?" Part of him didn't want to know the answer.

"Eventually. She said her life is here, but she needs to be with her family now."

He understood that. It's why he'd given up his place to move in with Dale. When your family called, you went. And you stayed as long as you were needed.

"Is she okay? I mean, as okay as…"

Andi gave him an understanding smile. "I'm not sure. She sounded kind of lost."

"Okay, thanks." He stood to go.

"Cooper?"

He looked back at Andi.

"She's vulnerable right now. She sounded more than lost. She sounded broken. I don't know her parents, but I do know she's daddy's girl. She doesn't need a SAR responder swooping in to save the day. Nobody can do that for her. Her father, her life as she knows it, can't be saved by someone else. What she needs is someone to let her know he's there for her, but don't make any promises you can't keep."

Andi was someone who understood the adrenaline

rush like he did, someone who was part of a team that plowed in, took risks, took control, and saved lives. She knew what he was feeling and what his instincts were. She'd also been on the other side of that pain. He'd heard Joe and Wade talking about Andi and Joe's brother, Jeremy, about how they were just falling in love when Andi listened to his last words as his SEAL chopper fell from the sky. She knew all about saving and being saved.

Cooper nodded. "Thanks, Andi. I appreciate everything you've said and passed along."

He left the bakery and walked down the street just as a light rain began to fall. It broke his heart to know she wasn't there for him to run into.

***

Amanda tucked her empty suitcase into the closet of her childhood bedroom. All her clothes were back in the drawers just like they had been all her life. Only the dresser wasn't the same because she took her furniture with her when she first moved out of the house. The room didn't look the same either. She'd always rolled her eyes when a woman in a Hallmark movie returned home from a full life in the big city, and her bedroom remained untouched. Amanda's mother waited less than a year before she turned Amanda's room into a guest room. There were three guest rooms now, enough for the ever-flowing tide of grandchildren swelling the house back to what it had been all those years ago. In addition, her mother had an office in the house as did her father, and there were several other offices in the east wing.

She wandered down the hall and looked at all the memories suspended on the wall. Wasn't that photo just taken last year? The eight of them on Easter when Amanda was still in elementary school. She smiled at the one with almost double the amount of people, taken on Christmas over ten years ago, her senior year of high school. Derrick had just gotten engaged, and Paul and Missy were waiting for baby number two to arrive. Was it really that long ago?

Her trip down memory lane was interrupted by the buzzing in her pocket. She reached for her phone and felt her heart flutter.

I heard about your dad. I'm so sorry. Let me know if you need anything. Anything at all. I'm only a plane ride away.

Amanda felt her throat constrict. That had been happening a lot over the past few days. Anxiety, she knew, but that didn't make it any less uncomfortable or disconcerting. His words were kind, but there was nothing he could do. There wasn't anything any of them could do. With her fancy degree, mounds of loans, and letters after her name, even she had no answers or ways to make things better.

Thank you.

Her finger hovered over the keyboard. Should she say more? What more could she possibly say to a man she barely knew but who made her feel like no other man had ever made her feel? She hit send and pocketed her phone. She had other things to worry about right now.

"Hey, Sissie. You okay?" Peter was watching her from the doorway. She didn't know how long he'd been there, caught up in her own world as she was. She tried to smile.

"As okay as I can be." She lifted her shoulders, feeling the helplessness she knew they all felt.

He entered the room and sat on her bed, pulling her down next to him. "How are things in Arkansas? Still like it?"

"If that's your way of asking if I'm staying home, the answer is no. I do like it. I love the people, the town, the area." She sighed. "It's become home to me. Not that I don't miss you," she rushed to add. "I do. I miss all of you, but…"

"You have your life as your own person and not the baby of the Morgan-Pierce family."

She smiled. "Yeah, that pretty much sums it up."

"Am I allowed to ask if there's someone special?"

Cooper's face floated before her, but she waved it away with her hands. "Not really. Not technically."

She found herself smiling despite her intentions not to mention Cooper. Dating was never easy for the younger sister of five boys. Each brother had to do his part in finding out everything he could about the guy in question and then scare him to death if he so much as thought any impurity about their baby sister.

Peter nudged her. "Come on. It's me you're talking to. I see right through you."

She shook her head. "Honestly, there's nobody.

There's a guy I'm talking to, but…"

"But?" He dragged out the word, waiting for her to fill in the sentence.

"I don't know. He's a search and rescue responder, and I've helped him with some of the people they've rescued. I even went with him on a rescue and delivered a baby in the middle of the forest during a fire." She was exhilarated just talking about it, the fear and panic of the night absent from her memory.

"That sounds dangerous." He frowned. "Not exactly the kind of date he should be—"

"Don't be ridiculous. These weren't dates of any kind. We've never gone on a date at all. We went hiking one day. That's it." She regretted telling her brother. As far as she knew, there really wasn't anything between them but her overactive imagination.

"But you like him," Peter said, dismissing her thoughts as if she'd said them out loud.

Amanda sighed. "I think I do. I mean, I know I do, but I don't know if it would work. He doesn't do commitments, and neither do I."

"He told you that? Came right out and said, 'I don't do commitments'?"

Amanda punched her brother in the arm. "No, silly. He has a reputation. Something happened in the past." She stopped. "You know, I never did find out what it was. But something happened, and ever since, he's dated, but nothing serious." She shrugged. "And we're both working all the time. No time for relationships."

"Sounds like you're both making excuses."

"Since when did you become the love guru, psychoanalyst of the family?"

"Since meeting Tricia," he said with a smile.

"Wait, are you—"

"Soon. I was going to ask a few weeks ago, but then, well, you know."

"It's hard to make plans for future happiness with Daddy being sick?"

"Yeah." He looked down.

"You know, I think it would make Daddy happy to know that you're happy and settling down."

"Maybe." He lifted one shoulder. "But I could say the same about you."

She mimicked his gesture. "Maybe. We'll see."

"Hey, you two," Mason said from the doorway. "Mama says dinner's ready."

Peter stood and reached out to take her hand. He pulled her from the bed and wrapped her in a hug.

"For what it's worth," he said as he held her, "life's too short to invest all your time and energy into a job. Being happy and sharing that happiness with someone else should never be too hard to fit into your life."

Amanda pulled back and smiled at her brother, her lifelong best friend. She'd think about what he said, but whatever happened or didn't happen with Cooper wasn't only up to her.

***

Cooper stared at the text until his vision blurred. He

put his phone on the counter and turned just as his mother walked into the house with a large, covered basket on her arm. He could smell the lasagna and garlic bread, the meal she always made when it was prepared specially for him. Even that didn't help his mood.

"Hi, Mama," he said, hearing the sadness in his own voice.

"Cooper, baby, what's wrong?"

"Just some bad news, that's all. About a friend. What brings you by?"

"Can we talk?"

Cooper stiffened. What was this about? His mother never sought him out for a conversation.

"Me? Or everyone? Dale and the kids are at the movies."

"Just you," she said, walking past him to place the basket on the kitchen table. She gave Scout some loving before she opened a cabinet and retrieved two glasses, took them to the fridge, and filled them with iced tea. He followed her lead and set the table for two, then sat down. She took a seat across from him, and they bowed their head to pray.

"I talked to Dale earlier," she said once she had served them each a slice of lasagna and large piece of bread.

His body went on high alert. He might as well have just gotten a call from the sheriff.

"What's wrong? Are you okay? Is Daddy?"

"Yes, yes, we're fine. It's you I'm worried about."

The fork stopped in front of his mouth. "Me? Why?"

"Dale tells me Dr. Pierce's father is sick and that she's gone home to Nashville."

"Yes, but I don't know why that would make you worry about me."

She gave him the look, the one he'd seen a million times—when he broke the cookie jar and tried to tell her a ghost had knocked it down, when he blamed a scratch on their car on Dale who hadn't even driven the car since he bought his own piece of junk, when he told her his heart wasn't broken over Lauren Davis breaking up with him—the look that always made him back up and recant whatever story he'd just told her.

"Mama, I don't know what Dale has told you, but Amanda and I work together. Kind of. I mean, she's helped me out a few times when—"

"Stop right there." She held her hand up. "Don't even think about trying that with me. I saw the look in your eye as soon as I mentioned her name." She wiped her mouth with her napkin and placed it back in her lap before looking him in the eye. "I don't know Dr. Pierce very well, but I know you. From what I hear, that woman has a lot going on right now. She's about to experience the biggest heartbreak of her life, and she doesn't need someone being wishy-washy about his feelings for her. She's going to need support and compassion, and she can get all that from Andi and their other friends, so don't offer it if you can't commit to being there when she needs you. If this is another one of those times you're going out with someone to make the world think you're okay when inside, you're not still beating yourself up over something you couldn't control, then back off. Let her friends help her heal. She doesn't need her heart broken twice."

She reached for her tea and took a long drink, letting everything she'd said settle into his brain.

"On the other hand," she started again. "If you're ready to make a commitment, if she's the one who is somehow breaking down that wall you've erected around your heart, then don't let her think there's nothing for her here because that will keep her right there in Nashville where someone else will swoop in and help her glue back together the fragments of her heart. Do you understand what I'm telling you?"

A slow, easy smile dragged across Cooper's face. "Mama, sometimes you talk around your point like it's a riddle that needs to be solved, but yes, I understand."

"Good. Then you've got some thinking to do." She started eating again but paused between bites. "But don't go rushing up there to declare your love and stand by her side. She needs her family right now, not some big romantic gesture."

"Mama, in case you haven't noticed, big romantic gestures aren't exactly my thing."

"Cooper, no romantic gesture is your thing, big or small. You've got a heart with such a great capacity for love, but you've let it sit dormant for five years. Talk around town is that it's finally starting to come alive again, to put out some shoots. Maybe by the time the good doctor comes back, it will be ready to blossom."

Cooper almost laughed out loud but managed to

chuckle. "You know what? Even the Lord Almighty could learn a thing or two about parables from you."

He took a bite of lasagna. "Mama, can I ask you a question?"

"Of course. You can always ask me anything. You know that."

He put his fork down and looked at his mother, whom he loved more than anyone on earth.

"Mama, when you and Daddy used to fight over his job, why did you stay?"

She flinched. "Baby, how could you ask me that? Your father and I love each other."

"I know you do, but you used to fight all the time. You were always angry with him for spending all his time at the station instead of at home, for going on all the night calls and holidays. You never seemed happy."

"Oh, Cooper. I was never angry with your father. I was young, you boys were young. We were all young. Your father had been volunteering at the station since he was fourteen. We got married at eighteen and had you boys right away, first Dale and then, well, you, but in between…" She stopped and dug her fork around her food before she looked at Cooper. "Before I had you, when Dale was around five, I had a miscarriage. Your father was on a call, and the ambulance was there, too. My mother had to drive me all the way to Mountain Home, and by the time we got there, I was in a bad way. They didn't think I'd ever be able to have another baby, but you proved them wrong." She smiled at Cooper.

He was stunned. "I never knew that."

"No, not many people do. You didn't talk about things like that in those days. Anyway, your father blamed himself for everything even though there wasn't anything he could've done about it. Rather than making him stay home more, the situation caused him to throw himself into his work."

"This is beginning to sound familiar."

She nodded. "Yes, and I should have had this talk with you years ago. I'm sorry about that."

He reached over and patted her hand. "It's okay, Mama. I'm sure it's not easy to talk about."

"It's not so hard now, all these years later. But here's the thing, Cooper. Your father and I didn't know how to make ourselves feel better, so we just fought. People didn't go to marriage counselors or anything like that, they just worked through it. Eventually, we did work it out, but I know it was hard on you boys."

"And you weren't angry that Daddy was always gone?"

"Oh, I was, but I knew why he was doing it. I just didn't know how to get him to stop doing it. I was as angry at myself as I was at him for not talking to him about it. After he hurt his back, I told him how I felt, and you know what he said to me? He said, 'May, why didn't you just tell me you wanted me home more?' That was it. That was all I had to do."

"But he loved firefighting. Don't you think he would've resented missing out on all those fires?"

"Cooper, if I asked, and he stayed home more, I wouldn't have cared if he kept fighting fires. As long as

I knew he'd have stayed if I wanted him to."

Cooper shook his head. "Mama, sometimes I just don't understand married people."

"You will someday, Cooper. You will. Now, eat that lasagna before it gets cold."

The rest of their meal was filled with general conversation about the weather, the kids, Scout, and things happening in town. After they did the dishes together, Cooper walked his mother to the door. He hugged her and told her goodnight before stopping her in the doorway.

"Mama," he said, taking a breath. "Thank you. For your advice and your guidance."

"It's always available to you Cooper. All you need to do is ask. Or not," she said with a bright smile and a twinkle in her eye. "I'll offer it either way."

He watched her leave and thought about all she said. He walked back to the kitchen and picked up his phone from where he'd left it just before his mother arrived over an hour prior.

Thinking about you. Try to have a good night. And get some sleep.

***

Amanda's head was spinning. The bombshell her brothers had just dropped on her was still exploding, and her brain was reeling from its impact.

"I can't believe you're even bringing this up right now. Daddy is still here, and Mama is smart, capable, and strong. This isn't our decision to make for her."

"She doesn't want to stay here," Mason told her. "She keeps talking about how big and lonely it will be when it's just her. She's mentioned a few friends who moved once their spouse died and how happy they are."

"But this is our home. She and Daddy have lived here their entire marriage. Nobody does that anymore. They've always been here because this is where they always wanted to be."

"They," Derrick said. "This is where *they* always wanted to be. Together. That's about to change."

"But don't you think she should take some time, think it through, try to make her own life here, before this drastic decision is made by her or any of us?"

Peter shook his head. "You don't understand, Sissie. She doesn't want to stay here. She's told us that."

Amanda looked around the house. It was nothing like her home in Buffalo Springs. On the contrary, it was the exact opposite, a typical Southern planation house with a winding staircase overlooking a marble foyer that was an actual, honest to heavens, rotunda. There were more rooms than she could ever fill even with all the grandchildren her six children would be able to provide. It still boasted its original kitchen with a stone floor and hearth, but the room had been doubled in size with a renovation that would make both Joe and Gordon Ramsey jealous. The dining room rivaled that of the White House, and the parlor, sitting room, and added-on family room boasted antique furniture that had been in her mother's family since the days after the Civil War when the family had fought to keep their house from carpetbaggers and went from planting cotton to soybeans and raising cattle.

Nobody in Buffalo Springs, including Joe, knew how Amanda had grown up, with society parties and debutante balls and a silver spoon in her mouth. Amanda's parents paid for her college, but she paid her own way through medical school at her father's insistence, and Amanda understood why. It was one way they taught her how to value the dollar, how to portion part of her income to pay off her debts, and how to manage her own finances. Her parents wanted her to be financially savvy and independent because the bulk of their family wealth wasn't available to her or her brothers except through modest trust funds they would each inherit upon marriage. Even Joe, her own business partner, didn't know that one of the clinic's biggest donations wasn't just a random grant but a gift from her mother's family foundation. Without that money, they never would have been able to rebuild and expand the clinic after the fire a few years back.

"This home has been in Mama's family for generations. We can't just sell it," Amanda protested.

A wave of looks rose and fell around the table, and Amanda felt like she was drowning in whatever they weren't saying.

"Abby and I are moving in here," Derrick said. "I'm going to take over the business."

"He means, he's going to oversee the cattle, and I'm going to help run the foundation," Abby clarified.

"It's too much for me to do alone," Mason told her. "It has taken on a life of its own, and I need help from someone I can trust."

"It's a medical foundation, overseeing billions of dollars given out to hospitals and clinics, and nobody thought to ask me if I wanted to be part of it?"

Unwilling to meet her gaze, some of her siblings and their wives looked down or away, but Peter didn't.

"Come on, Amanda," he said gently. "Would you want that responsibility? Would you have given up being a doctor to run the foundation? Would you have left the life you have now to come home and sit in an office all day, attend board meetings, and travel without seeing anything but hotels and hospital meeting rooms?"

She knew he was right, but it still stung.

"Why didn't anyone ask me?" She looked at each of her brothers, waiting for a reply.

"Because I told them not to," came a voice from the doorway. Her mother entered and took her place at the head of the long mahogany dining table. "I knew you never loved Nashville, never loved the idea of working for the foundation. You could have been part of it, but you went to medical school instead, following your father's footsteps instead of mine. You hated working in the big hospital. It's not who you are. You've taken root in that little town in the Ozarks and have blossomed there in a way you never would have or could have here."

Amanda felt a tear run down her cheek. Her mother was right, but for some reason, it hurt to hear her say it.

"I love you, you know. I love all of you." She looked

around the table. "I just felt suffocated here. I needed to—"

"We know, Sissie," Peter said, covering her hand with his. "And that's partly our fault. We always saw you as our little sister who needed protecting, but you needed to be your own person who could stand up for herself and make her own decisions. And look at you now! Delivering babies in forest fires."

Several gasps went up from around the table, but her mother smiled.

"I was so proud of you when you told me about that. I wanted to reach right through the phone and hug you. You've made quite the life for yourself, but I know you. With your medical background, you would have felt obligated to come home and take over, doing something you would hate, and leaving behind the life you love. So I told everyone that you were not to know of our plans until everything was in place. I didn't know it would be now, when you're home to tell your father goodbye. We didn't know the cancer would come back or that he'd have so little time." Her voice cracked, and Amanda felt that closing of her throat again.

"Hey," Paul said to her. "If it makes you feel any better, Missy and I are staying put in Alabama. And Peter's still practicing law."

"Well, I do represent the foundation," Peter said.

"But you don't work for it," Derrick said. "But I think what Paul is trying to say is, don't feel bad for living your life. Not everyone has to work for the family business. Technically, I'm not even working for the foundation. I'm just a cowboy."

They all laughed. Cattle ranching in the 21ˢᵗ Century was a far cry from the old Westerns. Derrick spent his days in a three-piece suit looking out the windows of his fancy, high-rise office, making deals to sell the best bulls and following the cattle market closely to take advantage of the futures, things Amanda admitted she would never fully understand.

"So, you guys all have this pretty much planned, don't you?"

"Mostly," Mason told her. "Just some minor details to wrap up."

"Anything I can do?" she asked.

"Spend time with your Daddy," her mother said. "He's missed you so much."

Amanda bit back tears. That's what she came home for, and she wouldn't let him, let any of them, down.

Fourteen

I'm coming home.

That's all the text said, but Cooper read into it so much promise. Amanda was returning, not just to Buffalo Springs but to home. She'd said home. He knew he might be putting too much meaning into one little word, but there were a million other things she could have said that would have meant everything he didn't want to hear.

I'll be here. I've missed you.

He stopped and read the text three times before backing it up.

I'll be here. We've all missed you.

He stopped again and decided to go with his gut and his heart. He hit the backspace some more.

I'll be here. I miss you.

A swarm of emotion buzzed through him as he hit send. His stomach, a nest of bees buzzing round and round. How would she respond?

The word *Read* appeared, but there were no dots indicating she was typing back. It was as though his insides were being stung over and over, and the taste in his mouth was anything but sweet honey.

He tried to sleep, but Amanda's face kept stealing its way into his mind's eye. Maybe she was busy. Maybe she was spending the night with her family and didn't have time to text him back. He flopped over onto his back and stared at the ceiling. He thought about his feelings for her and his desire to spend his life with her. There, he admitted it. He wanted to spend the rest of his life with Amanda.

He turned over, and his gaze landed on his nightstand. For the first time in five years, Cooper opened the drawer and took out the velvet box. He opened it and stared at the ring for several moments. He closed the box then closed his eyes, holding the box against his chest.

"I will always love you in some way, Jessie, but I love Amanda in a way I never thought I could love anyone. I hope you understand." Cooper put the ring back and closed the drawer, knowing it was time to finally let go.

He hadn't been asleep long when the call came, and he never thought to look at his text messages. He was focused on pulling together his team and doing his job.

A mother and daughter were lost somewhere on the trail to Hemmed-in-Hollow Falls. Most of their calls took place there, so Cooper's team was well-versed in knowing where to look and how to find lost hikers, and Scout was getting better each time in finding people even without knowing their scent. It didn't take long for the pair to be located. They were cold and hungry but no worse for wear.

It was just after midnight when Cooper fell back into bed and realized he'd never looked at his phone other than to answer calls from the sheriff while they searched. There was a text notification, and he opened the app to find a message from Amanda.

I hate to ask, but are you able to pick me up at the Springfield airport the day after tomorrow? Andi dropped me off, but she has a full schedule this week with the holiday this weekend. I don't mean to be a bother, but I don't know who else to ask.

Cooper frowned. Did she not understand what those three words meant? He didn't just miss her. He couldn't wait to see her. He'd run all the way to the airport if she asked him to.

It's no bother. I'm happy to pick you up. I can't wait to see you.

No, her father just passed away. She wasn't coming for a casual visit.

It's no bother. I'm happy to pick you up. I'm glad you're coming home. Send me your flight info.

He hit send. He hoped she read into the word 'home' the same thing he did. He put the phone down and rolled over. He was asleep within minutes, Amanda's radiant smile and beautiful, gold-flecked, hazel eyes luring him into his dreams.

The following morning, he had a text from Amanda with her flight information. She would be home the next day. Cooper let the sheriff know he needed the day off as soon as he arrived at the station. He never took off, and the sheriff asked if he was feeling okay. Was there a problem? Were his parents well? Cooper laughed and explained he was picking up a friend at the airport, but he didn't expand when the question arose in his boss's eyes.

He arrived an hour early and sat in his car, scrolling though search and rescue stories on Reddit. Every once in a while, he participated in one of the threads, but he mostly just read what others experienced and gained knowledge from their triumphs and tragedies.

When Amanda texted him she had landed, he headed into the airport. Unlike most airports, her walk to baggage claim would be a short one, and her bags would be unloaded in only a few minutes' time. He hurried into the baggage area and watched for her to emerge from the secured part of the small airport. When she appeared, the sound of his beating heart flooded his ears, and he forced himself not to run to her.

She obviously didn't expect him to meet her inside because she picked up her phone and start typing as she walked toward one of the two carousels. His phone buzzed, and he read the message that she was waiting for her bag. He waited until she was standing at the carousel and made his way over to stand behind her. When she reached for her bag, he reached around her and closed his hand around hers on the handle. Their eyes met, and he smiled.

"I've got this."

She smiled back at him and let him take the bag for her. When he put it down and turned toward her, he finally understood the expression, *her eyes danced with excitement.*

"I've got one more," she told him. "I gate-checked my carry-on." He nodded, and they stood next to each other, watching for her bag.

Once he had both in hand, they walked outside.

"Thanks for doing this. I really appreciate it."

They reached his truck, and he placed the bags in the backseat of the cab before turning to her.

"I'm happy you asked me. You know, I'd do anything for you." It was the greatest admission he'd made to a woman in five years. Maybe ever, considering the amount of weight those words held. Amanda looked deeply into his eyes before nodding.

"Thank you," she whispered before she fell apart.

*****

"I'm sorry," Amanda said, her head still buried in his now-drenched shoulder. His strong arms were around her back, and she never wanted him to let her go. She felt safe there, sheltered from all the pain and heartache.

"Don't be sorry," he told her, running one hand down her auburn hair, the other protectively cradling her back. "You're allowed to cry."

She pulled back, expecting him to release her, but he kept a firm hold.

"I haven't cried. I mean, before now. I wanted to. I

felt terrible that I couldn't cry, but the tears wouldn't come. I cried when I said goodbye, of course. In those last few moments before and after he slipped away, I cried more than I've ever cried before, but after that, the tears just weren't there. I don't know why. My sisters-in-law cried more than I did." She gave a little laugh, not that it was funny.

"Grief is like that," he told her. "Sometimes it takes hold of you so strongly, you can't breathe, not to mention cry. It's like it sucks all the emotion out of you, and you feel hollow, unable to feel anything at all. Then, suddenly, it hits you with such force, you have to let it all out."

"You sound like an expert on grief. I guess you've had to deal with that a lot on your job."

He stared at her for a moment, his eyes searching hers, and she remembered weeks back, almost months now, when Paige and Allie were talking about what he'd been through. He nodded.

"Something like that," he said. "You ready to get home?"

"I am. Thanks."

He opened the door and helped her into the truck before closing the door for her. For some reason, Amanda felt nervous, but she didn't know why. It's not like she'd never been alone with him before. But somehow, this felt... different.

Once he was settled in the driver's seat, Cooper started the engine and turned to her.

"Have you eaten? Do you want to stop for lunch

before we make the drive home?"

Right on cue, her stomach growled. "I'm starving."

Cooper smiled and backed out of the parking space. "Let's stop in Branson. It has the most choices, and it's on the way."

"That sounds good. Do you mind if we stop at the store on the way back? I need to pick up a few things. I have nothing to eat tonight or in the morning."

"I wouldn't be so sure about that," he said with a smug smile.

"What do you mean?"

"You have a lot of friends, Amanda. One of them is Helena."

"She didn't."

"She did. Most of the town pitched in to stock your refrigerator. They also weeded your garden, planted the flowers Andi's mom had ready for you, and cut your grass."

Amanda closed her eyes and laid her head on the back of the seat. "This town is amazing. None of that would've happened in the city, or even out where our house is, especially where our house is." Not that they would have needed that kind of help when her mother had a paid staff to do it all for her.

"You've spent the past three years taking care of everyone in town. It's the least they could do to show their appreciation. And everyone loves you, Amanda. You're one of us."

She opened her eyes and looked at him, her heart swelling. He reached over and took her hand in his, and

Amanda felt it again, something was different between them.

"Do you want to talk about it?" he asked, and she blinked a few times trying to figure out what 'it' meant. "Your dad, being home, any of it?"

Of course, that's what he meant.

"Not really," she said honestly but found herself talking anyway. "A lot happened. My family is going to go through a lot of changes, but it's all good. Nothing that really affects me. The funeral was nice. Most of the greater Nashville medical community was there, and Dad would've appreciated that." The giant funeral with a procession to rival that of a Kennedy was covered by all the society pages, but she knew he wouldn't know that. Despite not wanting to talk about it, she continued to tell him about the roles they each played in the service, her brother's eulogy, and the poems her nieces recited. She didn't tell him that the governor attended—he played golf with her father—or that her mother's dear friend and high school classmate, singer Amy Grant, was in attendance. It wasn't until they arrived in Branson that Amanda realized she'd been talking the entire hour.

"Well, so much for not really wanting to talk," she said, trying to hide her embarrassment.

"I didn't mind. I like hearing about your family."

They chose a restaurant and went inside, each having a burger. Amanda hadn't eaten much in the past three days, and her hunger hit her all at once.

While they were eating, a little girl bounded across the room and threw herself at Cooper.

"It's you! I knew it was you!"

Amanda and Cooper looked at each other, both at a loss for words.

"Bridget! Oh, my gosh. I'm so sorry. I'm so—"

"Mama, it's him! It's the Rain Man!"

"I'm sorry, Sir. Ma'am. I don't know what she's talking about."

Before he could reply, the girl looked up at Cooper and said, "Thank you for saving us. That night in the storm when our car got caught in the flood. Thank you for getting us out."

Amanda saw recognition, or at least understanding, dawn on his face.

"You're welcome," was all he said, his cheeks turning pink.

"You're the search and rescue guy," Bridget's mother said. "I didn't recognize you."

Amanda felt chills run down her arms as the woman's expression changed from horror to gratitude.

"She's right. Thank you. Thank you so much. We tried, my husband and me, to find out your name. We called the park and the sheriff's office, but they refused to give it to us."

"That's standard, Ma'am. We were just doing our job." Amanda heard the emotion in his voice.

"Well, it wasn't standard for us." She looked at Amanda. "He's a real hero."

"I know," she said. "I've seen him in action."

"Well, we won't bother you any further, but thank you." They walked away, and Cooper took a drink of his tea.

"That was nice. Does it happen often?"

He shook his head. "First time for me."

"Nobody comes back to thank you?"

"No. And I wouldn't want it if they did. It's my job. Seeing someone reunited with their family or knowing they're going to recover, that's all the thanks I need."

"I understand that," Amanda said.

He looked at her and nodded. "I knew you would."

"The Rain Man," she said with a smile. "It fits."

"Because I look like Dustin Hoffman."

Amanda laughed so hard, she choked on her water, not even having time to be embarrassed about the drops that flew through her nose.

"I hardly think so."

Cooper joined her in laughter. "The Rain Man, huh? I kind of like it."

"Me, too," she said, still chuckling.

When they finished and asked for the check, they were told the bill had been paid. They looked around for Bridget and her mother, but they were already gone.

"Sometimes, you just have to accept it and know you made a difference," Amanda told him. She wanted to say more. She wanted to tell him what a difference he made in her life, but she kept it to herself. There would come a time for that, and she'd know it when it happened.

***

For the first time in his life, Cooper prayed there

would be no calls for the next few hours. He'd gotten a haircut and shaved, no nicks, which was a miracle in itself. He had on a shirt his mother gave him for Christmas she said would bring out the green in his eyes, whatever that meant. He wore his best jeans and pulled on his favorite dress boots. He assessed himself in the bathroom mirror before heading downstairs.

"Wow! Uncle Coop, you look awesome!"

"Thanks, Bean." In the past couple weeks, Suzy had squelched her baby talk and said things in a manner more befitting an eight-year-old. She wasn't jumping on him to get him out of bed and had started reading to herself at night. Part of him felt wrecked, and another part was happy she might finally be growing up and maybe even moving on from her mother's death, not that she ever fully would.

"She's right," Serena said. "You look quite handsome."

He blushed. Who wouldn't? She was Serena Blake after all.

"Thank you, both. Serena, I really appreciate you coming over to stay with the kids. Dale said he shouldn't be too long."

"Sugar, you know I don't mind." She smiled at Suzy. "You know how much I love these kids."

"When do you go back to Houston?" He asked as he picked up his wallet from the counter.

"Just a few more days."

"But she's coming back," Suzy affirmed.

"I sure am, Sugar. I'll be back in a few months, after

I've settled everything at home and ensured everything properly transfers here."

"I can't believe you're opening your business here," Cooper said. A couple months back, he'd have been willing to carry her luggage all the way from Houston. Now, he was just happy for her, as a friend.

"And I've already got clients lined up," she said with a sparkle in her eye. "I can't wait to get started."

He looked at his smart watch. "Gotta go. You guys have a great night." He kissed Suzy on the top of her head and waved to Jamie, who barely acknowledged him.

There was a spring in his step as he walked down the sidewalk. He'd debated taking the truck, but the skies were clear, and the night was warm, and he knew Amanda preferred walking. As he reached up to ring the bell, he suddenly felt nervous, but nothing prepared him for what he awaited him when she opened the door.

He'd seen Amanda in pants with a lab coat, her hair in a bun. He'd seen her in dresses and dress slacks at church with her long hair neatly arranged down her back. He'd seen her in workout leggings and t-shirts, a ponytail bobbing behind her head. He'd never seen her looking like she did now.

Amanda walked onto the front porch, her hair loose in large curls, wearing a hunter green dress that accentuated every curve. There was a two-inch strap on one shoulder and a regular sleeveless cut on the other. The dress hung just above her knees, which peeped through an inverted V that began a split from the front of the dress, crossing over to her waist. The split managed to make the dress modest and sexy at the same time. She wore teardrop earrings and a few silver bangles but no other jewelry with low-heeled silver sandals to complete the outfit.

"Everything okay?" Amanda asked, and Cooper realized he had stood there gawking at her for too long.

"Everything is perfect," he said, his heart caught in his throat. "Ready?" He held out his arm to hers. She looped her arm through his and let him lead her down to the sidewalk.

"I'm sorry I can't take you anywhere fancier than La Forna. Next time, maybe we can go to Alpena or Eureka Springs."

"What do they have that Buffalo Springs doesn't have?" she asked with a smile. "I like it fine right here."

Several people greeted them on their way to the restaurant, and Cooper noticed their stares, not at him, of course. Walking down the street, with Amanda's arm in his, made him feel ten feet tall, and he was sure the grin would never leave his face.

"Hello, Cooper, Dr. Pierce."

Cooper smiled at the former mayor, Imogene Baker. She was a town legend and never missed anything.

"Good evening, Mrs. Baker. Nice night for a walk."

"It is, and I see you're taking advantage of it." She looked at Amanda. "I'm so sorry about your father. It's one of the hardest losses in life."

"Thank you," Amanda said, her voice strained.

"I'm glad to see you two finally getting things right.

Don't screw it up." She looked at Cooper when she said that, and he nodded.

"Yes, Ma'am."

Amanda laughed once she was out of earshot. "She's amazing."

Cooper agreed.

They talked about almost everything that came to mind over the course of the night, topping off their pasta dishes with gelato and decaf coffee. Cooper didn't want the evening to end, so after dinner, he proposed a walk to the town park where the tents were already erected for the big Memorial Day festival that Paige and Allie had planned for Helena, the town's official festival organizer.

Under the moonlight, they sat on a bench and looked up at the stars.

"Did you know that Joe can name every constellation in the sky?" Amanda asked.

"I did not know that," Cooper said. "I bet he was able to woo a few girls with that skill."

"I know it impressed Helena."

Amanda shivered.

"Are you cold?"

"A little. I should have brought a wrap."

"No need," Cooper said, putting his arm around her and pulling her close. "Better?" he asked, his voice sounding deeper than normal.

"Better," she whispered, not looking at him.

On the contrary, he couldn't take his eyes off her. Without realizing he was doing it, he reached up and curled a strand of hair around his finger. "I've never seen hair this color except on actresses."

"You must not get around much," she said with a smile.

"Not much. College in Missouri, but not much farther than that. Not that St. Louis is far."

She turned to look at him. "I didn't know you went to college, not that it matters. I just…"

Cooper laughed. "It's okay. Most people wouldn't think someone in my job would have a four-year degree."

"What did you major in?"

"Emergency Management. Thought I might like to work in the Rockies, but decided the Ozarks would always be home. And believe me, I see plenty of action. Buffalo River is the thirteenth busiest SAR park in the country."

"Really? That high? Wow."

"Definitely keeps me busy."

"No wonder I see you so often."

Cooper was quiet for a moment but then said, "Amanda, I'd actually like to see you more often than that. More than just after I've rescued someone."

She nuzzled closer to him.

"I think that can be arranged," she said quietly, laying her head on his shoulder.

He rested his head against hers and closed his eyes. He could feel the pulse in her neck against his shoulder, and his own heart seemed to find the rhythm to match it. He never wanted the night to end.

When Amanda yawned, Cooper gently nudged her with his shoulder. "Come on, time to get you home."

"I'm so sorry," she said as they stood. "I didn't mean to—"

Cooper turned her toward him, pulled her against him, and kissed her. It wasn't planned, and it wasn't the gentle, romantic kiss he'd imagined, but she kissed him back until they were both out of breath.

He held her against him, raking his hand through her hair, with her head on his chest.

A chuckle escaped his lips. "Do you know how many times you've apologized to me in the past few months? You need to stop telling me you're sorry, or I'll think you don't want to be around me. I don't know what you're sorry for now, but I had to show you that I'm not sorry. Not for a single minute we've spent together."

She giggled against his chest before turning her face to his.

"I'm not really sorry. I'm tired, but I'm not sorry," she said, repeating what she'd said to him that first night he encountered her in the rain.

"Good. I don't want to hear it again unless there's a real reason for you to say it."

"Okay, I'll remember that. But Cooper?"

"Yes?" His eyes held hers, and in them was the reflection of all the stars in Heaven.

"I'm going to be sorry if you don't kiss me again."

This time, he leaned in slowly, grazing her lips with his own, teasing, probing, until he gave in to his desire and claimed her mouth with his.

***

"Well?" Melanie asked when Amanda walked into the clinic after the early Mass on Sunday.

"Well, what?" she said coyly.

"Come on, how was it?"

Amanda grinned. "The best night ever."

"Oh, I knew it would be. Every female in town from twelve to ninety is going crazy over the way he looks at you, and every one of them, married and single, has imagined themselves in your shoes at one time or another."

Amanda laughed and kept walking to the lounge. "Oh, come on."

"I mean it. Trudy would die if Cooper looked at her like that. I mean, we all knew it wouldn't last. He's so much older than she is, and besides, he never..." Melanie clapped her hand over her mouth. "Never mind."

"He never commits," Amanda finished.

"Yeah, but he also never asks anyone out either. He goes if they ask, but he never asks, not since Jessie."

Amanda placed her coffee cup in the machine, popped in a pod, and pushed the button before she turned to Melanie. She leaned back against the counter and folded her arms across her chest.

"I wish somebody would tell me who Jessie is and what happened. Did she break his heart?"

Melanie's eyes went wide. "You don't know?"

Amanda shook her head. "I know nothing. I heard that something happened a while back that made him stop dating. I don't know what it was. I keep meaning to ask Andi, but somehow, the timing has never been right, or the subject just hasn't come up."

"You really don't know?"

"I really don't know," Amanda said, trying—and failing—to keep the annoyance from her voice.

"She's in a coma, has been for five years."

Amanda blinked in confusion. "What does that have to do with Cooper?"

"Jessie was Cooper's partner, his SAR partner, before he was lead responder. But she was more than that. There was talk about them getting married. I was working for Wade's family at the time, and everyone knew how they felt about each other. Cooper has always been the most eligible bachelor in Buffalo Springs. Anyway, they were helping the fire company battle a wildfire in the national forest. Somehow—and this is the part I don't really know the details about because nobody really talks about it—he and Jessie got separated. I think, maybe she went off on her own for some reason. Bottom line, the fire turned, and Jessie was trapped. She tried to outrun it and ended up going off a cliff. When Cooper found her, he thought she was dead."

Coffee forgotten, Amanda slunk into the nearest chair.

"Oh, my gosh. Poor Jessie. Poor Cooper. No wonder." So many things made sense. His lack of commitment, his allegiance to his job and his team, his carrying her from the fire like Superman.

"Yeah. He was in a bad way for a long time. There was never any hope, from what I remember, but I think her parents still pray she wakes up. I heard from Cindy that he went to see her not long ago. I didn't know he still did that."

"Do you think he still loves her?" Amanda heard her voice crack, felt her heart do the same.

Melanie looked pained as she lifted her shoulders. "I don't know. Maybe? I mean, he's never dated anyone seriously since then, but then again, there was never you. This seems…different."

Different. The same word that kept coming to Amanda's mind each time they were together. Something was different between them. Certainly, now that they'd kissed. But…

Was he still in love with Jessie, and would he be for as long as anyone held hope that she would wake up?

***

How was your day?

The text was short and straightforward, but she hadn't answered, and it had been an hour since she read it.

"What's wrong?" Dale asked when he walked into the living room after putting the kids to bed.

"Nothing," Cooper replied, tucking his phone into the sofa cushion.

"Doesn't look like nothing. Looks like you were

trying to use telekinesis on your phone."

"Not quite. Just checking my messages."

"Everything okay?"

"Sure. Why wouldn't it be?"

"I don't know. You just look like someone just told you your dog died."

Scout lifted her head as though she understood, then laid back down in front of the woodstove.

"I'm fine."

"You said the date went great."

"It did."

"So?"

"So, why is she ghosting me?" he said sounding more resentful than he meant.

"What makes you think she's doing that?"

"Because she read my text an hour ago and hasn't answered."

Dale laughed. "You stupid, love-sick idiot. It's been one hour. Maybe she had an emergency at the clinic. Maybe she's talking to her mom, giving her every last detail about last night. Give her the benefit of the doubt."

Cooper's phone rang, and he hurried to answer.

"We've got a hurt hiker on Centerpoint Trail. We know where he is, and the rangers are there, but he fell over a ledge and can't get out. Sounds like he broke something. He's out of reach of the rangers."

"Copy. On the way."

"Good luck," Dale called as Cooper grabbed his gear and headed out the door.

As he drove to the EOC, he wondered if the wish for luck was for the rescue or his relationship with Amanda.

***

A few hours later, Cooper met Amanda at the clinic. The young man he rescued leaned heavily on him.

"Thanks for meeting me," Cooper said when Amanda opened the clinic door.

"Of course. It's my job." She smiled, but it didn't reach her eyes. "Let's get you inside," she said to the hiker who was barely putting weight on his right foot.

Cooper waited in the lobby for Amanda and the man to finish. It was the first time he'd waited after dropping someone off and the first time he'd wondered why he ever thought it was okay to leave. As he sat in the empty room, he realized how quiet it was, how dark the rest of the building was other than the light seeping from under the bottom of the closed door where Amanda treated the hiker. No nurse showed up. No second person to lend a hand or be there, just in case. He didn't want to think about 'in case.'

Cooper stood and looked outside. The streetlights were out. Were they always out at this time of night? Were they on timers? Did Amanda enter and leave here in the dark?

"Be sure to follow up with an orthopedic doctor next week," Amanda said as she opened the door. She led the man down the hall and stopped when she noticed

Cooper, her mouth open in surprise.

She said goodnight to the patient, closed the door, then turned to him.

"I didn't know you were still here."

"I wanted to talk to you, and then I started thinking. Are you always here alone when I drop someone off to see you at night?"

"Yes, when I'm the one on call. Why?" She walked around the other side of the counter and made a notation on a piece of paper on the desk before straightening up and looking at him.

"I didn't know. You're here all alone, and I'm dropping these people off without knowing anything about them. I should be staying."

"Cooper, it's not your job to stay once the patient has been turned over to me."

"But it should be. I'm going to say something to Sheriff Wilson. We shouldn't be leaving you, or anyone, alone with someone at night with nobody else here."

"Cooper, nothing has ever happened. We're perfectly safe."

"But you're not. You might not be. Don't you get it? I could be putting you in danger by walking away."

Amanda bit her lip. "Cooper, if this is about—"

"This isn't some weird, we're dating so I own you thing. And it's not a macho, you need a man to save you thing. I genuinely think you shouldn't be alone with any of these people. What if that hiker was a drug user who suddenly had some kind of hallucination and attacked you? Or what if he was a serial killer?"

Amanda laughed, and Cooper reeled back.

"This isn't funny."

"I'm sor—. No, I mean, I know it's not, but really, a serial killer?"

Cooper wanted to shake her. He was furious. How could she be so naïve?

"Just do me a favor, no, do yourself a favor, okay?"

She nodded, trying not to smile. He took a deep breath and told himself to calm down. He moved closer until they were almost touching. His anger spent, and his desire taking hold, he cupped her chin in his hand and turned her mouth up to meet his. After several minutes, he pulled her to himself.

"Oh, Amanda. I don't know what I'd do if something happened to you. If you got hurt because of me."

Like a switch had been flipped, Amanda jumped back.

"What did you just say?"

"I don't know. That I'd be upset if something happened to you. I mean it. Please, don't let anyone leave you here alone again. Okay? Or else, every time there's a call, you're going to come out of that room to find me sitting out here, and I'm not going to get any sleep. Ever. And I'm going to be a walking zombie and not be able to do my job. Do you want that on your shoulders?"

She shook her head, reached for her keys, and walked to the door. "I need to go. You need to go."

He stepped out of her way. "Amanda, what's wrong?"

"I need to lock up. You need to leave. I'm sorry." She turned to him as she opened the door. "I mean it. I really am sorry."

Fifteen

"You never told her?" Dale said in disbelief. "Why the heck not?"

"There was never a time to tell her. How would you have done it? Thanks for helping save Helena's life. By the way, my ex is in a coma, and I've been blaming myself for it for five years? Or how about, isn't it beautiful here on the bluff? Speaking of bluffs, did I ever tell you my ex fell from one?"

Dale exhaled. "Okay, but there had to be some point when you could've told her."

"Does it matter now?"

"I guess not, but I thought you needed to know." Dale shuffled some papers on his desk as Cooper paced.

"The wireless companies sure save a lot of money here in Buffalo Springs. I think there are still tin cans connected with string that connect your house with Wade's and his with Jackson's and, wait who did you say told her?" He stopped pacing and looked at his brother.

"Melanie. Then Melanie told Cindy who told Jackson who told Wade. Oh, never mind. The point is, she knows, and Melanie said she was pretty shaken up by the news."

"But I think it's more than that. I tried to talk to Amanda the other night about not being alone with patients at night, and she freaked out. Told me to leave and closed the door in my face. I don't get it."

"Wait. Amanda works alone at night with patients?"

"When she's on call and there's an emergency or when one of my team drops off someone after a rescue. I know," he said at the look on Dale's face. "I was freaked out when I realized it."

"Why didn't any of us think about that before? Why hasn't Joe ever said anything? Even he shouldn't be left there alone. He knows better after what happened to him back when he opened the clinic and his ex-girlfriend broke in. We don't know anything about the vast majority of the people you rescue."

Cooper rushed to the chair opposite Dale's desk and sat, nodding his head enthusiastically. "I know, right? But why be angry with me about it?"

"I don't know, Coop, but it sounds to me like you two have a lot to talk about."

"But she's not talking. I've tried texting, and I tried talking the other night, but she's shutting me out."

"Kind of like you shut everyone out?"

Cooper sat back and heaved a frustrated breath. "I'm trying not to do that anymore, and I've never shut her out."

"You think she feels that way after hearing about Jessie?"

Cooper hung his head and cradled it in his hands.

"Go. Talk to her. What have you got to lose? If it's already over, then it ended before it really started. If it's not, then save it."

"What if I'm already in too deep?"

Dale smiled, "Then I'd say, it's about time, and why are you still sitting in my office?"

Cooper started toward the door but stopped and turned back. "Hey, Dale. Whatever happened with that abandoned tent you sent me to check out? Anything ever turn up?"

"Nothing at all. And I talked to Joe discreetly about Serena being alone, and he laughed. Said Serena could protect herself with her bare hands better than I could with a gun." Dale shrugged. "Maybe it was nothing."

"Weird," Cooper said with the shake of his head. "But weirder things have happened out there."

"Agreed. Now, go. You have some things to fix."

***

Amanda wasn't typically the last person to leave the clinic, but she had some paperwork to finish and then got held up on a call from a frantic mother whose child had eaten a glow stick left over from the Memorial Day festival.

It was after six when she engaged the alarm, walked

outside, and turned her back to lock the door.

"Can we talk?"

Amanda's scream pierced the quiet of the early summer evening. She held her keys out like a weapon as she spun around, ready for a fight.

"My goodness, Cooper. You scared me to death. Is it a habit of yours to go sneaking around behind people, giving them heart attacks?" She took a deep breath and pocketed her keys after fumbling to lock the door, her hands still shaking from the fright. Or from seeing Cooper. She honestly wasn't sure which.

"I'm sorry. I didn't mean to scare you. I just want to talk. Please."

She'd already decided to tell him no, but the pleading in his voice and the worry lines on his forehead tugged at her heart. She sighed.

"Where do you want to talk?" Surprise and hope flashed in his eyes, and she instantly regretted her compliance. She'd made up her mind they would never work. No matter how much she might have wanted them to.

"Wherever you want. Here. Your house. We could drive somewhere."

"My house is fine, but meet me there. I don't want anyone to see us walking together and add fuel to the gossip."

His face fell, and she knew she'd hurt him. He didn't deserve that after what he'd been through. But she needed to establish boundaries.

"And please give me ten minutes to change."

"Fine. I can do that. Do you want me to use the back door?"

Obviously his hurt was leaning toward anger, but she wouldn't rise to the bait. If he was itching for a fight, it wasn't going to happen here.

"Just let me change clothes. Then we'll get this over with." It was harsh, and she knew it, but she pushed her way past him and walked with purpose—a phrase she picked up at Girl Scout Camp years ago that meant get there as fast as you can without running—and tried to use the short walk to calm her temper and her nerves.

After twenty-five minutes passed, she assumed he'd changed his mind and began rummaging in the fridge for something to make for dinner. When the doorbell rang, she wasn't sure if she was relieved or irritated.

After a few cleansing breaths, she opened the door to find him standing on the porch with a takeout bag from the BBQ Pit.

"Mama always told us never to show up at someone's house empty-handed, and I thought we could use a change of pace as far as food."

The aroma of barbecue sauce and fresh cornbread went straight to her head, and she opened the door to let him in. Her stomach immediately growled, and she resented its interference. Cooper knew chances were she wouldn't have anything already prepared, and he knew from their dinner date conversation, as much as she loved Rick's burgers, she sometimes craved well-cooked beef brisket with a side of cornbread.

Cooper went right to the table and began unpacking

the food while Amanda went to the refrigerator and pulled out two beers. She held one up, and Cooper nodded, mumbling a quick, "thanks."

They ate in silence, but Amanda felt the words, the accusations, the rebuttals hanging in the air around them like speech clouds in a meme. Finally, Cooper wiped his hands and face, took a long sip of beer, and cleared his throat.

"I heard through the grapevine that you know about Jessie. Can I explain?"

Amanda squeezed her brow and studied her dinner plate. So, this was why he was there.

"Jessie," she said, not knowing what more to say.

"My partner and almost fiancé."

Just hearing the word was a knife to her heart, and she realized, no matter how angry she was, she still had deep feelings for him. She nodded.

"I guess you know what happened."

She spoke quietly and carefully. "I know she was your partner, she fell during a wildfire, that you found her and thought she was dead. Now she's in a coma, right?"

He nodded. "For the past five years."

Her heart ached for him. His voice, his eyes, his whole body showed her how much it pained him. How much he still loved her. She pinched her lips together and willed herself not to cry. Mostly because she didn't know if the tears were because she felt his grief over Jessie or because of her own belief he could never be hers.

"I'm sorry," she managed to whisper.

A smile slowly appeared on his face. "There you go again."

She found herself smiling back but quickly wiped it away. "I meant, I'm…it's…"

"I know. I understand what you meant. It's what we say when we don't know what else to say, 'I'm sorry.' Like it will somehow convey everything that can't be said or done."

"You still care about her."

Cooper blinked, and his Adam's apple bobbed. "I do, but I don't love her. Not like I did back then. I was different then. My life was different. My view of the world was different."

Different. "But you still visit her."

Cooper's eyes popped in surprise. "Once. A couple months ago." He looked down, ran his hand through his thick hair a few times, then looked back at her. As he spoke, his voice became hoarse with emotion. "Something happened a few months back. I had a moment of poor judgement on a rescue. My state of mind was called into question, rightfully so, and I knew I had to do something about it. I went to see Jessie to tell her…" He looked away, cleared his throat, then turned back to Amanda with a grin. "I went to tell her I was sorry. For not going to see her before then, in all those years, and for not being able to save her." He sighed a long breath and shook his head.

"I blamed myself. I thought if I had done something differently, not let her go alone, made sure she stayed out of the path of the fire, she wouldn't have fallen."

"But Melanie said the fire turned."

"It did, but that didn't stop me from questioning my decisions. She was my partner, and I let her go off on her own."

"Would she have done that anyway, even if you'd told her not to?"

He shrugged. "Probably. Yeah. I mean, I did try to stop her, but she was so determined, so stubborn and self-assured. A lot like you were the other night."

Amanda closed her eyes and felt her temperature rise but breathed deeply through her nose until she was calm. It was her turn.

"When I was growing up, there was this unspoken rule that I needed to be looked after, protected, guarded even. Everywhere I went, everything I did, every date I went on, every party I showed up at, there was a Pierce brother, ready to go to battle for me or scare off anyone who looked my way." She looked pointedly at Cooper. "I didn't need protection. I didn't need my brothers sleuthing behind my back to discover the details of every date I went on so they could take turns 'coincidentally'," she used air quotes, "showing up wherever I was. It was humiliating, and after a while, nobody wanted to take me out."

"Which is why you went to college out of state."

She nodded. "Yes. I had a choice in that. My parents," she hesitated, "they could send me anywhere I wanted to go, and they understood why I wanted to get away for four years. Medical school was another issue. I had to pay for that myself, so it was back to Tennessee." She laughed. "It would've been cheaper to go out of state, but I had a nice scholarship, so I went to Vanderbilt. Even though Dad was there, I knew he'd let me get through on my own, and he did."

"The other night, when I was upset that you were working alone, was that—"

"Because of my brothers? Yes, and this time, I really am sorry. I was already upset about Jessie, and then when you talked about me needing to be protected, I was projecting after all those years of trying to escape being guarded like a child unable to care for herself."

"I wasn't trying to treat you like a child."

"I know, and I did talk to Joe. We're going to work something out, even if it's asking you or one of the others to stay until we finish treating the patient."

"Amanda." Cooper stood and walked around the table. He pulled out a chair and sat beside her, taking her hands in his. Amanda felt no urge to pull away. "Can we try again?"

"What about Jessie? Are you still in love with her?"

"No, and I don't know if I ever really was. If I'm being honest, a part of me will always love her in a way, but we were kids. She was my partner, and I saw in her all the same things that are in me, so I thought it was right. We had a good time together, worked well together, all that. But I didn't know what I wanted back then. Asking her to marry me just felt like the right next step. Would it have lasted? Maybe. Maybe not. I've changed so much in the past five years, but maybe I wouldn't have if she hadn't been hurt. I don't know. What I do know is that the man I am now is not the man I was then, and the woman I loved then isn't the woman I love now."

Amanda swallowed. She didn't ask him to expand on that. She didn't know if she was ready to talk about love, but she knew she wasn't the same person she was when she graduated from college and went to work in the ER, when she was not much older than he and Jessie were. What she did know was that the circles he was tracing on the top of her hand with his thumb were replicating themselves in her abdomen.

"Can we try to make this work? At least see where it's going?"

Amanda closed her eyes. Her whole body felt alive at his touch. Nobody else had ever made her feel this way, and she knew, without a doubt, these feelings weren't just physical. She owed it to herself to try. She opened her eyes and nodded.

"Yes, I want to give it a try."

Cooper's worried frown grew into a wide grin, and he took her hand, pulling her to him, wrapped his arms around her, and held her tight. She breathed in the scent of him, musky with a hint of pine and dirt, and all the smells of the Ozarks. She let herself relax in his arms and knew that after all these years, she finally allowed herself to give into the peace of feeling safe and protected.

✳✳✳

"Ever gone fishing?" Cooper asked Amanda after dropping off a female hiker, Olivia, with a broken ankle.

"Honestly? Never."

It was the first time Cooper had seen her since the night at her house. He'd had one call after another, and the rescues were only going to become more frequent as the summer went into full swing. He wanted to take every opportunity he had to spend a few minutes with Amanda between calls. They stood in the lobby, chatting while she waited for the hiker to fill out paperwork.

"A couple of my brothers hunt and fish, but Dad was more into golfing. And my mother doesn't touch anything before it's cooked."

Cooper laughed, realizing how easily laughter came when he was with her. No more broodiness or the desire to be left alone. He wanted to be happy, and he wanted to make her happy.

"Your mom doesn't cook?"

Something flashed across her features before she nodded and simply said. "Nope. Not her thing."

"Want to give it a try? Fishing, I mean. I'm off Saturday, at least I'm supposed to be."

"I'd be game for that. But I might not be any good."

"I'm ready," Olivia called from the wheelchair behind Cooper.

"I'll call you later," he said before saying goodbye to Olivia and wishing her luck. He waved goodbye to the office staff as he walked out the door.

He walked to his truck from the clinic and never stopped smiling the entire ride to the next town where the sheriff's office was.

"You're in a good mood," Sheriff Wilson commented.

"It was a good day. It was an easy rescue, and I got the hiker to the clinic with nothing more than a broken ankle, hopefully. Anything you need me to do besides paperwork?"

"Actually, I'd like a sit-down if you don't mind."

Cooper's smile faltered. "Sure. Everything okay?"

"Everything is fine. Just something I need to talk to you about."

Cooper followed Beverly into her office and took a seat in front of the desk. She took her seat and folded her hands in front of her.

"Your work has gotten the attention of the higher-ups."

Cooper sat back and assessed her. "What does that mean?"

"The guys from FEMA were impressed with how you handled the landslide a couple months back. Of course, they didn't pick up on what happened with Lucy."

His face flushed, and he nodded.

"Anyway, since then, they've been keeping an eye on you, following your rescues, asking a lot of questions about the way you operate. Which is a good thing," she said, holding her hand up when he leaned forward and opened his mouth to ask what she meant about how he operates. "The accident and the fire, the lost hiker, even the smaller incidents, they've followed up on. With me, with your teammates, with the people you rescued."

Cooper sat back again but didn't relax. What was going on here? Was he under some sort of investigation? And why hadn't his crew said anything?

"I haven't done anything wrong," he began to protest.

"On the contrary," Sheriff Wilson said. "You've done everything right. To a T. Which is why FEMA agent, Arthur Mills, and Director Gary would like a meeting with you."

"I know Arthur. Worked with him a few times. He's a good guy." He cocked his head to the side as her words sunk in. "Director Gary? As in ADEM Director?

"The very one."

"But why do they want to meet with me?"

"I think Director Gary has something to ask you, something I hope you'll consider, though it pains me to admit it." She looked at him intently, her dark brown eyes shining. "I'd hate to lose you, Cooper, but these things aren't up to me."

Cooper's mouth hinged open just a bit as she went on to explain what all this might mean for him and his future.

***

Amanda returned to the exam room after Olivia had her x-ray—courtesy of Amanda's family's foundation—which confirmed the break.

"He's so hot," the young woman said.

"I won't disagree," Amanda said.

Melanie choked back a laugh, and Amanda shot her a look. She gestured toward the patient, and Melanie put her arm around Olivia's other side. "You're going up on the table on three."

"Are you two, like, an item?" she asked, once she and Amanda were alone. Olivia was settled on the table, and her words were a bit slurred. Amanda assumed the pain medication was taking hold. She smiled as she pulled up the x-rays on the lightboard.

She turned to her patient. "I don't think that's what we're here to talk about." She pointed at the pictures. "See this bone, here?"

"I mean, you should be if you aren't. The way he was looking at you, he's totally into—"

"Ms. Webb. I'd like to show you the break and talk about what I see."

"Oh, sure. Sorry. I guess it's none of my business."

Amanda shook her head and pointed out what was on the x-ray, breaking the news that Olivia would probably need surgery.

The rest of the day went by quickly, and Amanda was surprised when she noticed the rest of the staff shutting everything down. Joe wandered down the hall, looking stronger and healthier than she'd expected him to only a few weeks after the accident.

"I think I'm ready to be back full-time."

"Are you sure?" Amanda asked, looking him over with the eye of a doctor. "I don't want you overdoing it."

"I'm sure. I feel great, and Dr. Shepherd said I can do whatever I feel up to doing. At least, here at work."

She knew he was still undergoing physical therapy for his heart and his body would still require a few more weeks to recover from surgery. Overall, though, she had to admit that he looked great.

"Can I get a doctor's note stating you're ready to take on more work?"

Joe gave her a hard stare. "I'm ready to take on more work."

Amanda sighed and rolled her eyes. "It's not a note, and you can't be your own doctor, but I think you're ready. Is Helena okay with this?"

"She's fine with it. Tells me that my being out of the house only half the day is driving her crazy. Her mom is there all the time anyway, so she has help."

"It's not Helena I'm concerned about, but I trust you know your body, so if Dr. Shepherd says you're ready, then who am I to argue with two doctors I know and trust?"

"What's going on?" Ashley asked.

"Joe's coming back full time," Amanda told her. "So you and I will finally have a normal schedule."

"Phew. I'm glad to hear it. I really like working here, but I'm beat."

"You've been a fabulous addition to our team," Amanda encouraged the young physician's assistant. "I'm glad you stuck it out."

"Thanks. I'm glad you're getting better," Ashley told Joe. "Mind if I cut out?"

"We're all cutting out," Joe said. "Right, Amanda?"

"I'm right behind you," she said. "I just have some paperwork to finish."

Joe eyed her wearily. "You remember what we all talked about?"

"Yes. I'll be out of here long before dark. It's only five-forty-five now. I'll be done by six-thirty at the latest."

"Okay. Ashley, let's get out of here so Amanda can get her work done. I'll see you both tomorrow."

Amanda told them goodbye then locked the door behind them. She settled in at her desk and unlocked her laptop. Before she got to work, she pulled her phone from her pocket, remembering that it had buzzed during her last exam.

I have to head to Little Rock for the night. Some meeting Wilson wants me to attend. I'll talk to you before Saturday. ♥

Amanda smiled and texted back, telling him to have a safe trip. She added the kissing emoji.

Amanda turned to her laptop. She had never been so behind on paperwork. With all the extra patients she and Ashley had been taking on, she barely had time to breathe. She was more than happy Joe was returning full-time.

She lost herself in work, not noticing how the time slipped away. When she finally looked at the clock, she was shocked to see it was almost nine. She looked out the window and saw that darkness had set in. She was rolling her shoulders and stretching her neck when she heard the glass break.

They'd had a break-in once before, not long after Amanda joined the practice. Joe's ex set fire to the clinic in an attempt to set him up for insurance fraud. Thankfully, nobody had been in the building at the time, and they'd had no incidents since then.

Amanda stood and walked slowly and silently toward her office door, which was at the top of the stairs in the old, converted house. She tip-toed out into the hall and peered over the banister. A shadow fell across the patch of moonlight on the hardwood floor below. She pulled back and flattened against the wall. She reached into her pocket for her phone, but the pocket was empty. She pictured the phone on her desk where it had been ever since she texted Cooper hours ago.

She crept back into the office, not turning her back on the door. The shadow appeared on the wall along the steps, and her heart ratcheted its rhythm. There was no place to hide. They had removed the closet doors in the office during the restoration so they could have easy access to office supplies. All medications were secured in a closet downstairs with a biometric lock. Only she, Joe, and now Ashley could access it with their thumbprints. Maybe that's what they were after.

She frantically looked around the room, lit only by the reading lamp on her desk. Ah, her desk. It had a panel on it that shielded her legs while she was working. Amanda dove to the floor, grabbing her phone as she tucked herself under the desk. Her hands shook as she tried to unlock the screen.

Need help. At Clinic. Someone's here. Hurry.

She prayed Dale would see the message, but she knew he was off-duty, home with his kids, and Cooper was well out of town by now. But she didn't dare call, didn't make a sound. Who else could she text?

She heard a light footfall on the floor just outside her office. Maybe the lamp would scare the person away. She held her breath and tried not to move. The door creaked as it was pushed opened, and she was certain her thundering heart would give away her hiding place.

Suddenly, she heard a steady buzzing noise and closed her eyes. She couldn't answer the phone, but he would hear it. He would—

The buzzing stopped, and she realized it wasn't her phone.

"What?" The question was hushed and harsh but sounded booming in the night. "I'm still sick. I'll be back at work in a couple days."

Amanda wouldn't be able to hold her breath or stay in this cramped space much longer, but he was standing in her office, just feet from where she cowered.

"Yeah, I know. I get it. Yeah, of course I'm in Houston. Where else would I be?"

She heard a board creak. Was he leaving or coming closer? His voice came from the hallway.

"I gotta go."

She waited another twenty minutes before she moved, watching the minutes tick slowly by on her phone. The text to Dale still showing *Delivered*, not *Read*.

Amanda took a chance, dialed his number, and

waited for him to answer.

"Hey, Amanda, what's up?"

She burst into tears, unable to form words.

"Amanda? Where are you? Are you hurt?" She could hear him moving, giving directions to Jamie to call his grandmother. "Amanda, can you answer me?"

"Clinic," she said between tears.

"I'm on my way. Are you in danger?"

"I don't know," she whispered.

"Stay with me, okay? I'm in the car now. Lights and sirens on. Can you hear them?"

She listened, heard nothing but her own heart beating, and then answered, "Yes." She sniffed and took several breaths. "Are you here?" The sirens were loud, and suddenly lights bounced off the office walls.

"I'm here." She heard him close the car door, run up the front steps. "It's locked. Where are you?"

"Upstairs. My office. I'm coming."

"Amanda, don't move. Stay where you are." He shouted away from the phone. "Police! I'm coming in!"

She heard another voice from somewhere.

"Tim, cover me." Then she heard the door crashing open. "Amanda, we're in."

She listened as they went through the downstairs and crawled out from under the desk when she heard his footsteps on the stairs.

"Amanda!"

"Here," she called, using the desk to pull herself to standing. Her legs were shaky, and a pain ripped through her back as she straightened. She wasn't quite upright when Dale wrapped her in his arms. "Thank Heaven. Cooper would never forgive me if I hadn't gotten to you in time."

A thought struck her as she leaned back and looked Dale in the eyes. "He's going to be furious with me."

"You've got that right," Dale said soberly. "What happened?"

"Building's clear," Officer Tim Rhodes said from the doorway. "I saw your car go by with the lights and sirens and followed you. What's going on?" He looked from Dale to Amanda and back to Dale who was still embracing her. Dale quickly let go.

"Amanda was just about to fill me in." He looked at her and asked, "Amanda, do you know Tim? Tim, this is Amanda, Cooper's, uh, friend."

Tim chewed the side of his lower lip. "Yeah, I know Dr. Pierce. What happened?"

Amanda took a deep breath and relayed to the officers what happened and what she heard. "Dale," she said, looking intently at him, "He said something about Houston. Could he have been looking for Serena?"

***

Cooper left the meeting in stunned silence. He didn't know what to think, what to say, how to answer. Luckily, they'd given him until the end of the following week to get back to them, though he had a feeling they wanted an answer before then.

He nodded at the woman exiting the elevator before

he entered and pushed the button for the ground floor. He wiped his hand down his face and stared at his distorted reflection in the door until the elevator came to a stop and the doors opened.

He walked outside into the bright sunlight and followed the path to the parking lot. He nodded at the servicemen in uniform and smiled at the suits, government officials who worked on the base where the Arkansas Department of Emergency Management was housed. He'd visited the base before, done some training with the department, and attended a meeting or two. This was the first time he'd ever been summoned there to meet with its head, and certainly the first time he'd met the Governor. He considered the fact that the highest-ranking man in the state had gone to meet Cooper rather than having Cooper go to him at the Governor's Office.

This was a big deal. The offer was a big deal. One that indicated a future he'd never imagined. The pay alone was enough to have him hyperventilating, but he'd maintained his cool.

Once inside his truck, he sat and stared out the windshield at the building in front of him. Somewhere in Northwest Arkansas there was a satellite building connected to this one. It wasn't far from Buffalo Springs, but it was a far cry from the sheriff's office. More pay, yes, but also more responsibility, and less danger, less in-the-field. Cooper didn't know how he felt about that.

There would also be frequent trips to Little Rock,

which wouldn't be too bad. He kind of liked the drive. But he didn't like the city. Hated cities. An office in the Ozarks with scheduled, mandatory meetings and trainings on the base or in the capital was a good compromise.

The sun beat down on the dashboard, and Cooper started sweating. He could blame it on the heat, but he knew part of it was the question they'd asked him to consider. Would he take the job?

*****

"We need to talk," they said in unison. It should have led to a moment of laughter, but they were both silent, the air between them hushed as they waited for the other to speak.

Amanda stood in the kitchen, rubbing the tension in her neck with one hand and reaching for her glass of wine with the other. The phone teetered on the counter, and she pushed it away from the edge.

"You first," Cooper said, for which she was grateful.

"I asked Dale not to call you."

"Dale? Call about what?"

She wished she could see his face, read his expression as she carefully told him what happened. The dead air after she finished said enough. She could imagine the tightness in his jaw, the crease in his brow, and the daggers in his eyes.

"Joe left you alone? At night? After we talked about—"

"Cooper, it was my fault. I told him I'd be out of there by six-thirty, but I lost track of time. I was so absorbed in work, I didn't even notice it had gotten dark."

She heard him take a deep breath, knew he was trying to maintain control. She imagined his white knuckles bracing the steering wheel.

"Thank the Almighty you're okay."

"I won't ever let it happen again. I promise. After you voiced your concerns, even though I was angry, I knew you were right. A bit overprotective, if I can be honest. I never thought there was a real cause to worry." She let her last few words fade but added, more forcefully, "Please don't be angry with me or with Joe."

After a few beats, he answered. "I'm not angry with either of you. But if I get my hands on whoever—"

"We think he was looking for Serena."

"What?" he asked, his voice awash with incredulity. "Serena? Why?"

She told him what she'd heard. "I wasn't sure at first. It wasn't much to go on. Then Dale contacted her in Houston, and she's been staying at her mother's because her house was broken into while she was away. She didn't know until she got home, and she didn't tell anyone but her parents. She didn't want Joe to worry with all he and Helena have going on."

"How did Dale take the news?"

"Um, Fine, I guess. Why?"

"Never mind. Are you okay? Not physically, I mean."

She smiled. "I'm okay. I was more nervous about telling you. I mean, once it was over." She gripped the counter before picking up the phone and walking into the living room. She lowered herself onto the couch. "Cooper, I was petrified. I didn't know…" She couldn't finish the sentence.

"I'm so sorry I wasn't there. I mean that. I hate that I wasn't there to hold you when it was over. I hate even more that I wasn't there waiting for you to finish working. If I'd been there, you wouldn't have been alone, and he probably wouldn't have broken in."

"I probably wouldn't have been there at all," she said honestly. "But it's over, and I won't let it happen again. I told Joe I'd pay to replace the window and the door. Dale said the department will take care of the door, and Joe said insurance will cover the window." She puffed out a breath. "Anyway, your meeting. How'd it go? You said you wanted to tell me something."

"It's something I want to talk to you about before I make a decision. I've been offered a job."

Her heart stopped. "In Little Rock?"

"Yes and no. Near Beaver Lake at the Army Corps of Engineers. It's the base for the ADEM."

"ADEM?"

"Arkansas Department of Emergency Management. They want me to take over the entire Northwest Arkansas SAR Division. I'd oversee all the teams, coordinate events between SAR, ADEM, and FEMA, and train new responders for action."

"Wow." Amanda stretched out on the couch and

tried to imagine what this would mean for Cooper. A huge jump in responsibility for sure. "Would you work more hours?"

"Hard to say. Doesn't sound like it. More of a desk job except for the trainings. I'd be on scene for big things like wildfires and landslides like the one back in April, but otherwise, it's more management and coordination."

"Here's the big question," she said. "Would you like it or hate it?"

"Well, that's the thing. I've been thinking lately about how long I want to do this and if I want to do it when I'm married, when I have kids."

Her heart constricted, and her stomach clenched. "You've been thinking about that lately?" She bit her lip as she waited for his response.

"I have, and I don't want to go rushing out during the night every time someone is lost or hurt. I don't want to leap across gorges or drop from choppers. I mean, I love it. There's a rush like no other, but there's also the danger. I don't know if I want to be in that kind of danger anymore, outrunning fires and dropping onto cars in major floods."

She heard the doorbell and wondered who could be stopping by at, she looked at her watch, seven at night.

"Hold on, someone's at the door."

She carried the phone with her but dropped it when she opened the door and Cooper rushed in, taking her in his arms. He kissed her with a ferocity she'd never experienced, and she kissed him right back.

"How did you do that?" she asked, her breath

shallow and her limbs weak.

"Kiss you like I've been away too long?"

She smiled. "Get here so soon."

"We talked for half the drive," he said with a grin. "And I wanted to finish the conversation in person."

He took her hand and led her to the couch where he sat and pulled her down beside him.

"The fact is, I love the training part. I've been involved in that to a degree, and I'm good at it. I'd take the job and sit behind a desk all day just to be able to lead the trainings. Parts of those are in Little Rock, but the hands-on stuff is right here, along the river and in the park and forest. I'd only have to be in Little Rock a few days a year. The rest of the time, I'll be right here."

"I like the sound of that," Amanda said, still holding his hand. She took her other hand and cradled it around the one she held. "I like that a lot."

"I've got a few days to think about it, talk to my parents and Dale, to my team, but I think I'm ready to try something new. And if I don't like it, I can always go back to SAR."

He lifted his free hand to her face and tucked a loose strand of hair behind her ear. "What do you think?" he asked, his voice barely above a whisper.

"I think I want you to do what makes you happy."

"Being able to do this every morning and every night would make me happy." And he crushed her mouth with his.

Sixteen

"You've got one!" Cooper yelled, jumping into the water and splashing his way to where Amanda stood on a rock. "Hold the line still."

"I can't," she said laughing. "He's too wiggly."

She held the rod high in the air as Cooper tried to catch the fish swinging in the air. She almost lost her balance, but she steadied herself. Cooper grabbed hold of the line, and she watched with interest as he tugged the hook from its mouth. He held it up for her to see.

"This one's a beaut. A smallmouth bass. Over fourteen inches for sure." He made his way to the shore where his measuring stick was still in his tackle box.

Amanda carefully made her way off the slippery rock and went over to watch.

"So, I win?" she asked with a broad grin.

Cooper looked at her and smiled. "Fourteen point eight. Possibly a win, but only the first one, so we'll have to see."

He dropped the fish into the cooler and pulled her

to him. She quickly moved the rod to her side, so it wasn't between them.

"Nice catch," he said before giving her a celebratory kiss.

"Thanks," she said, "but I've got another chance to win. Two fish each, right?"

He laughed and released her. "That's the law."

"Then let's get back to it. Amanda, one. Cooper, zero."

She bounded back to the rock and climbed up, ready to resume casting.

Cooper climbed on his rock and steadied himself as he cast his line.

"Are you sure you haven't done this before? I've taken people fly fishing who've had lessons, and they still can't get the hang of it. You're a natural."

"Must be the skill of a doctor's hands."

"Must be," he said before he turned back to his rod. "I've got one!" he yelled, and Amanda stopped to watch him bring the fish close to himself and reach out to grab it. He slipped from the rock, into the water and Amanda let out a belly laugh.

"Agh!" he screamed, which made Amanda laugh harder. "Amanda, help!"

She stopped laughing and watched as he dragged himself to the side of the river. She hurried from the rock, throwing her rod to the ground.

"Cooper, are you hurt? What's wrong?"

"Get us away from the river," he yelled frantically, and Amanda grabbed his arms, but he screamed and yanked his right arm away. She took hold of the other arm and dragged him as far from the riverbank as she could.

"Let me see your arm." Amanda grabbed his arm, and, again, he screamed in pain.

"Jeez, it burns. Burns like the dickens, like a fire on the inside burning its way out." He cursed, something Amanda had never heard him do.

She looked closely at his arm. "There are two punctures," she said before it dawned on her. "Oh, gosh. Two. That means—"

"Amanda, listen to me." His breathing was rapid and shallow. "I don't know how long I'll be awake. I need my phone."

"I have mine," she said starting to call 911.

"*My* phone," he insisted through raspy breaths. He reached for his pocket, but she leaned over him and pulled it out before he got that far. "Code is zero-three-nine-one-one-six. He laid his head back and closed his eyes briefly. He cursed again. "Lucy," he said.

Amanda nodded and searched for Lucy's number. She put it on speaker and held it to his mouth.

"Hey, Coop. Got a call?"

"Yeah," he said, his breathing even shallower and more rapid than before. "Cottonmouth. Need. Antidote."

"Coop! Where are you?"

Amanda held the phone close to her face. "Lucy, it's Amanda. We were fishing. He fell in, and then he screamed in pain, and, and—"

"Amanda, calm down. You can do this. I'm on my way, but I need you to forget that this is Cooper and do what I tell you. Got it?"

The phone shook uncontrollably, but she nodded.

"Amanda, you with me?"

"Yeah, yeah, I'm here. What do I do?" She put the phone on Cooper's chest and willed herself to calm down, to concentrate. *Do what Lucy tells you. You've got this.*

"First, where are you?" Amanda told her the best she could. "Okay, what's his pulse?"

Amanda laid two fingers on his throat and counted, relaying the info to Lucy.

"Is he swelling?"

She looked back at his arm, and her fear skyrocketed. "Yes! Oh, my gosh! So much! So fast! And it's turning black. It's already red and purple. Lucy, it's bad, really bad." She looked at his face. He'd gone as pale as his arm had gone dark. "Cooper, Cooper, can you hear me?" She slapped his cheek, and he mumbled a response.

"Is he conscious?"

"Barely."

"Amanda, I need you to do what you would do for any patient."

"Clean the wound."

"Yep. But first, make sure his shirt sleeve isn't tight. If it is, cut it so it's open and lose"

"Okay." It didn't seem tight, but Amanda didn't want to take any chances, so she looked for the tackle box, retrieved the knife, and cut his sleeve from the cuff to the shoulder. "Done."

"What arm is it?"

"Right."

"So, no watch."

"No. Other arm."

"Good. He doesn't wear jewelry, so we're good there. Go ahead and clean the bite. Consciousness?"

Amanda tried to rouse him. "None." She checked his pulse again. "Pulse racing. Breathing rapid and shallow. He's got antibacterial wipes in the tackle box. That's the best I can do."

"We'll see how out of it he is," Lucy remarked. "Move, darn it. Out of my way." She honked her horn, but Amanda barely noticed, in full doctor mode now.

She dabbed the wipe on the wound, and Cooper's body jolted. He screamed, but Amanda kept wiping.

"You're doing great, Cooper. I know it burns. Just stay with me."

Even barely awake, he spat a string of words only Amanda's toughest patients ever said to her, and only when they were in extreme pain.

"I'm going to cover it now, Cooper. I'm going to have to move your arm some to get the bandages around it."

Only, what bandages? She took the knife and cut off the bottom of her t-shirt in a three-inch band. Worried about infection, she placed a clean wipe on the area before she began wrapping it.

"Amanda, what's going on?" she heard Lucy ask.

"I've got it cleaned and covered. Cooper's heart rate is still high, and he's in and out of consciousness." She looked around for anything to use to cover him. "I need to leave him to look for his kit. If it's in his truck, I can cover him with a mylar blanket."

"How far away is the truck?"

"Not far. Maybe five minutes if I hurry. I'm elevating his legs now. Arm with the bite is on the ground, below his heart. I'm going to leave the phone. Can you talk to him?"

Before she could move, she heard a siren. It sounded like it was getting closer.

"I hear a siren."

"I texted Lance when you first called. He was calling Dale and 911. I didn't know which one of us could get there fastest."

"Amanda!"

"Dale!" she screamed. "Over here! By the river!"

When Dale crashed through the trees, Amanda thought she would burst into tears, but she stayed strong. Her job was not done.

Dale dropped to the ground beside Cooper. "Coop! Coop! Can you hear me?"

"Stop…shouting…you big…dope," he slurred.

"He's in shock. I need a mylar blanket. I'm thinking in his truck."

"I've got one. Hold on." Dale jumped up and raced into the woods.

"Dale's getting a blanket," Amanda said, maybe to Cooper, or Lucy, maybe to herself. She was just talking at this point, trying to keep him awake, Lucy informed, herself calm.

"I'm almost there," Lucy said, but her voice was drowned out by more sirens.

"Ambulance is here," Dale said, ripping open the blanket and dropping it onto his brother. They both worked it under him, but Amanda left the arm out to keep off pressure. Dale was back on his feet and running toward the trees.

When he returned, he had the paramedics with him, Lucy fast on their heels.

Amanda filled them in on his vitals as best she could, told them what she did and how he reacted. She sat back and let them work. Lucy raced to her side and wrapped her arms around Amanda. They watched without saying a word.

"Inserting IV," said the one with the butterfly needle as he punctured Cooper's arm.

Amanda watched the other EMT tear open the serum.

"Administering CroFab," he said as he emptied the hypodermic needle into the prepped IV.

"Administering oxygen," said the first one, pulling a mask onto Cooper's face and hooking him up to a portable oxygen machine.

When Cooper was loaded onto the stretcher and carried to the ambulance, Lucy said, "I'll get all your stuff. You go with Cooper."

"His truck," Amanda began.

"I'll send a couple guys to get it," Dale said. "Go."

Amanda didn't argue. She turned and ran behind the paramedics, praying the entire time they sped to the hospital.

***

"She was incredible," Lucy said. She was standing on one side of Cooper's hospital bed, next to Lance. Amanda stood on the other side, holding his good hand and blushing.

"I was a mess," Amanda said.

"At first," Lucy agreed. "But you snapped to it and never faltered. You saved his life."

"I have to admit. I've never treated a snake bite, and definitely not one I watched happen."

"Coop, man, you're a legend," Lance said. "The greatest SAR responder there ever was, and now a cottonmouth survivor. Man, the stories they'll tell about you."

Amanda and Cooper exchanged a look.

"Guys, I've got something to tell you."

"Yeah, we know," Lucy said. "We've known for a while."

"You do?" Cooper asked, his tone one of sheer surprise.

"Of course. You and Amanda are more than responder and doctor. It was obvious way back when she saved that hiker's life on the trail."

"Then you just happened to have her with you the night of the accident," Lance added, pumping his eyebrows in a way that made Amanda's jaw drop.

"Hold on," she started.

"I picked her up at her house," Cooper said, leaning up in the bed.

Amanda put her hand on his chest. "Down, cowboy. You're supposed to be resting." She looked at Lance. "I was in bed, my bed in my house, alone, when he came pounding on the front door telling me to hurry, grab my bag, and get in the truck."

"I was nicer than that," Cooper protested.

"No, you weren't," Amanda said. "You were very pushy."

Lucy laughed. "He can be pushy, all right."

"Is there room for more in here?" Dale asked, ushering Suzy and Jamie into the room.

"Uncle Coop!" Suzy yelled, and Dale caught her just before she climbed onto the bed.

"What did I tell you about being careful?" he warned.

Suzy ignored him and went right to her uncle. "Did you really get bit by a snake? And Dr. Amanda saved you? And you rode in an ambulance?"

"Well, you seem to know all the details already, Bean," Cooper said with a smile.

The room filled with more people when Cooper's parents arrived, followed by Paige and Jimmy and more Mackenzie cousins.

"We should let you rest," Lucy said, once they were squeezed in like sardines. She leaned in and kissed him on the cheek. "I'm glad to see you're okay."

"Hey," Coop said before she could go. "Amanda was there, but you kept her going. Thank you."

There was no jealously on Amanda's part. She knew she couldn't have done it without Lucy. The two women smiled at each other, acknowledging their growing bond.

After several retellings of the story and others about family members who'd suffered worse injuries, everyone left, two by two, until only Dale remained. The kids went home with their grandparents, but Dale wasn't ready to leave even though Cooper had drifted off to sleep.

"Thank you, Amanda," Dale said quietly. "I don't know if I've said that already."

"Dale, you don't need to thank me. I'm just relieved he's okay."

Dale looked at his brother. "He loves you, you know. He may not have said it yet, but he does."

Amanda smiled. She'd be darned if she said it to Dale before she said it to Cooper, so she just nodded. "Thanks."

Dale eyed her for a moment before nodding and turning to leave. "See you tomorrow," he told her as he walked out the door.

Cooper mumbled something, and Amanda leaned down to put her ear close to his mouth.

"What did you say?"

"He's right," Cooper said lazily, a smile tugging at his lips.

"I know," Amanda whispered before kissing him goodnight.

Six Months Later

A light snow clung to the pine trees in the national forest and dusted the rocks along the bluff. Deer roamed the woods while bears slept peacefully in their caves. All was quiet as Cooper walked the trail, Scout by his side. His cadets had concluded their training that afternoon, all passing with flying colors.

After they left, Cooper and Scout took some time to meander through the forest, basking in the peace and quiet. Though Cooper wasn't officially employed by the sheriff's department anymore, they still participated in search and rescues where Scout's services were needed.

Cooper enjoyed his job more than he thought he would. He knew he'd love the teaching part, but he didn't think he'd like the desk part. He was pleasantly surprised. Rather than a slow, pencil-pushing position, it kept him on his toes, coordinating field operations, visiting EOCs, and providing backup when the searches warranted. He had access to impressive software and large monitors that allowed him to follow the responders in action using GPS satellite systems. He liked the way his department worked with the local sheriff's offices and with FEMA and discovered none of the discord one saw on television and in the movies.

There was only one area of his life where he was discontented. Every night, he told Amanda goodbye and returned to Dale's house where he continued to help with the kids, but he had it in mind to change that. Soon.

As he and Scout climbed the final stretch before the bluff, Cooper took in the view, one he'd forgotten how much he appreciated until that day last May when he'd been there with Amanda. He reached into his pocket and took out the velvet box he'd been carrying with him since he bought it the week before. He opened the lid and smiled as the winter sun glistened off the diamond. He'd sold the other ring, the one Jessie never even knew about, and he bought one he knew was just what Amanda would like. He couldn't help but smile as he thought about how it would look on her finger.

They didn't stay long, he and Scout. It was cold, and the forest was not kind after dark on a day like today. Christmas was a week away, and Cooper had big holiday plans. For the first time in his life, he wasn't spending it in Buffalo Springs, and he was a little sad at the thought, but he was looking forward to seeing all the lights and sounds of Christmas in Nashville.

To say he'd been shocked would be an understatement to describe how he felt when Amanda confessed who her parents were—honestly, the names and the foundation meant nothing to him—and the kind of childhood she'd had. When Amanda knew her two worlds were going to collide once she took Cooper home, she revealed her trust-fund secrets to both him and Joe. She and Cooper were both surprised to find that Joe had known all along where the money came from each time they received another anonymous donation for the clinic. Every doctor in the South knew the name Dr. Ronald Pierce as well as his wife's family foundation. Joe put two and two together soon after he brought Amanda in as a partner and grants started rolling in.

Cooper didn't care about Amanda's family or her money. She could've sprouted from a hole in the forest floor, and he'd still love her more than anything in the world. He was a lucky man, knowing she felt the same.

"Let's go," he called to Scout as he made his way out of the forest. He hummed an actual Christmas tune on the way back to Buffalo Springs, something he hadn't done since he was no older than ten.

It was dark by the time Cooper pulled into the house that would eventually become his home, and he and Scout both bounded up the walkway, both excited to be there.

"I'm home," he called, just like the husband and father in an old 1950s' television show.

"In here," Amanda called, and he found her right where he knew she'd be, her head stuck in the fridge.

Cooper stifled a laugh and held up the bag in his hand. "How about a Bogart burger and sweet potato fries with a side of slaw, two pickles?"

Amanda closed the refrigerator door and turned to face him, a broad grin on her face. "Now, there's a man I could fall in love with."

"Could?"

She smiled, and it sent his heart into a gallop.

"Did," she confirmed as she went to him. "How do you always know when I won't have dinner planned?"

"I don't know. Does today end in a y?"

She swatted at him, and he jumped out of the way. "Be careful. I'm holding the food."

"I knew I kept you around for a reason."

"And I know exactly what that reason is," he growled as he tossed the bag on the table and pulled her into a hungry kiss that no food could satiate.

***

"Here's to another Christmas in Buffalo Springs," Helena said, raising her glass. "And to a first Christmas here for some." She smiled at Serena and clinked glasses with her sister-in-law.

"I'm just happy to be with y'all." She turned to her parents. "And to have you, Mama and Daddy, here with us."

"We wouldn't have it any other way," her father said, smiling at her and then at Joe.

"To future Christmases in Buffalo Springs," Joe said, making another toast.

Serena smiled, and tried to squelch her growing unease. The texts had started up again, the threats growing with increasing intensity.

When she announced she was closing her Houston-based business and no longer catering to the stars, the messages stopped for a while. But ever since she started work on the new store, her phone pinged at least once a day with a message or graphic or meme, some laughable and some horrifying.

She gazed at the fire, recalling the wedding that ruined her reputation and her career. She was ready to start over again. She was ready to plan real weddings for real people, and she wanted to involve the whole Buffalo Springs community in each celebration.

"I hear wedding bells may be in the future for everyone's favorite couple," Helena said, pulling Serena's attention from the blaze.

"Oh, really?" She turned and smiled at Helena.

"Yes. I heard from Andi who heard from Wade, who was told by Dale that…"

Helena chattered on, but Serena's mind zeroed in on one name in Helena's list. She shoved aside all thoughts of texts and threats and the world she left behind. She was starting over, and impeccable planner that she was, she already had the perfect picture of how the new year was going to progress.

To be continued…

Acknowledgements

Several years ago, one of my very best friends told me she thought the Arkansas Ozarks would be the perfect setting for one of my book series. I had two problems with that. I had never been to Arkansas (Tammi and I met in the Holy Land and instantly bonded, but I had yet to travel to her home), and I wrote stand-alone novels and trilogies, but not series. Eventually, I took Tammi up on her invitation, only because I wanted to visit her, but still had no intention of writing a series. I spent a week in the fall with Tammi in those beautiful mountains and valleys witnessing, as Cooper said, "their autumn glory."

Tammi took me to one small town after another, regaling me with stories about each place; but it was the town we drove through with broken windows, cracked sidewalks, and a dry fountain that tugged at my heart and cried out to me for salvation. My week with Tammi was more than a research trip. It was a joyous few days spent with someone I love, and I truly am grateful for her friendship, hospitality, and insistence that the Arkansas Ozarks were the perfect setting for a series. It was also the beginning of a journey for me, and for you, to the small town of Buffalo Springs, a journey I hope will continue for many years (and books) to come.

Thank you, Tammi, for knowing just the inspiration I needed before I knew it myself. That's how true friends operate, and it's friends like Tammi who make up the small towns in my books. Each person I write about is based on someone I know and love, so it's only right for me to thank my wonderful friends for their love and support. Debbie, Cheryl, Anne, Ronnie, Jeanne, Donna, Victoria, Sharon, and Tammi have all read every book I've ever written, and that means the world to me. Librarians and friends, Shannon and Mindy, read and recommend my tales, and I truly appreciate their friendship and encouragement.

My parents both read my books, recommend them to everyone they know, and hand out my business cards to friends, strangers, store cashiers, and anyone and everyone they meet. Mom reads every book from the time I begin writing, giving me her unbiased (truly unbiased) opinion and advice. She is my top critic, biggest supporter, and very best friend.

Another one of my best friends, Anne, also reads every book from the start. She never fails to lead me in the right direction and tells me when she feels something needs to be changed or fixed. Her honesty is invaluable in giving you, my readers, the books worthy of you. Mary Ann, a dear friend and a pilgrim on two of the journeys I led, lent me her college English professor talents, and I am so grateful for her edits and suggestions.

A few years ago, I switched editors because my first (and quite wonderful) editor specialized in nonfiction, and she always told me I should consider going with a fiction editor. Cayley Ross stepped in and took the reins in steering me down the right road. Her skill with plotlines and eye for loose ends and contradictions never cease to amaze me. I am blessed to have her and encourage others to seek out her services. You won't regret it. Thank you, Cayley, for taking me on as a client. I love working with you!

I'm writing these acknowledgements as my husband

drives us (and our two dogs) to my parents' house for Thanksgiving. This is what he does, whatever I need him to, so I can finish a book in time for you to receive it on the date I've promised. Without his love and support, I could never do what I do—write full-time and travel for inspiration—and I'm eternally grateful for his support. Thank you, Ken, for always knowing what I need, for encouraging me to visit places like the small towns of Northwest Arkansas, and for giving me the time and space to do what I love to do.

My three girls, Rebecca, Katie Ann, and Morgan, have lived most of their lives with a mom who "writes books." They live alongside my characters (some based on them) without complaining that I give these other personas more time, love, and attention than I give to them. They help me with plot ideas, assist me with book sales, and tell their friends to suggest my books for their book clubs. I am blessed to have been gifted these three beautiful women.

Most of all, I must thank you, my readers. Without you, I would have no reason to keep writing other than to empty my brain of stories and characters only I would ever know. I write because I am called to write, but I publish because you are called to read.

With all my love,

About the Author

Amy began writing as a child and never stopped. She wrote articles for magazines and newspapers before writing children's books and adult fiction. A graduate of the University of Maryland with a Master of Library and Information Science, Amy worked as a librarian for fifteen years and, in 2010, began writing full time.

Amy writes inspirational fiction for people of all ages. She has published two children's books and numerous novels, including the award-winning Desert Fire, Mountain Rain and Sapphires in Snow, two books in the Buffalo Springs series. A former librarian, Amy enjoys a busy life on the Eastern Shore of Maryland.

The recipient of numerous national literary awards, including the Illumination Award, LYRA award, Independent Publisher Book Award, International Digital Award, and the Golden Quill Award as well as honors from the Catholic Press Association and the Eric Hoffer Book Award, Amy's writing has been hailed "a verbal masterpiece of art" (author Alexa Jacobs) and "Everything you want in a book" (Amazon reviewer). Amy's books are available internationally, wherever books are sold, in print and eBook formats. Follow Amy at:

http://amyschislerauthor.com
http://facebook.com/amyschislerauthor
https://twitter.com/AmySchislerAuth
https://www.goodreads.com/amyschisler

Book Club Discussion Questions

1. Cooper Mackenzie quickly became one of my favorite characters (next to Zack in my Chincoteague books). Like Zach, he struggles with guilt from past mistakes. How would you counsel him to move on? Do you have personal experience in putting your past behind you from which Cooper could benefit?

2. In some ways, Amanda Pierce is also trying to escape her past. As much as she loves her family, she found that she had to move away to find herself and live her own life? Have you ever felt that way? What did you do, and how did it turn out?

3. Cooper often finds himself in church, praying before the tabernacle, when he is seeking peace. Do you have a place where you go to find peace? How does that particular setting bring tranquility to your life?

4. Like so many of us have done (or are doing), Cooper begins discerning his future and what God's plan is for him. Have you been there? How did you find the answers? Are you still pondering the direction your life should take?

5. Are you a hiker? What is the most challenging hike you've undertaken? How did you feel upon completion?

6. Buffalo Springs grows with each novel that is added to the series. What businesses would you like to see added to the town's landscape?

www.ingramcontent.com/pod-product-compliance
Lightning Source LLC
Chambersburg PA
CBHW030916300726
48970CB00001B/183